better lands – The Discoveries

Susan Clawson

Trenton, Georgia, U.S.A.

Paperback ISBN: 978-1-64719-645-5
Ebook ISBN: 978-1-64719-646-2

Published by Abuzz Press, Trenton, Georgia, U.S.A.

Artwork by RJ Heredia

The characters and events in this book are fictitious. Any similarity to real persons, living or dead, is coincidental and not intended by the author.

Library of Congress Cataloging in Publication Data
Clawson, Susan
better lands – The Discoveries by Susan Clawson
Library of Congress Control Number: 2021939844

Printed on acid-free paper.

Abuzz press
2021

Meet the Author

Susan Clawson grew up in the Burlington, Vermont area and, for the past 14 years, has resided in a rural town in northern Massachusetts with her husband. They plan to move to the Kentucky area when they retire. Their children are all grown, and living throughout the U.S. Susan has worked in sales, marketing and training for most of her career. She is excited to present book 1 of a 5-book suspense *pandemic* series to her readers.

Look for Book 2 – as the story continues - this Fall:

'better lands – The Southbound Journey'

#151 Lilly! Enjoy the journey! S

DEDICATION

I'd like to dedicate this book to those who encountered COVID 19's deadly wrath. To all the families, friends and those I don't even know, who fought so bravely to survive and continue to do so, my prayers are with you. Just know, there is light at the end of the tunnel, there always is.

To my husband-Kerry, my mom and my oldest daughter-Nikki, who endlessly listened to continual revisions of this story. Also to my youngest daughter, Lindsay, for your encouragement. A huge thank you to everyone for all your dedication, love and support.

To RJ Heredia, my future son-in-law, who graced the cover of this book with his awesome artwork. Thank you!

To my dedicated editor, Katie Elizabeth! Thank you for your helpful eyes and advice! You've been a rock through this venture!

Here's to better lands and to a hope that it is not our future.

PROLOGUE

It finally happened; the world had morphed almost overnight, recreating itself into a place of constant sickness, uncertainty, and endless mortality. The metamorphosis was like a roller coaster with no stops, soaring through everything in its path. Those that survived it would never know life to be the same again.

It had been four years since the pandemic made its first debut, creating ungodly havoc and injecting itself into the ecosystem. Initially, the spread of it triggered poverty, destruction, and mass confusion, along with enormous collapses within families, cities, states, and countries. As time went on, the necessities became harder to get, some completely gone. The pandemic bled disastrous infrastructure failures within all the technical networks.

Most modes of transportation were extremely limited or non-existent. Gas, oil and propane resources were scarce. There were no longer enough people to run and maintain the facilities that kept businesses alive, so they closed down. The necessary essentials, such as food, water, and other supplies that folks couldn't find on their own, were transported in by boats and sporacdically dropped off at distribution hubs located on larger bodies of water.

Some farmers' lands and various facilities remained untouched by the virus, and for a short while, were able to produce some of the much needed necessities distributed to the hubs. The sparingly disbursed supplies caused despair and anger among many surviving communities, especially when they didn't get enough. Most food manufacturers had permanently closed down production causing prices to soar on rarity items, some only available on the black market while supplies and money to purchase them lasted. All overseas exchanges were discontinued and for the most part, even from county to county. Nobody was willing to share.

By the time the second virus wave blew through in early 2023, the world had experienced its most severe pounding, dwindling down the global population of 7.7 billion by over two-thirds. In addition, the new strain, stronger than before, no longer needed a human host for its survival, only the DNA. It found its source in abandoned houses, apartment and office buildings, retail shops, boats, RVs, cars and more, then ran amok within them, multiplying itself like rabbits. Any breathing inhabitants that came within a few feet of its existence sadly met their demise. It was mandated that all abandoned structures were to be burned to the ground, to help terminate its localized existence.

Even though two waves of the deadly virus had already taken out a majority of the planet's breathing population, an incoming stronger third wave was expected to wipe out even more. On top of the pandemic, global warming had set the world in motion for other drastic changes, and only intensified due to the downsized population that left no manpower to control or maintain its ongoing destruction. The fires, floods, hurricanes, along with the extreme temperature changes, left most areas without operational power grids or cell towers. Technology was dying. Some regions, less prone to the climate devastation, were lucky enough to receive sporadic services. Existing solar and wind energy helped in some places, but maintenance remained the biggest downfall.

Those that were fortunate enough to escape the pandemic's deathly grip and the wrath of mother nature, lived, with no other choice, in a new uncertain world. They were evacuated from the security of their own homes, forced to live on the streets, in tents, in fields, in forests, wherever they could assure future survival. In the more populated areas, the smells from the smoldering structures were prevalent in the air, some so extreme it wasn't breathable. There was little to no escape from any of it, until a new hope emerged.

Spring 2024 – A Four Year Reflection

Among all the world wide chaos created by a 4-year fatal virus, sat the once-bustling city of Burlington, Vermont. Its soul resting in a quiet solitude, tattered and lost from being beaten by the unseen enemy that stole its livelihood. At the end of the Church Street Marketplace, stood a famous icon the city was known for, a dilapidating faded brick church that had once triggered the street's name. Several yards in front of it a corroding bronzed life-size deer guarded a waterless fountain that was filled with decaying rodents, molded leaves, and garbage that created a stench so strong, one could barely pass by it without gagging.

In the midst of the charred remains of the marketplace, a young girl sat alone, gazing upon the church. Her heart beat heavily against her chest, knowing it was the last time she would lay eyes upon it. She had been destined to become a visionary leader for thousands of survivors and would take some of them with her to the better lands, a place rumored to be virus free. The better lands had given them hope that there was a chance to bring back a sense of normalcy into their lives, one they hadn't seen since 2020.

It had been over four decades since Church Street converted from vehicles to foot traffic. Many huge boulders were brought in by cranes and placed randomly up and down the newly bricked road. They symbolized rugged individualism and were a compelling site, resting near some of the booming retail shops and restaurants. Even after the pandemic arrived, they stood unscathed, as the rest of the marketplace collapsed around them.

A few blocks down the street was an old mall entrance leading to an unfinished ten-story apartment complex. It had been under construction before the pandemonium had started, but unlike the surrounding buildings, its structure still remained intact. It's size and location made it difficult to burn down. Parts of it was occupied by the homeless, those willing to take chances that the virus wasn't hiding within it.

Just outside the mall entrance, upon one of those massive boulders, sat the girl, Rosa Rochelle Wells. She was all by herself, knees pulled close to her chest, rocking back and forth, staring at the church as the evening sun bore the last light upon it, before disappearing into the night. Her bare, blistered feet peeked out from underneath the ragged, soiled, green dress that draped over them. It was hard to identify she was in her mid-teens as her long, blonde strands of hair partially covered her face. A frayed, cotton, tan scarf was loosely wrapped around her neck, one she'd occasionally cover her face with to prevent soot from getting into her lungs from the constant smoldering debris.

Rosa was 16 and, not by her choice, going on 30. So much had happened in her young life. So many losses. So many changes. They all made her stronger and determined, despite all the devastation, that it wasn't the end for her, or for the others she now shared her life with. They hoped the better lands were the answer for their continued existence on the earth. As she sat and reflected over the last four years, she couldn't believe the once privileged life that had sheltered her from its darkest moments, were now her daily encounters. She wanted so badly to escape them and the next morning was her chance, along with those that chose to follow her. But for that moment, she tightly wrapped her arms around her legs and continued to reflect back on what the last four years had saddled her with.

The marketplace sat silent from any chatter and laughter it had been used to. In its heydays, the street welcomed many people who'd stroll up and down it from dusk til the early morning hours, but all the attractions were gone. The shops were mainly demolished; there was no street music or outside cafés revealing the smells of coffee, steaks, and pizza. All was replaced by the burned building remnants that had cast a permanent scent in the air and an eyesore for the few that roamed about. The airwaves were occasionally graced with whooshes of skateboard wheels and infrequent clatter of rusted grocery carts rolling over the uncared-for bricks that lined the street. As the sun began to set, the sporadic surges from the power grid caused the streetlights to flicker randomly, casting a dim light over the grim surroundings.

Rosa felt her eyes fill with tears as she thought about her parents. She missed them terribly and still couldn't believe they were gone. Especially her dad. It had been four years since she last felt his arms wrapped securely around her. She missed his smile, his laughter and how he made her laugh. He never judged her, he just loved her. She'd never forget that horrid day, the last day she ever saw him.

Spring 2020

With sirens loudly blaring, the ambulance whipped down a long, paved driveway that led to a large residential home just yards from Lake Champlain on Shelburne Bay. The late spring sun shone brightly over the polished landscape, slightly reflecting off the clear, calm body of water that signaled afternoon was approaching. The emergency vehicle came to rest under a beautifully sculptured gazebo-type carport just near the front door. The flower gardens that surrounded the entrance way were filled with hundreds of tulips of all colors. Potted plants displaying daffodils and daisies lined the outskirts of the porch.

The red lights were left flashing, but the siren silenced as two men, suited up like astronauts, jumped out from the front of it. The back doors swung open and two more EMTs hopped out with a gurney full of medical equipment. They raced toward the wide open double doors that were anticipating their arrival.

Once inside the large glass entranceway, the men stopped to gauge their surroundings. The humidity level was high from all the tropical plants that greeted them. A thin layer of moisture quickly covered the outside of their plastic face shields, slightly fogging them. To the right of the foyer, they saw a huge, Victorian-style living room displaying several oversized paintings by John Michael Wright, a British baroque-style artist from the 1600s. Straight ahead of them loomed a beautiful white marble staircase. Its golden brass railing sparkled as the sun's rays beamed in through the floor-length windows lining the stairwell. As their eyes continued to look about, pleas for help came from the upper level.

"Up here! We're up here!" shouted a trembling, high-pitched voice, "Please, hurry! Up here!"

Without hesitation, the four men immediately raced up the stairs with the gurney. Upon arriving on the second-floor landing, they spotted a young girl, clearly terrified as she stood with her back braced against the wall. She looked to be about 11 or 12. Her long, blonde hair was pulled back in a ponytail and a pink headband had slightly slipped down onto her forehead. Her teary blue eyes blinked profusely, as she watched the paramedics approach.

Before they had a chance to ask her where to go, the familiar pleading voice shouted from down the hallway, "Hurry, please!"

At that point, they abandoned the girl and followed the voice past four bedroom doors to the last room at the end of the hall. The pleas subsided as two of the EMTs grabbed the medical bags off the gurney and rushed into the room to assess the situation.

The bedroom chamber was almost as large as a dance studio, with high ceilings and detailed molding that elegantly framed it. The French décor mimicked times from the Victorian era, with more Wright paintings hung about. The thick, gold velvet curtains were drawn open to let light in from the floor-length windows. On the far side of the room, situated between two sets of stained-glass French doors, was a king-sized Victorian canopy bed, sporting matching gold velvet attire. The bedspread was falling off its side.

One of the French doors was open, filling the room with a scent of fresh air. Just outside of it was a large balcony overlooking Lake Champlain and, just across the water in New York, a picturesque view of the Adirondack Mountains. The area was a prime and prominent place to live, and those with means inhabited it. The medium-sized mansion-type homes were spread far enough apart so that neighbors didn't see or hear each other when they were outside.

The bay, located in the town of Shelburne, offered great outdoor recreation in the warmer months, such as swimming, fishing, and boating. A private yacht club perched at the end of the cul-de-sac road with nearby walking paths that took hikers through the woods to the tip of Shelburne point, opening up to panoramic views of the lake.

The 120-mile, eighth largest freshwater lake in the United States, had played an important role in the Revolutionary War. It had allowed movement from colonies to its nearby neighbor, Canada. The oldest known fossil reef in the world was found housed in Lake Champlain, dating back 450-480 million years.

The town itself, established in 1763, was named after a member of the British Parliament, Earl of Shelburne, and in the 20th century became home to the famous icons, Vermont Teddy Bear Factory and the Shelburne Museum.

In the middle of the bed, lying on his back, was a middle-aged frail-looking man gasping for air. Both of his arms rested tightly across his chest. The sheet and blankets were off to his side; his t-shirt and boxer shorts appeared to be dripping in sweat. Standing next to his bedside was a distraught, well-dressed lady in her mid-40s, gently rubbing his upper arm and forehead. Noticeable red blotches covered her face, most likely from crying, and her body trembled as she looked over at the EMTs approaching the bedside. She became more hysterical as they got closer.

"Please, please, over here! Please help him! Please, hurry!" Her voice was anxious yet a bit weaker than when they first arrived.

"Ma'am, we really need you to step away from the side of the bed so that we can get closer to him," one of the paramedics loudly stated, stopping for a moment, waiting for her to move.

It had become apparent that she wasn't going to give them the immediate access they needed, as she stood firmly by the bedside, clinging even tighter to the man's arm.

"Ma'am, we really need you to let us over there," the EMT said again.

Meanwhile, one of the other paramedics, who was standing at the foot of the bed, asked, "Ma'am, would you mind coming over here so

I can get some more information? I at least need you to confirm his name. Can you do that for me?"

She looked over at the man then attempted to catch her breath, still not moving and finally answered, "Bill … Bill Wells. Please, please, help him. He's my husband. He's so sick; you have to help him … please."

One of the paramedics got close enough to lightly rest his hand on her shoulder then softly said, "We're going to do the best we can, but you have to let us do our job, and you'll have to move away from him," he paused for a moment, watching her teary eyes staying focused on her husband, then continued, "I'm Mike, and I assume you're Rochelle, the one that made the call to us?"

Rochelle Wells was a petite, slender woman dressed in black yoga pants and a red cashmere sweater with a silky pink scarf tied loosely around her neck. Her blonde ponytail bounced about as she hesitantly acknowledged Mike and eventually let him guide her to the other side of the room. It was easier than he had anticipated.

Her once bright blue eyes, now swollen and red, despairingly looked at him as she softly asked, "Yes, I'm Rochelle Wells. You can help him, right?"

Rochelle's eyes fixated back on her husband as she slowly tried to nudge her way back to the bed, but Mike blocked her attempt. He told her she needed to stay out of the paramedics' way, but knew she wasn't in a state of mind to listen, so knew he'd have to stay close by while his counterparts worked on Bill.

There was nobody around to comfort Rochelle as she watched the EMT jam the big blue breathing tube down her husband's throat while the other man punched needles into his arms. It was too much. She grabbed her stomach and keeled over, gagging as if she were about to vomit and worked herself into enough of a frenzy that it took Mike a few minutes to calm her back down. Shortly after the tube settled and the surrounding machines turned on, Bill let out a few hoarse gasps. His face, which had previously reflected dire pain and stress, seemed to relax as his darkened eyes closed and his breathing calmed.

It all was so surreal to Rochelle. Just a month earlier, the three of them had been at their second home in Barbados during their daughter's spring break. It was a short welcome getaway at the small yet cozy beach house located on prime, oceanfront property. Just 15 years earlier, Bill's parents, after enjoying it themselves for a couple of decades, gave it to them as a wedding gift. As a kid, Bill had spent many summers there and was excited to bring the same tradition to his own family. His parents continued to spend some summers there with them until they passed away, just a few years before the pandemic had hit.

Rochelle felt a momentary calmness surround her as she recalled the mesmerizing sounds of the waves and smells of the ocean. She slightly smiled as she thought about the local culture and welcoming residents. Then there were the tropical drinks they had on their private balcony as the island's sun set for the night. She felt a pit form in her stomach as she remembered dreading their departure, feeling uncertain and fearful it was the last time they'd all be there together. There were rumors of a virus that had hit parts of North America, like it already had in a few other countries, resulting in extreme devastation for those in its path. Bill tried to assure her that they'd be okay and had many more years ahead to enjoy their getaway, and all its creature comforts. Even though he told her not to worry, she did, and upon arriving home, her worst fear was confirmed. It was complete chaos.

The pandemic had arrived and spread quicker than anticipated. Suddenly businesses were closing, transportation slowed down, some essentials were scarce, and thousands of people were already dying. Medical care was overwhelmed, and there weren't enough health care providers or supplies to keep up with the growing, sick and dying population. Everyone was ordered to wear gloves and face masks in public to avoid the airborne virus as much as possible. Vermont, along with many other states and countries, eventually shut down. It never got better.

Since Rochelle married, she wasn't an income generator. Instead, she had devoted her time to her family, church programs and volunteered at a local women's shelter. Rosa was their only child who excelled in her studies at a local private school. As parents, they couldn't have been prouder of their daughter. At just 12-years-old, she was captain of the school's soccer team and had lead roles in a couple of school and church plays. Rosa also helped her mother with a lot of the church activities and even sometimes at the women's shelter. On her own, through the church, Rosa had started a fund-raising campaign that brought much needed programs to local nursing homes; then, she helped solicit some community members to run them. Rochelle and Bill supported Rosa's future aspirations of wanting to become a leader to help make a difference in others' lives. They credited her compassion to Rochelle and her ambition to Bill, who had a long line of leaders in his family.

For 20 years, Bill had been the CEO at a local family-owned, deluxe soap manufacturer. His grandfather had originally started it in the early 1940s, only to hand it over to Bill's dad, who eventually handed it over to him. Bill had always been known as a fair employer, providing his employees with good medical benefits, more than enough PTO, and the ability to work flex schedules as needed. During the initial pandemic outbreak, his business was classified as non-essential and required it to temporarily close its physical doors, shortly after 23 of his 350 employees tested positive with the virus. Bill furloughed most of them with continual benefits while the management team worked from their homes, as he did. It was just three weeks later Rochelle dialed 911.

As the paramedics lifted Bill onto the gurney for transport, the room filled with Rochelle's relentless pleas that drowned out the monitor beeps, "No, oh God no… please, can't you just take care of him here? I can't be with him at the hospital… please," she begged, pausing as she tried to catch her breath. "He can't be alone! Please… I need to be with him."

Rochelle hastily moved toward Mike who was standing near the foot of the gurney, then grabbed one of his arms, hoping her pleas would stop them from leaving the room. From the moment Bill became bedridden and she dialed for help, her biggest fear was once he left their doorstep, she'd never see him again. It was all over the news that visitors were limited in the hospitals but restricted from patients' rooms who were diagnosed with the virus. There were no exceptions and because of that, many victims were left on their own to fight for survival, many dying without loved ones by their sides.

Simultaneously, Mike gently grabbed both her arms and replied, "Rochelle, it'll be okay. Please, let us get him out of here now so we can give him the best chance to fight this. I promise, it'll be okay and someone will contact you once he gets settled in."

Then, after he sternly gazed into her swollen, tear-filled eyes, she slowly backed off, and he softly said, "It'll be okay, I promise."

Then Mike grabbed one of the monitors and walked beside the gurney as they began to wheel Bill out of the room. Rosa had been standing in the doorway, watching everything that was happening to her dad. She felt like she was caught in a dream, one she couldn't wake up from. With eyes wide open, she tried the best she could to decipher what was going on and what it all meant for him. She saw her mother falling apart, crying and begging the strangers not to take him away.

"Please, sweetie, you need to move aside. We have to get your daddy to the hospital as soon as possible," one of the paramedics softly said as she unintentionally blocked the doorway.

Rosa momentarily froze, not knowing which direction to move in or if she even could move. She heard her mother's frantic voice ringing in her ears, and panic set in. She mustered up the strength to move aside and caught a close up glimpse of her dad surrounded by all the tubes and needles stuck in his frail body. Her heart sank as he laid there, so still, with his eyes closed and pale face completely dominated by the breathing tube. The monitors continually sang, keeping the paramedics informed of his stats.

Rosa always thought of her dad as a strong man. She recalled how every time he came home from work, she'd run to greet him. He'd immediately put down his briefcase, pick her up, swing her around, then hold her tight in his arms. After he softly kissed her cheek, he'd ask how her day was. Then there were all the times she'd watch him chop and pile up firewood with little to no effort. She'd catch glimpses of him working out in their gym, lifting heavy weights, sweating profusely and seemingly never out of breath. The father she knew was far from the meek, vulnerable man who was hustled past her, lying so flat and motionless on the gurney. She had never seen him that way and it scared her.

Through it all, deep down Rosa knew what was happening and it made her feel even more alone and afraid. When her family got home from that spring break vacation and were surrounded by the 'new normal', her parents made sure she understood what was going on. There were so many changes they had to quickly adjust to. Rosa had to attend school online. They no longer went to church or participated in outside activities. She couldn't play with her two best friends that lived just down the street. They had to wear gloves and face masks when they left the house. Then her dad started working from home, and her mother stopped volunteering. It was a lot for Rosa to take in, but she tried to be brave until she overheard her parents talking about things getting worse. The news emphasized death daily. Everything was different. She was frightened because she really didn't know what it all meant.

Her parents saw how it was affecting her, but all they could do was promise her that in the end, everything would be okay. Then her father started coughing. He couldn't stop. It looked like it hurt him. But he told them it didn't. And then it got worse. His body ached. And then he got a fever. But he said it would go away. Her mother wanted him to get some help. But he refused. He feared the moment he left the house, not only would he be alone, but it would be a burden on his family. He got insufferably worse, to a point where he couldn't breathe well, so her mother dialed 911.

Rochelle rushed by her as if she didn't exist, following the paramedics as they scurried further away down the hall. All Rosa heard were the sounds of shoe soles clicking against the marble stairs as they swiftly went down them. Her mother's faint voice echoed in the stairwell, constantly telling Bill how much she loved him and that everything was going to be okay. Rosa stood in the upstairs hallway outside of her parents' bedroom, unable to move again, unable to run downstairs after them to tell her dad that she loved him too, and didn't want him to go. She tried hard not to cry and told herself he'd be back soon. After all, he had promised her everything would be okay no matter what.

She never did see him again. Three days later, he died.

***

As she continued to gaze upon the church, Rosa finally felt a sense of peace flood through her after all the years of turmoil and loss that she had encountered. With both her parents gone, she had been left to fend for herself. Even though the past few years were like a blur, the things that happened remained clear. Things she wished she could forget, mainly the four people that died at her hands, even though she knew it was for the right reasons. They all were in a better place for it and it was time to move on.

Rosa felt good about what was next for her and the people she now lived among. But the need for them to move immediately had become necessary. The third wave of the virus was inevitable and rumored to be just months away. It was time to find a safer territory and migrate to the better lands, in hopes it was there. She and Jean-Pierre had already prepared the others for departure. Rosa was so thankful he and Darcy came into her life, just months earlier.

The Boys… Jean-Pierre Berger

Jean-Pierre Berger and Darcy Couture arrived in Burlington, Vermont in the Fall of 2023. At that time, Jean-Pierre was 17, a transient from Stanstead, Quebec, just north of the Vermont border. The town had only been around since 1995 but was considered one of the jewels of the Canadian Eastern Townships. The pandemic raised havoc within it during its initial three year reign.

Jean-Pierre was the oldest of five siblings, but by the time he had arrived in Burlington, he was the only one left. The others had fallen victim to the fatal virus. Jean-Pierre's two five-year-old twin brothers were the first of his family to contract the virus in early 2020. He was only 14 at the time and it had happened so quickly, before anyone realized how deadly it was. The boys started with a small cough, then within a day, a fever set in with temperatures pushing 104-degrees. They were bedridden and miserable. Both parents thought it was a case of the flu and weren't worried since they all had their yearly shots. Everyone was shocked when the very next day, both boys died within hours of each other.

Overly distraught about their death, Jean-Pierre's mom locked herself away in her bedroom for several months, rarely joining in with the rest of the family. She wasn't able to function as a mother or wife as she couldn't get past the loss of her twin boys. Jean-Pierre's dad did the best he could to make ends meet, but the added responsibility of assuming both parental roles forced him to take a lot of time off from work. It eventually led to losing his janitorial job at the local college. Things were tight for a bit, but eventually his wife came around and he was able to find a new job nearby. But several months later, just after normalcy found its way back to their household, the second wave struck with much more vengeance.

The virus implanted itself in both Jean-Pierre's parents and his four-year-old sister, at the same time. They experienced extreme breathing issues, high fevers, and severe headaches. That same day they were rushed to the hospital but just two days later, within hours of each other, they died.

Jean-Pierre, then 15, and his nine-year-old sister, Kate, were devastated, alone, and frightened. There were no other family members nearby and a mandate to stay at home was in full force, preventing any neighbors from lending a helping hand. Some did come as far as the property line to wish them the best, occasionally leaving food and other supplies, but that was the extent. It was all up to Jean-Pierre to figure out how to take care of them and survive from the relentless killer.

Both the Berger siblings took online classes for a few months until they ceased due to sporadic power outages continually interrupting the internet platforms. Initially, Jean-Pierre insisted they keep up with their studies, but with no available mentoring, it went by the wayside.

The virus was tightening its grip. As time went on, the local food mart's shelves had fewer items as vendors supplied less. Prices were high, and only folks who had means were able to get what they needed when it was available. Luckily, Jean-Pierre's dad had stashed quite a bit of money away underneath a bed mattress, making it possible to continue to purchase the necessities for an indefinite amount of time. Others weren't as lucky and found themselves reduced to stealing for their survival.

Since the Berger home had long been paid off, Jean-Pierre had no major debt to worry about. The house was easy to maintain, and when the power grid was down, the wood stove kept it warm and came in handy for cooking and heating hot water for bathing. During those black-out times, Kate was scared. She didn't like the darkness or the extreme silence, but Jean-Pierre put her at ease by making it fun. He'd pretend they were on a camping adventure even though they were just inside the house. Those nights he'd sleep on the floor next to her bed so she could rest peacefully.

They both remained healthy, keeping a roof over their head, but Jean-Pierre constantly worried about it. He had no idea what they'd do if and when evacuation orders came down or where they'd go. Some of the surrounding neighbors had already left, their homes boarded up, but wouldn't stay vacant long. Transients would soon take them over, which was even more concerning for Jean-Pierre. He worried they'd try to break-in and take some of their goods. All he and Kate could do was keep their heads up, stay alert and try to stay positive. Six months into adjusting to the post-pandemic changes, Darcy Couture came into their life.

The Boys... Darcy Couture

Darcy Edwin Couture, a transient from the outskirts of Montreal, was 17 at the time he arrived in Vermont. The once bustling metropolis had an European charm surrounding it, officially founded by the French in 1642 which added to its romantic charm, attracting lots of tourists.

The Couture family had lived in one of its largest semi-suburban neighborhoods, just northeast of downtown. The single-family three-story buildings were made of cobblestone and brick. There were streets full of them, lined up side by side, with rod iron fences surrounding a small patch of grass in the front of each entrance way. Since there were no backyards, most of the neighborhood kids either played in the not-so-busy one-way streets or at a local park.

Darcy was an only child and lived with both his parents until age five when he lost his mom to cancer. His dad never remarried and they stayed together in the same house. They were close, almost like brothers, and did a lot of fun things together. On weekends and vacation times, they escaped the city to camp, fish, hike, attend ball games, and ventured on short trips exploring the Canadian lands. Other than that, they spent their free time at home playing video games, watching movies and hanging out.

In the early part of 2023, just as Darcy turned 17, his dad came back from a business trip with an uncontrollable cough. When he went to the doctor, he was immediately hospitalized. Due to the strict visitation policies that hospitals were bound by, Darcy wasn't allowed to see him. In fact, he never did see him again. He died a couple weeks later.

Five months later, the virus invaded nearby structures, including homes on his street. Before Darcy knew what was happening, a whole block of them were targeted to be burned, his included. Darcy had no choice but to leave. He threw a bunch of clothes and some other personal items into his backpack then headed out to the unknown. Some of his friends let him couch surf until stronger social distancing restrictions sent him to the streets to fend for himself.

Montreal's cell towers and power grids constantly experienced sporadic outages, making it difficult to stay informed about all the destruction the virus was causing throughout the planet. Hearsay from trusted folks who traveled around wasn't reliable, but it was the only information anyone had to go on. Unfortunately, some only shared what they knew others wanted to hear, so the devastation was downplayed. Rumors spread that the United States were less affected and had an abundance of food supplies along with plenty of safe shelters. The misleading news caused many to rush to the border only to find they were deceived. In many cases, it was worse. Most of them never made it back.

Being homeless and left to fend for himself was far from easy. Darcy felt alone and scared more times than not. Occasionally, a couple of his friends snuck him into their homes, giving him food and a place to get a restful night of sleep. He more than appreciated their generosity, even though they all knew the risk. Darcy knew he had a big challenge ahead of him and had to figure out what was next for his future.

Every day Darcy thought about crossing the border into the states. But to do so required proper identification, and he failed to grab his passport or birth certificate before his old homestead was demolished. Word on the street was that the border crossings were heavily guarded by armed forces, and those that tried to cross without any identification were detained or even shot. That meant he had little to no chance of getting onto US soil. Darcy wasn't sure how much of it was true and wasn't sure he was willing to take the chance to find out, yet he knew he had to find a safe place to call home and it was no longer in Montreal.

One night while Darcy was at his friend's home, he overheard a conversation between his parents. They were trying to figure out a way to get across the US border and mentioned two small towns that rested on either side of it, only separated by the Tomifobia River. Darcy had learned about the river in school, that it was a primary source of Lake Massawippi. The parents had talked about the 140 acres of woods and trails that ran along its west side, mainly between Stanstead, Quebec, and Beebe Plain, Vermont. They were pretty sure there were many easy, unguarded crossing points there.

After giving it much thought, and determining there weren't any other options, Darcy decided to embark on the journey. He figured the worst that would happen was he wouldn't make it across the border and would have to find a safe haven elsewhere, if he weren't shot first. Of all the things Darcy kept in his backpack after his father died, was an old North American map book of the New England states. His dad had collected many of them over the years. Darcy knew it would eventually come in handy, since the border was so close.

Like his dad, the United States had always intrigued him from an early age, especially New York City. Since Darcy spent his whole life living in Montreal, he wanted to experience life in a bigger place, the one that professed to never sleep. His dad had promised to take him there when he turned 18, and Darcy had been looking forward to sharing that experience with him. He decided that would be his end goal, even if it was solo. Darcy spent time mapping out a route to get to the river, then across the border and onward to The Big Apple.

The night before his planned departure, Darcy headed over to one of his friend's homes and was greeted by many more of them. They gifted him with plenty of essentials, including a new tent, backpack, sleeping bag, even new sneakers. A few others showed up the next morning for the sendoff. Everyone knew the chances of seeing each other again were highly unlikely.

Darcy calculated that the journey to the river would take between three and four days on foot, depending on what he ran into. Some challenges that put him at risk were mainly running out of money, weather issues, and just traveling solo. He wasn't sure where he'd find additional food if he ran out or shelter if the weather got bad, but stowing away in abandoned buildings and stealing from any available food sources was no longer foreign to him; only the territory would be.

Darcy was a small yet stocky guy who stood about five-foot-five-inches. He had sandy blonde hair, pulled back in a short ponytail, and bluish green eyes that glistened in the sunlight. His thin yet muscular upper body supported the heavy travel backpack that he carried around. Dressed in an old pair of worn-out jeans, a white t-shirt, and a blue plaid flannel shirt wrapped tightly around his waist, he looked like a backpacker off to conquer a wanderer's bucket list.

It was midday, and the sun was casting down its warm rays upon him. The town of Stanstead wasn't far. There wasn't a soul in sight. Most of the houses on his path had been demolished to prevent the virus from lingering; those that were still standing were boarded up. It was obvious many of them had been taken over by either homeless transients or vagrants. There were occasional disputes and physical fights over the properties when newcomers tried to push out current squatters and take possession. The illegal owners were always on guard and ready to fight to stay at any cost.

Darcy was well aware of suspicious onlookers as he passed by them and knew some were peeking out at him through the cracks of boarded windows. Others sat in plain view on porches and front lawns, curtly glaring at him. Some even sported rifles, picking them up as he got closer to the property, knowing the threat would keep him moving. It certainly worked and also warded off a majority of other trespassers. Darcy knew better than to slow his pace down or even look their way when he walked by the properties. Finding friendly neighbors, or anybody for that matter, that would help others out had long gone by the wayside. Darcy certainly learned it the hard way.

Even when he thought he was safe, and out of sight, he wasn't. Everybody was out for themselves and everyone else just had to fuck off if they got in their way.

The Barn

Darcy had found some abandoned properties to stay in while in the Montreal area. But that didn't mean they were always a safe roof to shelter under. He found that out early into his homelessness on one rainy, cool evening.

It had been drizzling a good part of the day, so he and his stuff were wet and cold. In an overgrown wheat field, about 500-yards off the main road, Darcy spotted a dilapidated barn that looked as though it had been abandoned for years, and decided to check it out. Small pieces of red paint still clung to parts of the worn gray wood on the crooked structure. A small muddy path led Darcy to the half-opened door.

As he cautiously approached, he hollered, "Is anybody here? Hello, anybody here?"

Not getting a response, he hollered a few more times then decided to make his way inside. The floors were worn, with some holes scattered about where the wood had broken apart, unprotected from the seasons' changing weather. Darcy tried to slide the door closed behind him, but it was locked in place by old rusty wheels that no longer moved along the top rail. Dusk had fallen, but the empty barn still had some natural light peeking inside from cracks in the wooden walls. It was enough to see around. Inside was slightly damp from the open door and glassless windows. The piles of loose hay were strewn about and filled the air with musty smells, causing him to sneeze As he surveyed the room, he noticed a couple horse stalls and a few pieces of rusty farm equipment off to one side. Above him, there was a loft but no ladder to it.

Convinced nobody else was around, Darcy walked to the far end of the barn and found a place in a corner, shielded from any cold or rain coming in from the open spaces. He decided it was an inviting enough place to rest his tired body for the night. After taking off his backpack, he grabbed a nearby pitchfork and began collecting some of the old dusty hay, heaping enough of it into the corner, creating a soft cushion for his sleeping bag to lay on. He got his last apple and a power bar from his backpack, ate it, then plopped down on his bedding and quickly fell asleep to the sound of the rain pounding against the tin roof.

A couple of hours later, after the darkness of night fell over the barn, six motorcycles arrived on the scene. The path was too muddy for them to drive down, so they parked on the main road and trudged through the muck to make their way out of the rain. They were already three sheets to the wind from chugging down shots of liquor they had stolen from a local store. The barn was one of the group's regular stomping grounds when they were in the area and, up until that night, were the only ones that used it. They were anxious to get inside, party and get some rest.

The six motorcycle guys had been hanging out in the vicinity ever since they were de-patched from the Montreal Sons of Arches motorcycle club. The organization and its 500 plus members had been around for a few decades but recently downgraded its headcount after being hit hard by the virus, and the mandated evacuation orders. They lost their building, and a lot of the club's soldiers.

As the club continued to dwindle in numbers, smaller groups formed and frequently traveled together to some of the motorcycle festivals and other activities throughout the region. The six street thugs were the most feared bunch that roamed about due to the merciless havoc they created wherever they went. They had no morals or boundaries, especially with women, were disrespectful of property, and rumored to have killed several folks in nasty fights over small conflicts. Their continuous controversial crime sprees created unrest among the club.

The Sons of Arches, as a whole, were friendly and accepted by civilians. They frowned upon any violence used to pacify a quick fix and were quite aware of the ill spread rumors regarding the street thugs' outlandish actions. Eventually, the Sons of Arches washed their hands of the thugs, banished them from the club, and took back their patches.

Shortly afterward, the six of them took off on their own, floating about the general area, quickly becoming well-known by the locals, who classified them as 'street thugs'. They bullied their way into houses claimed by other transients and fought, even killed, to gain possession of others, sometimes for as little as just one night's stay.

Jeremy, the leader of the six-pack, was the biggest bully of them all. He stood close to six-feet-five-inches, weighing close to 300 pounds. His looks alone were enough to get his way when he wanted it. Jeremy had a tight grip on his own small crew and had no problem handing out demands to them, executing extreme consequences when orders weren't carried out his way.

As the motley crew approached the barn door, Jeremy signaled for everyone to stop and pointed to Blitz, one of the less aggressive members, to go in and check it out. Once Blitz gave thumbs up that all was clear, Jeremy snapped his fingers and motioned everyone else to follow him inside.

It was raining cats and dogs, but some light still shone through the cracks of the barn wall, enough that they could see the familiar farm tractor, balers, and the outline of the horse stalls.

"We'll stay here tonight, boys," Jeremy stated. "The rain should be gone by morning."

"Sure, Boss! It feels like home," Blitz chuckled, happy to be back at one of their regular squatting spots and out of the rain.

"I'm fucking beat," Jeremy sarcastically snickered as he plopped down on one of the nearby hay piles. "So, whoever has the liquor, get your ass over here with it right now!"

For the next 45 minutes, they sat around chugging down more shots and shared obscene stories while they figured out where they were headed the next day.

"So, Jer, I'd like to get to the states sooner than later. We've been dragging our feet, and I'd certainly like to get myself some of that American pussy," Chug announced as he belched, then made a sexual hand gesture while slurping on his bottle of rum.

"You're an asshole," Blitz responded as he took a sip from his whisky bottle.

Chug had known Jeremy since they were kids and had become his right-hand man since they formed the small group. For the most part, he was mild mannered, at least until he filled his bloodstream with ounces of 80 proof whisky. Then all bets were off. Originally Chug had designs to run their newly formed group but decided to let Jeremy take the reins after he threw a couple volatile tantrums about it. Chug took the right-hand seat and ended up as the one who consistently cleaned up Jeremy's messes. Chug tried to keep the peace the best he could, that is, whenever he wasn't part of the madness.

"I'm with ya, Chugeroo," Jury piped in, mimicking Chug's sexual hand gesture.

They all broke out in laughter, getting more obnoxious by the minute.

"That's the plan, you bunch of punk asses," Jeremy replied, laying back against a couple hay bales, almost finished with his whisky bottle. "We're going to get the fuck out of here and hit the states! At this point, I hate to say it, but I think we've overstayed our welcome."

"Here, here," they all chanted, chugging down more alcohol.

Jeremiah Stanley Dubois was pushing 50 and never knew what an easy life was all about. He didn't have a sympathetic bone in his body for others who experienced the same type of harshness that had been handed to him. His behaviors didn't stray far from his upbringing, having been ignored, beaten, and abused through most of it. Both parents had been alcoholics, heavy drug users, and constantly partied. They left him to fend for himself before he could even walk, sometimes weeks at a time. His nine-year-old sister was left in charge, barely able to take care of herself.

Jeremy was a victim of physical and sexual assault by random transients who crashed at their apartment for weeks on end, partying the whole time. He was bullied and kicked around by peers. At age six, Some of partiers thought it was funny to give him alcohol and drugs and watch him spin out. It went on for years and got to the point he partied right along with them. By the time he reached his mid-teens, Jeremy had enough and had to get away from the constant abuse. He already spent most of his time on the streets but decided to live among the homeless, feeling safer there than in his own home. About a year later he found his way into the care of the motorcycle club.

Jeremy never carried a rank when he was with the Sons of Arches, so leadership was new to him when he and Chug formed their own group. He refused to take a club 'pet name' like all the other members; most called him just Jer. His uncontrollable antics occasionally landed him some stints in prison, which only hardened him more.

"I gotta take a piss," Bunyan announced as he got up to find a place to relieve himself.

Bunyan was one of the more abrasive out of the six, and got along well with Jeremy, both similar in nature. Since it was downpouring outside, Bunyan stumbled over to the far end of the barn, unzipped his pants, and started to urinate into a corner. Just as he zipped them back up, something caught his attention out of the corner of his eye. It was an unfamiliar sight and looked like a pile of blankets thrown on top of a bunch of hay. When he staggered over to check it out, he discovered someone laying there, sound asleep. Not sure what to do, he whistled for Jeremy and the others to join him so he could show off his find.

"Well, well, what do we have here?" Jeremy smirkingly asked as Chug grabbed the backpack out from under Darcy's head, ruthlessly waking him up.

It took a few seconds for Darcy's eyes to adjust to the lighting, he could barely make out the three thugs that were standing over him. As his eyes focused more, he saw their long, straggly hair and beards that almost touched his face as they leaned closer, over him. He smelled a strong odor of alcohol and saw a small skull tattoo on each of their foreheads. Darcy felt his stomach turn inside out. He knew who they were.

Bunyan had already picked up a pitchfork while Jeremy and Blitz were squatting down next to Darcy. Chug handed the backpack to Jury, who started ransacking it, throwing Darcy's stuff everywhere. Darcy knew they were most likely looking for money or alcohol, neither of which he had. He also knew they were bad news, which made his heart beat faster in his chest.

Darcy quickly sat straight up and forcefully yet cautiously said, "Hey, leave that alone. That's my stuff, and believe me, there's nothing in there you want!"

The thugs just chuckled as they glared at him. Darcy felt panic flood through his entire body. His hands were sweaty and he felt his body tremble as if he were cold, but he wasn't. The momentary fear that flooded through him was they were going to beat the crap out of him or even worse.

"Please! I'm no threat to you guys. I just found this place to get out of the rain and get some sleep. I won't bother you at all, and I'll be on my way first thing in the morning," his voice cracked with uncertainty, his vulnerability was obvious and he was afraid they'd take advantage of it.

"What did you say there, boy?" Jeremy gruffly asked as he shimmied himself closer to Darcy's face.

"I said I don't want any trouble, so please, just let me be. I'll even get my stuff and leave now if that's what you want," he sheepishly replied, then started to stand up to gather his stuff.

Bunyan had been standing off to the side, flipping the pitchfork from hand to hand, then decided to push the rusty metal spikes against Darcy's stomach and sarcastically said, "Whoa, hold your horses, little boy. You ain't going nowhere 'til we tell you that you can go."

Darcy quickly fell back on the pile of hay and tried to scoot as far away from sharp metal pressing into his skin, but the barn wall blocked his attempt.

Blitz stood up, then placed his black leather boot down on Darcy's thigh as he yelled, "Yeah, kid, you ain't going nowhere!"

They all started laughing as Chug went to re-check the torn apart backpack, poked around the stuff that was scattered about, and announced, "Yeah, Jer, there ain't jack shit in this piece of shit backpack."

Jeremy stood up to check it out as well, then chuckled before getting nose to nose with Darcy as he said in a frustrated yet playful voice, "What? No prize for daddy here? That doesn't make me very happy."

Jury mimicked him, then kicked Darcy's side hard, causing him to wince in excruciating pain as he rolled himself into a fetal position. Jeremy glared at Jury and told him to back off. After one more brutal kick to his side, Jury obeyed, not wanting Jeremy's wrath to turn on him.

"Well, let's say it's your lucky day, boy," Jeremy sneered as he glared at Darcy laying in a ball, cowering in the corner, then yelled at Chug and Blitz, "Get his punk ass and shit out of here now."

Blitz immediately bent down, grabbed Darcy, and heaved him over his shoulder, then carted him across the barn out into the cool misty air.

He recklessly dumped him down onto the muddied pathway while Chug and Bunyan threw all his belongings next to him.

With one more kick to his side, Blitz backed away as Chug screamed, "Now go! Get your punk ass out of here, you little shit."

"And don't come back!" Blitz hollered.

Then the six of them stood by the barn door, watching and waiting for him to leave. For a few moments, Darcy continued to lay in the cold mucky mess, stunned by all that had just happened, trying to figure out his next move. It was the middle of the night, and he was afraid the thugs weren't done with him, but he had to make his move.

As he started to get up, the excruciating pain in his side caused him to temporarily fall back into the mud puddles. The street thugs broke out in laughter, hollering obscenities at him until he finally got up, gathered his stuff, and faded out of sight. It was then he counted his lucky blessings to be alive but knew at that point, no place was really safe.

Stanstead, Quebec

The trek to Stanstead, for the most part, was smooth sailing. Darcy found some open fields where he put up his tent and rested alongside others who were on similar missions to find a better place to survive. As luck had it, they all had food to share with him. After about five uneventful days on foot, longer than expected, he arrived in Stanstead, where almost immediately and quite by mishap, he met up with Jean-Pierre and Kate Berger.

Shortly after arriving in town, Darcy found himself standing in front of the local college. Most of the buildings were still intact, with only a few piles of burned rubble scattered about. The Stanstead College dated back to the late 1800s and once was a private boarding school for grades 7-12 that housed about 240 boys and girls from around the world. The first wave of the virus closed its doors, sending kids back to their homes to continue with online courses until the second wave totally shut that learning platform down.

Darcy decided to check out the campus and find a building that he could chill in for the night. In the new world of homelessness and uncertainties, most abandoned school campuses were deemed some of the safer shelters for transients. Threats were much lower since the street riff-raff didn't have any interest in staying in them. But the campuses were just that, transient places, not meant to full-time in. Little to no security patrolled the areas. The stays were an extreme risk since at any time, the virus could find its way into the buildings and attach itself to the abandoned shells and wait for its prey.

Darcy found himself standing on the unmanicured green grounds just in front of the main campus building, then paused for a moment and took off his backpack. He breathed in some of the fresh air and was about to sit down to rest his weary legs when out of nowhere, a soccer ball rolled in front of him, stopping right at his feet. Not seeing anyone else around, he bent over and picked it up. Then, out of nowhere, he heard a young girl shouting at him.

"That's mine!" the high-pitched voice hollered, and the next thing he knew, she was standing right in front of him.

Kate was a short, mid-sized young girl with dirty brown hair worn in a long braid that looked as though it had not been maintained for a few days. She wore a pair of old jean shorts and an oversized blue t-shirt that hung partly off her shoulder. Her face and hands appeared like they had not been washed for some time. She looked up at him and smiled as she reached out for the ball.

Then, once again out of nowhere, a loud, angry, voice filled the air, "Kate, what the hell are you doing? Get over here now!"

Darcy quickly followed the soundtrack to his left and spotted a tall, lanky guy walking rapidly toward him from one of the clusters of overgrown spruce trees. Darcy watched his dark brown hair fall over his eyes and continually bounce about as he angrily shook his head back and forth demanding the young girl go to him. There was panic in the little girl's face, leaving some doubt in Darcy's mind that she even knew the furious guy. He was in no mood to get entangled in any type of brawl over a family issue or any other.

Darcy quickly asked Kate, "Do you know him?"

"Of course she knows me! I'm her brother! And who the hell are you?" the hostile teen blurted out as he got closer.

"Whoa, I mean no harm to her or anyone Bro," Darcy responded, feeling a lump form in his throat. "This ball just rolled over to me. I picked it up and was just going to hand it back to her, that's all!" He turned to Kate and said, "Here you go, little girl."

Before Darcy could blink an eye, the guy smacked the ball out of both of their hands during the attempted handoff as he shouted, "Don't touch that, Kate!"

As the ball bounced across the grass, Jean-Pierre pointed his finger at Darcy and yelled, "And you, get away from her!" Then he grabbed Kate and held her close.

Darcy was taken back by his abruptness even though he knew the guy was most likely only worried about his little sister talking to a stranger. Neither of them knew who he was, so Darcy decided to try to put them at ease before the situation got out of hand.

"Hey man, sorry to worry you. I mean no harm whatsoever! I'm Darcy and just passing through. I hoofed it down here from Montreal and plan to head into the states," he stated.

"So why are you standing here then and not moving on? And who else is with you?" Jean-Pierre rudely asked, still riled up as he held Kate tightly in front of him.

"It's just me. I've been on my own for about a year since my dad passed away. Really man, sorry for the scare," he said softly, keeping his eyes focused on Jean-Pierre, then continued, "I plan to head to New York City, you know the one that never sleeps." He chuckled as he noticed Jean-Pierre was smiling slightly. "Since this town rests on the river that has the easiest crossing, well, that's why I'm here and need to take a break before I head across it."

For a few moments, they stood in silence, basically sizing each other up. Darcy felt the tension subside as he watched Jean-Pierre's eyes welt up. A quick blink let one tear escape as he slowly let go of Kate and responded.

"Look, sorry about yelling at you and all but one can't be too careful these days. I'm sure you understand." Darcy nodded in agreement as Jean-Pierre continued, "And yeah, I get it. Lots of folks pass through here to get to the other side. Sorry again for my over the top reaction!"

Darcy felt relieved they came to an understanding and responded, "No worries. Completely understand. I'm just looking for a place to find some food and to sleep for the night. I've been on the road for five days, a day or two longer than I expected. I thought this campus might be a safe place to hunker down," he paused for a moment, watching Jean-Pierre's face soften, then asked, "Maybe you have some suggestions?"

Kate looked at her brother and asked, "Can I go get my ball now?"

They all laughed, pleased they found some common ground as Kate ran off to retrieve it.

Jean-Pierre extended his out to Darcy and formally introduced himself, "Hey, I'm Jean-Pierre and you already met my little sister Kate. Look, we have some food over at our place, and you can rack out there for the night if you want. It's about a ten-minute walk from here. And … I know what it's like to lose family members, so sorry, man."

Even though the border crossing into Beebe Plain, Vermont was only about two and half miles from the Berger home, Darcy didn't leave the next day as planned, or the next week. Months went by as the three of them settled into a comfortable routine in Stanstead. That was, until Kate got sick.

Kate

It started with a little cough. Kate came inside one day from playing by the Tomifobia River, where she spent most of her time during the warm months. The river that divided the two countries was just down the hill from their backyard. Jean-Pierre made Kate promise not to cross it or swim in it, especially if she was alone. He was most worried that she would get caught in an undercurrent, or get kidnapped, or even attacked by unknown transients constantly crossing over the border. Kate promised him she wouldn't step off of the riverbank, and he trusted her.

For the most part, she listened to him, up until she met some new friends from the other side of the river and started hanging out with them. The kids came from the Vermont side, and crossed the river at one of its shallow points, to play with Kate. Since most of Kate's school friends and town playmates had either moved or fell victim to the virus, the river kids were her only contacts left. Kate needed the contact, the laughter, the hugs, the fun times, and they became a welcomed staple in her little life.

After always playing on her side, the river kids eventually wanted her to cross it to play on their side. Kate knew she wasn't supposed to but had a weak moment and did. The whole time, she was worried that Jean-Pierre was looking for her and couldn't handle the anxiety it caused, so she never did it again. Kate expected the river kids to give her a hard time over it, but they didn't and continued to cross the river to play on her turf.

Kate had dealt with alot for her young age as so much had changed in her little world after the second wave of the virus hit, including Jean-Pierre. Initially, the two had gotten closer after the loss of their twin brothers, especially when their mother wasn't able to initially be around the family after their death. But as more of the Bergers were taken by the virus, Jean-Pierre carried the weight of the world on his shoulders, trying to deal with the transition the best he could. Kate knew that, but didn't know what to do to help make it better. She rarely saw him laugh and eventually, they started drifting apart, hardly spending any time together. He became stricter, even more so than she remembered her parents to be.

When Darcy arrived, things seemed to get better for a while. Jean-Pierre laughed a lot more, wasn't as strict with Kate and initially included her in some of their activities. But as the two boys got more into playing video games, she found herself entertaining herself. Jean-Pierre seemed less worried about what she was doing and rarely checked up on her. Kate didn't mind, it just meant she could play more with the river kids.

Despite Jean-Pierre's warnings for her to stay away from others, especially those she didn't know, Kate was never worried that anything bad would happen to her. Just a few days earlier, before the cough, a couple of her river friends didn't show up with the rest of them. The others shared that the two girls got sick and died. As distraught as Kate was when she heard the news, she had no concept of what it meant for the rest of them as they hugged and consoled each other.

It wasn't long after the cough when Kate became bedridden with a high fever and breathing issues. Jean-Pierre was beside himself, having seen the symptoms way too many times and couldn't believe it was happening to his sister. The Stanstead hospital had closed for lack of workers, along with a few other local medical facilities. There was no place to take her.

For the most part, Jean-Pierre thought he had done a good job taking care of Kate despite the variables that they had to deal with. He kept her sheltered, fed, and so he thought, away from any dangers that could have carried the virus to her. The day he caught her ready to take the ball from Darcy, was when he realized she disregarded everything he told her about taking risks. He had thought she understood what the dangers were, but apparently she didn't. He realized he never should have stopped checking in on her like he did or he would have known about the river kids. He hated himself for that.

Jean-Pierre knew his sister had always been overly trusting. Ever since she first learned to walk it had always been a challenge to keep her away from strangers. Kate wanted to befriend everyone that crossed her path. Even their parents had concerns that her sense of adventure clouded any judgment regarding right and wrong. She was far from a loner, even though her life eventually depended on it. She needed to be surrounded by lots of activity, and even knowing things were a risk, she didn't back off. All Jean-Pierre could do at that point was admire her for her strength and playfulness as he held her quiet, cold body in his arms. He felt he owed her that.

When his little sister passed, Jean-Pierre was devastated. The only person he had left was Darcy. Over the next couple of months, Darcy helped him bottle up his despair and convinced him it was time to find out what was on the other side of the river. They both hoped there was a better life out there, at least one away from all the pain they had been through over the last three years.

The Meeting

It was early fall, 2023, when the boys said goodbye to Stanstead. With Kate lying peacefully next to the rest of his family, it was time for Jean-Pierre and Darcy to cross the border. They fixed up a couple road bikes that had been stored in the garage and mapped out the best route to get to Burlington, Vermont. They heard that the city was the most densely populated in the state and hosted a large distribution hub. Their plan was to hang out there until the Spring, then head to NYC together.

Even though it was only an eight to nine hour bike ride to reach their destination, they decided to make it a two-day trip. Neither were in a big hurry, wanting to check things out along the way. Knowing once the house was vacant that it wouldn't take long for transients to break-in to take ownership, made Jean-Pierre sick to his stomach.

As he packed up a few of his personal items and looked around the house, he felt panic and uncertainty set in. It was the only place he ever lived. He could still hear his siblings running about, the clanking of pans in the kitchen as his mother prepared dinner and the tv loudly blaring as his father watched the evening news. He still couldn't believe they all were gone. But he knew it was time to leave all the pain and turmoil behind, and finally move on, especially before the third wave of the virus arrived.

"Well, this is it," Jean-Pierre said, closing the porch door for the last time.

Darcy felt his despair as he put his arm around his shoulder and said, "You'll always have the memories, Jean-Pierre. Nobody or nothing can take those from you. And, just know it's been a welcomed stay here for me, and I will carry that with me as well."

Jean-Pierre looked across the street towards the cemetery where his family was buried then said, "We probably should've gotten out of dodge when you first got here instead of getting too damn comfortable.

I know that had cost Kate her life. I just don't know how I'll ever get over that."

Darcy thought for a moment then responded, "Hey, I'm sorry what happened and that she's not making this trip with us, but come on, man, let's not go down that path. We have no idea if that's true. And never will, so just remember the good times and don't over analyze it." Darcy patted him on the back, paused for a moment then asked, "Are you ready, my friend?"

After one last glance around the property, they put on their backpacks, made sure all their supplies were secured on the bike racks they had built, hopped on the bikes and headed out.

In no time, they were staring across a shallow part of the river, at Beebe Plain, Vermont. It was already early afternoon by the time they crossed and got onto US soil so they decided to ride for only a few hours then find a place to pitch their tent. They decided to stop in Morristown, a small rural, mountainous town, in the middle of seemingly, nowhere.

There, they found a small field just across the street from an old boarded-up farmhouse that looked like a good place to rest. The back of the property opened up to a small body of water where several tents were already spread around it. The boys decided it looked safe enough to pitch their tent alongside the others.

The sun still had a couple of hours before it set, and the early Fall air guaranteed a cool, almost frosty evening. The leaves were almost at their peak colors displaying a picturesque site throughout the Green Mountain area. Once the tent was set up, they made a small campfire and sat around it watching the sun slowly disappear over the pond.

"Kind of all seems like a dream, doesn't it?" Darcy asked as they warmed their hands over the remaining coals, watching some of the neighbors put out their fires and retire for the evening.

"Yeah, this whole damn mess still doesn't feel real. I can't believe it's been almost four years since I lost my two little brothers," Jean-Pierre paused for a moment, stirring up some of the hot coals with a stick then said, "And my parents and my two sisters. What a fucked up world we live in right now."

"I hear you loud and clear," Darcy agreed thinking about his own dad as he watched the moon start to rise up over the mountains. "Let's just hope we've seen the worst of it."

"No shit," Jean-Pierre said, shaking his head. "There's got to be something better out there. I mean what the fuck."

The air was cool enough to add a blanket of frost across the field, so they unloaded the bike racks and put all their stuff in the tent to keep it dry. After they checked to make sure the campfire was completely out, they called it a night.

The next morning the boys woke up to people yelling just outside of their tent. They quickly got up to see what all the commotion was about. It took a minute for their eyes to adjust from the brightness of the frosted field glistening as the early morning sun danced upon it. Then they spotted several people standing outside of the other tents, yelling at each other. From what the boys gathered, somebody was missing some possessions.

They decided to check out what was going on. As they got outside Darcy suddenly yelled, "What the hell happened here?"

"What? Where?" Jean-Pierre asked as he went over to the side of their tent, joining Darcy standing by one of the bikes.

"Where is my fucking bike?" he yelled, discovering it was gone.

The other campers looked their way, then one of the men strutted over, and gruffly asked, "Don't tell me, you're missing something too?"

"Sure am! My bike's gone!" Darcy exclaimed. "What the fuck is going on? We're out in the middle of nowhere! Who the fuck would take it? Or is this some kind of sick joke?"

"Afraid it ain't no joke, son. It's those damn vagrants! They're as thick as fleas around here," the man loudly sputtered, checking out the remaining bike then strutted back to the others to fill them in.

"Vagrants? You've got to be kidding me!" Darcy barked after him, "Unbelievable! In the middle of fucking nowhere, vagrants?" Then he looked over at Jean-Pierre and angrily asked, "Do you think it was one of them?"

Jean-Pierre just shrugged his shoulders not knowing what to say. They both were aware of the few onlookers staring over at them. Jean-Pierre plopped down on the frosty grass, holding his head to his knees.

"Well, I suppose the positive is that at least they didn't take them both," Darcy said, trying to stay positive as he stood in front of Jean-Pierre, looking off across the field, "and all our other supplies are safe. We'll make this work. It'll just take us a bit longer."

The boys knew that meant the rest of the trip would be by foot, and another seventeen hours instead of five. It also meant at least one more overnight before reaching the city. They loaded most of the belongings on the one bike, planning to take turns pushing it.

Just as they were getting ready to leave one of the camp neighbors hollered over at them, "Hey guys, come on over for some hot coffee and pancakes before you head out."

At first the boys weren't sure if it was a good idea, not knowing if the thief was among them, but they were cold and hungry so they accepted the invite.

"Where are you boys headed?" one of them asked as they all settled around a big campfire.

"Burlington," Jean-Pierre replied.

"Well, we've met a few heading that way. Makes sense with the distribution center there and all," he replied.

"Where are you coming from?" another asked.

"Stanstead, just over the border, "Jean-Pierre answered again.

"That's a hell of a hike," another responded.

"Yeah, well if my damn bike wasn't stolen, it wouldn't be that big of a deal. It was supposed to only take us eight hours total, and if we hadn't stopped here, we'd be there," Darcy curtly said.

"Look at them," one of the women piped in, breaking the tension, "They're young bucks! They'll be just fine. A little walking has never hurt anybody!"

Everyone laughed and chatted as they finished up breakfast. Once the boys were finally ready to go, everyone wished them luck and bid them farewell.

Two uneventful days later, in the early evening hours, Darcy and Jean-Pierre finally arrived downtown Burlington. They stumbled upon a small park, near the lake, filled with about 400 people of all ages who were intently listening to a young girl standing on a half-dilapidated stage, addressing them through a megaphone.

Battery Park's grounds were covered with patches of green grass surrounded by stalky maple trees displaying their vibrant, rustic colors. Some of the folks were sitting on the crumbling stonewall that led to an embankment overlooking Lake Champlain's shoreline. There were a few worn totem poles still standing about that were carved out of the park's old trees by some transient tourists a few decades earlier. Some popup tents were at the further end, and several children ran around, oblivious to the message the girl was giving.

That was the first time the boys laid eyes on Rosa. They noted that she wasn't much older than they were and watched as her long blonde hair flowed about in the continuous cool breeze. Her small yet poised body stood firmly as she excitedly addressed the audience. Jean-Pierre and Darcy decided to hang out in the back of the crowd to hear what she had to say.

"We're all just living these moments in the endless scheme of time right now. Ones that we're unsure of and ones that are running out as the third wave of the virus gets closer. We must make these moments count. You've all been so loyal and supportive about the migration plan that we're about to embark upon. It's finally time we begin preparing for the journey to the better lands!"

The young girl paused for a moment looking around at the crowd as they cheered, then continued.

"I know it's crazy to believe that the better lands are virus free. I'm not even sure if the rumors are true or not, but with Spring just around the corner, we'll soon find out. From the information we got from random folks that passed through here and the articles we've researched at the library, I believe we're on the right path. It all must mean something, and that something is definitely worth checking out and taking a risk on, right?"

"Amen to that," shouted someone from the crowd.

"It sure is! We've got this," shouted another.

"Let's hit the road now," screamed another as excitement again fled through the crowd.

Once everyone settled back down, Rosa continued, "The only thing we really have to worry about is settlers that might already be there, and they may not want to share their territory. I have no idea which parts are claimed, if any, so we could potentially walk into some difficult situations. We just need to be prepared, one way or another!"

The crowd interrupted, shouting out encouragement.

"We got this!"

"We'll share with them!"

"Let's get the ball rolling!"

Rosa continued, talking a bit louder into the blow horn, "Okay, settle down, everyone! The plan is to head out of here in early March, and there's lots to get done between now and then."

The boys weren't sure what was going on, but the crowd got more energized, cheering and jumping up and down the more the young girl spoke. As they stood behind the bulk of the folks, Jean-Pierre noticed an older gentleman by himself, standing in front of them.

"Hey, excuse me," Jean-Pierre asked, tapping on the man's shoulder. "I was wondering if you could tell us what's going on here, and who's that girl on the stage?"

The man half turned around, sarcastically yelling over the unsettled crowd, "You don't know who she is?" Then, after briefly eyeballing the boys, responded, "You must not be from around here! If you were, you'd know that's Rosa! She's the one that put together a plan to bring us all to the better lands! Apparently it's something you may want to check out," then turned away to continue listening to her.

Darcy and Jean-Pierre looked at each other, still confused about what was going on. This time Darcy decided to tap the man's shoulder then asked, "Excuse me, sir, what are the better lands?"

The man was clearly getting a bit aggravated with the interruptions as he spun around, abruptly saying, "I already told you to check it out. Now, if you don't mind, I'm trying to listen!" Then he moved a few feet away from the boys.

That only made them more than curious as they continued to listen to Rosa's enthusiastic voice channeling through the hand-held speaker, "As I've shared with some of you before from all that I've read, these virus free lands can be found in Kentucky, Missouri, Montana, and Wyoming. I know they're far from here and not easy to get to, especially on foot, but there's no other way. The best choice for us is Kentucky, which, by my calculations, will take about 35 days or so."

The crowd broke out in jubilant rants, "Let's do this!"; "Kentucky rules!"; "better lands!"

Rosa waited for a moment, then continued, "I can't emphasize enough that this journey won't be easy. It'll be long and possibly treacherous at times. Most of our nights will be in tents. And we all can't go at once. We're way too big of a group and will need to break up into different teams which will be determined at a later date. Just know, for everyone who wants to go, you'll get there! Maybe not this first round so you'll need to be patient as we figure it out. But we are going to find these better lands and live better lives!"

The crowd excitedly cheered as if their team just scored in the Super Bowl.

Rosa continued, "In the next couple months, I'll share more about the migration plan. But here's some good information that I'm sure you'll all find interesting. These so-called better lands in Kentucky are actually surrounded by two huge lakes. The better lands, known as The Land Between The Lakes, is the largest inland peninsula in the US. I read that the area was initially evacuated when the pandemic first rolled through, unlike anywhere else. I don't know the reasoning, but I do know that nobody was even allowed back on the land until quite recently. I also read that very little property had been burned. Now, that is either good or bad as the virus could still be lurking about, but again, it's a risk you have to decide if you are willing to take. I believe that the better lands can very well be our destiny!"

Again, the crowd went wild, jumping up and down, chanting loudly over and over, "better lands; better lands; better lands…"

It was apparent the crowd was getting worked up, so Rosa decided it was a good time to end the meeting and shouted out, "To the better lands! And God willing that none of us will be subject to the virus ever again! Until our next meeting, stay safe! I love you all!"

At that, the crowd grew even more energetic, but once Rosa jumped off the stage, they slowly calmed down and started to disperse, heading off in different directions.

"That girl has got it going," Jean-Pierre said to Darcy as he shook his head, "I'm not entirely sure what's going on, but whatever it is, we should find out."

"Let's try to catch up with her," Darcy said as they both simultaneously started walking toward her.

Jean-Pierre couldn't help but to marvel at Rosa's spunk and youthfulness, and how she got the crowd to excitedly listen to her. He also was drawn to her beauty, her poise, and her ability to get so many of them to believe in the better lands. She knew something they didn't, and they wanted to find out what it was. So the boys waded through the leftover group gathered around her to introduce themselves.

"Excuse me," Darcy said, getting her attention. "We're very impressed with how you spoke to that large crowd."

"We sure were," Jean-Pierre agreed as he extended his hand to Rosa and said, "I'm Jean-Pierre, and this is Darcy. We just came across the Canadian border and landed here just in time to hear you!"

Rosa smiled as she shook their hands and replied, "I had no idea I had a fan base in Canada, and I guess you did make it just in time," she giggled then added, "I'm Rosa."

Upon first introductions, Rosa was a bit skeptical in carrying on a conversation with the boys as they asked a lot of questions about the better lands. Their faces were unfamiliar, and she knew there was a risk in telling the strangers too much. Spilling the beans was a good way to compromise everything. But the more they talked, the more she warmed up to them. Once she found out they had nowhere to go for the night, she offered to bring them back to the winter shelter until they decided what their next moves were. Jean-Pierre and Darcy gladly accepted. Rosa couldn't have been more thankful that they did.

Mr. Chuso

About a year after Rosa's father died, her mother received a foreclosure notice on their lakefront home. Rochelle no longer could make the large mortgage payments as funds were running out and she was already a few months behind. Given the circumstances the virus had thrust everyone into, the bank graciously gave her a six-month reprieve, but that had passed. Rochelle was between a rock and hard spot since her daughter was attending online school and had no childcare so she couldn't freely go find a job to support their expensive household. She tried to list the home with a local realtor, but it was no longer a sellers' market. It was inevitable they'd have to move.

There were no family members that Rochelle could rely on since both her and Bill's parents had died a few years earlier. Bill's younger brother, Jed, was the only one left, but they didn't have a close relationship and she hadn't seen him in years, since he moved to California.

Jed's free spirit was a product of the late 1960's flower child era. He never had a steady income or home base since graduating high school. Over the years, his dad had offered him work in their company business which Jed sometimes accepted, but his commitment remained sporadic, generally coming and going only when he needed money. Rochelle had suspected early on that he was heavily involved with drugs, due to his decreasing health and spending money as quickly as he got it. Then he'd disappear sometimes, months at times.

When Rochelle and Bill were first married, Jed periodically called Bill asking for money or a place to stay when he had nowhere else to go. After taking over the family business, Bill tried to get Jed to work with him, but he refused. Rochelle never understood why her husband continued to hand out money and a place to stay when nothing changed. Bill loved his brother and wanted to believe he'd eventually straighten his life out. Jed crushed that belief when stole a large amount of cash from their bedroom safe then took off in the middle of the night, disappearing for months. When Bill finally received a call from him asking for help again, he informed Jed that he was done. They never saw or spoke to each other again.

After Rochelle lost their home, she eventually moved into the Chuso family condo located on the outskirts of Burlington near Oakledge beach. Her and Rosa shared a bedroom and even though it was cramped and wasn't her own place, she enjoyed the fact it was close enough to the lake that at any given time, when outside, she heard the waves beat against the lakeshore. Those tiny moments made the circumstances tolerable despite all that was lost to get there.

Rochelle befriended Mrs. Chuso several years earlier, when they volunteered together at a local women's shelter. Livy Chuso was a spunky, short, plump lady in her mid-50s, filled with laughter and compassion for others. She also worked part-time as a bookkeeper for a local attorney's office to help with the household expenses. Occasionally, Rochelle and Livy grabbed coffee together at the end of their shifts and over time became good friends, yet weren't close enough to attend family dinners or events together. Their personal lives were completely opposite.

Right after Livy heard that Rochelle and her daughter had lost their home, she insisted on giving them a room in her condo, at least until they got on their feet. Livy didn't tell her husband about their new 'tenants' until the last minute, knowing that he would disapprove.

Mr. Chuso was never fond of any of the Wells, especially Rochelle. He generally referred to her as an uppity narcissistic bitch, mainly because of their upper-class status. He knew she came from money, even before she was married, yet never saw her dole out any to those in dire need at the shelter. Based on that alone, he felt she had no business volunteering there or even hanging out with his wife. He felt if push came to shove, Rochelle wouldn't give the shirt off her back to someone in need, quite the opposite of his generous wife.

Mr. Chuso was right. Rochelle did have money at one point. Not just from her marriage, but from her own family. She was born into a wealthy Canadian family, and grew up surrounded by maids and nannies, never having to lift a finger. In her later years, she was taken care of through a bottomless trust fund that was destined to be signed over to her daughter, but the pandemic's impact on the economy dried it up.

Despite Mr. Chuso's impression of Rochelle, she was kind and compassionate, and had donated thousands of dollars and items to the shelter, even helped furnish some of the victimized women's apartments. She also helped out with other community services, for those in need. After the pandemic arrived, and shortly after her husband's death, all the funds were frozen. She had no expendable cash, and then it was gone. But Mr. Chuso saw it differently and there was no changing his views.

Rochelle was always a bit uneasy around Mr. Chuso, knowing he didn't particularly care for her. But she felt the same toward him. He was loud, obnoxious, bossy, always dirty and smelling like whisky, when he'd pick Livy up from the shelter. There were times Rochelle questioned their relationship, occasionally spotting black and blue marks on his wife's arms, but never asked Livy about them.

Mr. Chuso saw how Rochelle looked at him anytime they were in each other's presence. He wasn't going to apologize for his blue cotton button-up and navy-blue khakis full of grease from a hard day's work at the auto shop. There were so many times she made his blood boil, that he had to contain himself from verbally lashing out at her. They never spoke, and both were fine with that. When Livy told Mr. Chuso that Rochelle and her daughter were moving in, he was beside himself.

The Chusos' two kids still lived at home and were finishing up online courses at a small, local college. They'd graduate that Spring. The family rarely went anywhere except to pick up food for the household; all other socializing was on hold due to the pandemic. Mr. Chuso was fortunate enough that where he worked at the auto repair shop, hadn't shut down so they had no issues paying their bills.

Despite the tantrums he threw about Rochelle and Rosa moving in, Livy finally convinced him to let them rent out the extra bedroom for a short time. Even though Rochelle was a bit concerned with the new arrangement, especially living under Mr. Chuso's roof, there was no other choice. Before the move, Rochelle had been able to sell off some of her more valuable possessions to help pay for their new living quarters. Again, having no seller's market, their Barbados retreat sat unoccupied, until it was burned down when the virus took over the island. All the monies that were tied up in it, were gone along with the millions of other dollars the Wells had in stocks and bonds. They had bottomed out and would never recover.

When the move day came, Rochelle's house was locked up along with the rest of her possessions still in it, destined to be destroyed. She had no place to store them and was forbidden to return to the property after that day. Since their new space was limited to just one bedroom, they had enough room for a couple of suitcases of stuff, but no more. Rochelle loaded them in the back of her Mercedes SUV, and the two headed to their new life at the Chusos, one she hoped to be short-lived. Eventually, her beautiful lake home was burned to rubble, as most of the ones along the lakeshore, with no monetary compensation.

Since there was no room to park her SUV at the Chusos, and the gas industry was drying up, Rochelle decided to sell it to one of Mr. Chuso's auto shop customers, while the selling was still good. The new place was close enough to downtown that Rochelle didn't need it anyways.

Once it sold, Mr. Chuso dragged his feet giving her the money and made up excuses that the customer had yet to pay him. Rochelle sensed he was lying, and after confronting him several times along with getting Livy involved, he finally paid her. There was never an explanation for the ordeal, but she learned the customer had paid Mr. Chuso several weeks prior. When he reluctantly handed the cash over, Rochelle wanted to give him a piece of her mind, but didn't want to rock the boat any more than she had to. She already was bound to bump heads hard with him if she didn't find a way to get out of there sooner than later.

Rochelle eventually found a part-time, paying job. Nothing great, but it was a start, working at one of the remaining fast-food restaurants within walking distance. She worried about leaving Rosa home with the Chusos while she went to work, but Livy assured her she'd look after her and help with her online schooling. It took a few months, but finally, the Chusos and the Bergers settled into some normalcy among the chaos that continued to grow around them.

The following year things only got worse. The second pandemic outbreak didn't disappoint and was, as predicted, more deadly than the first. Especially in the Chuso home. First, Livy got sick and died before anyone could get her to a medical facility. Everyone was surprised the virus was the cause as they had carefully followed the public guidelines to avoid its grip. Not long after Livy's death, both of Chuso kids fell ill and, shortly after being placed on ventilators, died within a few hours of each other.

Since the virus played havoc among the Chusos, Rochelle was extremely worried they were next on its list. Mr. Chuso's world had turned upside down, he was crippled by depression, and hid in his room for days on end. Not long afterward, the auto repair shop closed its doors until further notice, pushing him further over the edge. He found solace by drowning his despair in his go-to comfort of whisky; his consumption increased daily.

As time went on, things didn't get any better for Mr. Chuso. He couldn't cope with his losses and sat in the living room in his recliner for hours, day after day, barely moving, barely acknowledging Rochelle or Rosa. Each day was the same. He'd eventually pass out from too much alcohol in his bloodstream, then once he woke up, was belligerent and overbearing. Rochelle insisted that she and Rosa both stayed in their bedroom as much as possible, away from him until she could figure out their next move. Mr. Chuso's nasty side scared her, the way he sneered in disgust whenever he saw them. Even though the snide remarks were mainly under his breath, she didn't trust him.

As the weeks rolled by, Mr. Chuso took less care of himself and his surroundings. The overwhelming stench from dirty dishes, overflowing garbage, and even him, got to Rochelle. She tried to keep up with the messes, but his looming presence limited her from doing so. He had gotten to the point that his alcohol intake was about 1.75 liters of whisky a day. The only upside was once he hit his tipping point, he was out cold for hours. At that point Rochelle and Rosa could peacefully roam about. It was clear it was time to move out.

Just two months after the Chusos' household had collapsed, Rosa's life changed again. Her mother developed a slight cough. At first, it seemed it was from allergies, but it progressively got worse as the all too familiar symptoms developed. She insisted her mother get help right away, but Rochelle refused for fear of leaving her daughter alone in the house with Mr. Chuso, along with the reality that she might not return. It got to the point that Rochelle's breathing was intolerable, so reluctantly, and with no help from Mr. Chuso, Rosa dialed 911. She watched as they took her mother away in the same heart-wrenched fashion they had taken her father. Just a few days later, she received word that her mother had died.

Rosa didn't know what to do. She suddenly was an orphan. The same emotionless fear and confusion she had after her dad died crept back in. But this time, her mom wasn't there to comfort her. Nobody was. All she knew was that the last three years of her 15 years of life had been cruel and full of uncontrollable chaos. There was much to think about, like where would she go or would she have to stay with Mr. Chuso? Would she get sick and eventually die herself? Would Mr. Chuso die?

Rosa cried for her mom. They had just figured things out after the last disaster and were going to move. They were a team. She cried for her father. She missed how he made everything feel better when he hugged her. If she could only have just one more hug. She cried for herself. She couldn't make sense of any of it. The virus forcefully struck her family for a second time, but now it was worse. She was forever alone.

Over the next few months, Rosa mainly stayed upstairs in her bedroom, out of Mr. Chuso's way. He had shown no sympathy for her loss and had only gotten worse with his alcohol consumption, hosting his own pity parties. She was at a point where she feared him more. Many times, when she went to the kitchen, he got up out of his chair and followed her in. He was getting intolerably boisterous but at times just stood in silence, watching her fetch some food as he slurped on his whisky bottle. Rosa tried to ignore his presence, but it didn't end there as he generally tailed her to the foot of the stairs, blurting out various threats that her day was coming, and she'd get what she deserved. Then, she'd race up the stairs to her room and push a small bureau in front of the door, hoping it was enough to keep him out if he ever decided to follow her there.

Rosa knew Mr. Chuso blamed her for all that had happened to his family and wished it were her instead of them. He told her that on so many occasions, as he became more aggressive towards her. She worried that he'd eventually cross boundaries and end up either violently or sexually abusing her. He gave her the once up and down looks every time she'd walk by the recliner and started moving closer to her when they both were in the kitchen. The one thing Rosa could count on was that his routine never changed, except when he occasionally left the house to pick up food or his whisky. Those were the only times she truly felt safe under that roof.

Despite all she endured, she was momentarily grateful that there was even a roof over her head. She had no idea what her future held, but the very thought of being stuck living with him wasn't settling well. Rosa didn't want to be there anymore but, for the moment, had no other choice.

The second round of the virus had intensified as it ungracefully stepped up its game with no regard to all it destroyed along its path. Within three months, more people died. Nobody was prepared for the ghastly numbers. With no cures, failed vaccinations, and no insight on its continued progression, the world just sat hostage to its devilish, deadly antics. The first strain had already caused enough turmoil, but the second one tightened the screws as it took on a new life of its own, finding a way to implant itself inside more than just the human body. Surviving within vacant structures that had human DNA remnants was mind-boggling. It didn't matter if it was wood, steel, plastic, metals, even concrete, but the DNA kept the deadly killer alive for months on end. It multiplied and waited patiently, in the vacancies for its next victims to become its prey.

Due to the highly contagious spread, more physical businesses shut down, and soon, online businesses and schools also ceased. Much needed medical facilities completely closed their doors. Unemployment was at its all-time highest; funds were no longer available to help the jobless. Once it was conclusive what the virus was doing, evacuation and burn orders increased throughout the country, leaving more homeless people to aimlessly wander about and fend for themselves.

The number of structures and vehicles ordered to be burned were numerous. But even with the mandate in effect, there weren't enough people to help keep up with the volume of orders. So, a lot of the larger buildings like hospitals, high rises, and multiple complexes had no other choices but to be boarded up until there was enough manpower to burn them. It was becoming evident that the mandate contained and confined the virus more than it previously had been.

Food was everyone's main concern, and grocery stores had reduced their hours and limited the number of people allowed in as the infrastructure continued to close down. Dollar limitations were placed on each visit to assure that everyone was able to get some supplies. Eventually, most of those locations closed their doors, especially when the distribution hubs and black markets took over.

The distribution hubs were housed in large warehouses or stadiums big enough for huge supplies of essentials. They were mainly located near large bodies of water so boats could easily transport goods from city to city or state to state. Because of the limited locations, those areas became heavily populated with growing tent communities so folks were closer to the supplies. As the economy worsened, essentials, even at the hubs, were harder to get. It created a new havoc and soon looting was at its all-time highest, and the survivors' tolerance levels at their all-time lowest. Those lucky enough to stay in their homes or even those that squatted in them, constantly fought off vagrants who tried to take possession.

The world was twisted into an unstoppable chaos, creating a fear and weakness that there was no escape from. A third wave of the virus was predicted to run a harder, less empathetic course for the survivors, if they even survived.

The last morning at the Chuso house, Rosa kept her normal routine as she got up early and went down to the kitchen to get some breakfast before Mr. Chuso got up. But to her surprise, he was already sitting in his chair. His bare, hairy belly was hanging over his striped, cotton pajama pants. He was holding an open bottle of whisky and glared at Rosa as she scooted by. For the most part, Rosa had been able to count on the fact that Mr. Chuso didn't have his first drink until closer to the lunch hour, and since it wasn't even 9:00 a.m. yet, she knew something was off. She hurried past him and into the kitchen, hoping he wouldn't follow.

Just as she picked up a bag of bread to grab a couple of slices for toast, Mr. Chuso took her by surprise as he came up behind her, pushing his large, heavy body against her back. She felt a slight sting on her stomach as she slammed against the counter where a ragged metal border dug into her skin, slightly tearing it as he roughly thrust her forward. Despite the pain, Rosa became more aware of his bulging stomach and the heat of his sweaty body radiating through the back of her shirt. His obese six-foot-three-inch frame towered over her. She didn't know what was going to happen next except maybe that she was going to throw up from his overwhelming body stench and the metal still slicing into her. As she tried to push herself back from the counter, she felt helpless, unable to move the massive weight pressed against her.

Rosa was frightened for her life as she heard herself say, "Mr. Chuso, what are you doing? Please, let me go. You're hurting me."

Without responding, he pushed her harder against the metal that continued to dig deeper, causing moments of excruciating pain. Then his big hairy arm reached around her causing her to drop the opened bag of bread onto the counter. The putrid body aroma mixed with the air, made it harder to breathe. Rosa felt his hot sweat starting to meld with her skin as it soaked through her shirt. Then he moved his scruffy face across the back of her neck until his mouth got close to her ear; his hot breath reeked of whisky, his breathing grew heavier.

He moved his lips close enough to her ear that she felt the heat of his breath as he slurred in a low, gruff voice, "If I were you, I'd stop fighting me, or things will get worse." His voice faded into a whisper, "This is my place, and I'll do damn well what I want here. But you, well, you eat my food. You sleep under my roof. You do what you damn well want. You're an entitled bitch, just like that piece of shit mother of yours. You both thought it was yours for the taking. Well, let me tell you loud and clear; your free days are over. There's a price and you're gonna pay me."

Rosa felt his spit rain on her ear and the side of her face as he spewed out his ugly threat. Every time she tried to turn her head away, he firmly held it still, pressing it harder against his as he continued his rant.

"I should've never let you two in here. You cursed my family. Hell, they would've all been here if I had just put my foot down and said no. And that's the price you're gonna pay for my family… you owe me."

Mr. Chuso's body momentarily relaxed as he slightly stepped back, no longer pushing his weight against her. Rosa hoped he'd back off and go back to his chair, leaving her alone. But within seconds, his grip tightened, and as his body pressed even harder against hers, the metal cut deeper into her skin.

As tears streamed down her cheeks, he drunkenly snarled, "The only fucking person I have to worry about now in this whole world is me. So, you best listen up and listen closely. As long as you're under my roof, you've got two choices. For starters, you're not my kid, and it ain't my job to support your scrawny ass, so I sure as hell don't want you eating the last bit of my food. You find your own shit elsewhere. Or if you want to eat my food, then you'll pay my price." He laughed as he slowly ran his tongue up her cheek then said, "By all means, I'll be your daddy. Either way, your free ride is over."

"Please, Mr. Chuso, I won't touch anything, please just let me go," Rosa pleaded, no longer able contain her sobs.

He laughed, then wrapped both his arms around her, hitting her slightly in the head with the half-empty whisky bottle as it flailed about. She thought for sure he was going to rape her or even kill her, so she just closed her eyes, knowing it was a battle she couldn't win, no matter what the outcome was.

"You hear me, girlie? As much as I despise you, I'd have no problem sinking myself into your young ass. I'll gladly take your cherry from you and don't think I haven't been thinking about it. At least you'd be good for something around here. Don't wait too long to decide, or I will," he whispered loudly in her ear, shoving his groins hard against her then exercising a few dry pumps.

Moments later he slowly backed away, grabbed the bread bag, chugged down some whisky, and staggered back to his chair. Rosa just stood still, frozen and unable to move. As the tears rolled down her cheeks, she tried hard to compose herself. The last thing she wanted was for him to turn around and come back after her. She took a deep breath once she heard his heavy body plop down in the recliner.

Her ear felt cold and clammy from the absence of his hot breath. She looked down at her stomach and saw some blood had soaked through her t-shirt from the cut yet the pain had momentarily subsided, at least until she began to move. She knew she had to make a decision to either run out the front door and get help or race past him to her bedroom and lock herself in. Neither were inviting, but those were the choices.

After a few moments of replaying in her head what had just happened, Rosa made a decision and mustered up the courage to dart for the stairs, hoping he wouldn't chase her. As she briskly moved past him, he threw the opened bread bag at her, scattering it everywhere.

Mr. Chuso started hysterically laughing and said, "That's right, you little bitch, you run. Just remember I'll be watching you, and I'll be waiting."

Once in her bedroom, Rosa quickly pushed the bureau against the door, sat on her bed, crying uncontrollably. Her whole body trembled and she had dry heaves over the thought of what could've happened to her. It was no secret that Mr. Chuso had always been a bully, and even worse when he drank, but until that day, she never thought he'd ever consider touching her sexually. She chose not to run out the door to get help for fear she'd still end up back under his roof, only to accelerate things. Either way she was scared and knew she'd never be able to fight him off.

There were several times Rosa had either seen or heard him verbally, even physically lash out at his own family. Many nights she'd lay awake and hear Livy and Mr. Chuso scream at each other. Often, she heard things thrown about, furniture shoved around, and doors slamming. Livy yelled at him to stop his craziness and sometimes demanded that he leave the house and not come back until he sobered up.

Rosa knew that he had raped his wife many times in his drunken stupor. So often, she heard Livy scream for him to get off her. But he never listened. Sadly, when Livy wasn't around, he'd lash out at his own kids and sometimes toss them around but nothing sexual as far as she knew. Rosa felt bad for the kids, even though they never developed a relationship with her beyond the occasional pleasantries when all of them were in the same room.

There were several times Rosa witnessed Mr. Chuso in the backyard screaming at his neighbors for one reason or another. It would get to the point that he'd grab empty liquor bottles from the recycling bin and throw them in their yards. The cops were called several times, and Mr. Chuso had been issued many citations, even threats of arrest.

Rochelle thought that he knew somebody in a higher place because his absurd, abusive actions never landed him in jail.

It would've been a different story if someone had called to report the physical abuse that he put his kids through. But the tormented chose to remain silent, like most do. It was clear that Mr. Chuso's drinking was attributed to the root of most of the evil that lived under their roof.

That morning, his threats took on a whole new life. Rosa was the last one left in his line of fire and was scared to death. As she managed to get her tears under control, she couldn't help wondering why the virus had killed off all the good people in her life and left behind nasty and undeserving ones, like Mr. Chuso.

Over the next hour, Rosa tended to her wound, which was more superficial than it felt, and just laid in her bed feeling defeated about what to do next. Then she heard the front door slam. The sound of the garage door opening and closing filtered through her open window. She looked out just in time to watch Mr. Chuso's Jeep Cherokee back out of the driveway and spin-off down the road; she was sure he was off to buy another bottle. That gave her about 20 minutes to at least hoard some food from the kitchen, so she pushed the bureau aside and slowly crept down the stairs. She noticed the bread still lying on the living room floor, and his stench that dominated the air as she walked past his chair. At that moment, she realized she still had some of it on her and planned to shower as soon as she got back upstairs. After a couple more dry heaves, she made it to the kitchen.

Rosa grabbed a small plastic grocery bag and packed it with a few apples, some saltine crackers, peanut butter, and some stale chips. There wasn't much else around, so she opened the refrigerator and saw a couple of bottles of iced tea that her mother had bought shortly before she got sick. Rosa had made a point not to drink them. It was the only thing left of her existence besides what was in their bedroom. She threw them in the bag and headed back upstairs.

Once safely in her room, it took a few minutes for her heart to stop racing. She tried not to imagine what would've happened if Mr. Chuso had come home and caught her, but the thoughts ran wild. As Rosa sat on the bed munching on an apple, her thoughts were also fixated on something she saw on her way to the kitchen. Just as she had passed Chuso's recliner she saw a quick, bright flash that momentarily blinded her. When she stopped to see where it was coming from, it was gone. Not being able to stand the stench, she had proceeded to the kitchen.

On her way back, she saw it again and, this time she decided to investigate it a little further. As Rosa got closer to the recliner, she was startled with what she saw. Sitting on the nearby end table was a handgun. More specifically, a silver Beretta M9 handgun, which she knew all about since her father had a couple of them in his personal collection. It laid there, surrounded by a stack of gun magazines and some balled-up tissues. She realized that the sun's rays had come through a nearby window and reflected off the shiny metal, causing the blinding flash. Guns didn't scare her, at least not the ones her father had. But, this one did. She shuttered, then ran upstairs.

As Rosa continued to think about the gun, she recalled how her father had first shown her, at just six-years-old, how the safety latch worked and how to handle it with caution in case there was ever a need to use it. He demonstrated how to load and unload the clip every time he had it out and promised when she got older, he'd teach her how to shoot it. For a brief moment, her eyes filled with tears realizing she would never get that chance with him.

Then the thought of the shiny gun took over, and Rosa wanted to get another look. She knew time was running out before Mr. Chuso returned, so she hurriedly went back downstairs to check it out. In her mind, there was no reason for the gun to be out in plain sight or even be in the house. She had to find out if it was loaded, so she slowly picked it up, both nervous and excited to hold it in her hands. For just a moment, she closed her eyes and envisioned the first time her father put it in her hands and how heavy and cold it had felt. It still felt that way. She remembered him showing her how to hold it properly.

When she opened her eyes, the gun was pointed directly at Mr. Chuso's chair. It frightened her. She quickly lowered it and was about to put it back when she noticed three boxes of ammunition on the floor next to the stand. Her hands got sweaty as she reached down and picked them up. They were full. She froze, not knowing what to do next, but then something came over her that made her tightly grasp the discoveries and race back to her room with them. Rosa thought she had gone mad as she stared at her new possessions. Without a doubt, she knew she should put them back before Mr. Chuso got home; otherwise, there would be hell to pay.

"Maybe I should just sit here and wait for him to barge in then shoot him," she said aloud, nervously chuckling.

Shocked at hearing her own words, she picked up the gun and checked to see if the safety switch was locked. To her relief, it was. Then she remembered how her father had shown her how to use the thumb release for the clip. She followed his instructions, and out it popped into her hand, and to her surprise, was fully loaded. Rosa quickly pulled back the slide on the top of the gun to see if the chamber was loaded. Her dad had always told her that most gun accidents happened because people failed to empty them. Sure enough, one lone bullet was sitting there, waiting for it's time to shine. Her heart skipped a couple beats as she couldn't think of one reason why it would be there. Then she felt another dry heave coming as she wondered if maybe it was meant for her.

After shaking off the thought, Rosa quickly put the loaded clip back in the gun, then held it tight in her hands as she aimed directly at the bedroom door, envisioning Mr. Chuso walking through it. That was the moment she decided she really needed to kill him before he got to her first. Rosa saw no other way out as her own life flashed before her, at the mercy of his hands.

She took a minute to shake off the horrid thought, as she rehashed his regular routine after he got back from shopping. She'd hear the kitchen door slam, then a couple bottles of whisky banging down on the counter along with any bags of food he picked up, then he'd stumble into the bathroom, then grab one of the bottles and make his way to the recliner. There he'd stay, drinking until he passed out.

She played out the scenario of what could happen once he realized the gun was gone. Long before that welcomed time when he'd pass out, she knew he'd look over at the empty end table and briefly check around for the missing gun. Then he'd become enraged, realizing the only other person that could have it, was her. He'd bolt up out of his chair then stagger up the stairs to confront her, once he forcefully pushed through the blocked door. To his surprise, she'd be sitting on the bed, with the gun pointed right at his head. He'd be so drunk and enraged that it wouldn't scare him, so he'd charge toward her, demanding the gun. Just as he got close enough for her to smell his stench, she'd pull the trigger and stop him dead in his tracks. She'd watch as he grabbed his chest in disbelief, still spewing out demands to hand the gun over. She'd keep shooting until his last breath.

The longer she sat there, playing out the gruesome scene in her head, the more she changed her mind. As angry and scared as she was, Rosa knew she couldn't take somebody else's life, regardless of how cruel and undeserving they were. At that point, she knew it was time to leave the house and had to get out before Mr. Chuso returned. There was no time to shower. In fact, she lost track of it and wasn't even sure how much time there was before he got back. She quickly gathered some of her stuff and put it in a backpack, then looked at the gun still sitting on the bed. After taking a few deep breaths, she picked it up, put the safety back on, then shoved it and the boxes of bullets into her bag.

With her hand on the doorknob, Rosa took one last look around the bedroom. She couldn't help the tears as she remembered how, within those four walls, her mother had lovingly protected her from the harsh realities of the pandemic's torture that flooded the world. She still didn't know its full extent, but was about to find out for herself. As she quietly said one final goodbye to life as she once knew it, a sense of sadness passed over her. Rosa took a deep breath as she opened the door, ran down the stairs, through the house, out the front door, and into the driveway.

The crisp-mid morning air smacked her in the face, but the sun's warmth immediately hugged her. Rosa had no idea what was ahead or how things would end up, but she knew it had to be better than living under the Chuso roof. Without any desire to look back, she adjusted the backpack on her shoulders, then strode down the driveway and headed toward the inner city in hopes of finding something better.

The Beach Community

For the next couple hours, Rosa wandered aimlessly around downtown Burlington, lost, alone, and scared. All she could think about was Mr. Chuso coming home, finding the gun and her both gone. She envisioned him chugging down the new bottle of whisky as he figured out his next moves. It wouldn't surprise her to see his jeep patrolling the streets in hopes of finding her, so she knew getting out of sight as soon as possible was necessary; she just didn't know where.

Even though she had grown up around the area, she was on unfamiliar grounds by herself. She finally decided to take a break near the once popular floating boathouse restaurant. In its pre-pandemic days, it was a hot spot where tourists and local folks enjoyed food, drinks, and the serenity of Lake Champlain's gentle waves lapping against the docks, as well as views of the New York Adirondack mountain's landscape. It closed during the first round of the virus and stood boarded up, just waiting for its demolition like most of its surrounding neighbors.

Rosa decided to sit down on one of the rickety wooden benches, and after checking on her wound that had finally stopped bleeding, she watched a pack of seagulls fly overhead. Occasionally, some of them landed on the rock barriers of the shoreline, scrounging for any type of food that might be about. She took in the warmth of the noontime early summer sun and was momentarily soothed by the waves continually flapping against the rocks. She closed her eyes, trying to forget about Mr. Chuso and the world she was about to face, alone.

Other than the birds, the only other signs of life were a few homeless transients and local folks meandering by. Rosa could see a few yachts and smaller boats anchored offshore, just rocking back and forth on the small waves beneath them. A nearby sign forbid anyone to take residence on them, yet there was no visual security around to ward off someone from doing so. On occasion, a cyclist or skateboarder passed by her, barely acknowledging her presence. A nearby public parking lot had been barricaded off to prevent any homeless folks from vagabonding in the vacant cars, vans, and buses that had yet to be burned.

Later that afternoon, after eating some of her crackers and throwing a couple to the seagulls, Rosa decided to head north in hopes of finding shelter for the night. About a mile and a half up the street, near an abandoned high school, she saw a sign that read: 'North Beach Tent Community,' with an arrow pointing down a long street that seemed to lead back toward the lake. Since Rosa's family had access to their own beachfront, they seldom, if at all, ventured to any public beaches. On occasion, she had visited North Beach a few times with her best friend, so she felt somewhat familiar with the area. At the very least, she thought it might be a good place, out of sight from Mr. Chuso, where she could stay for at least the night. So, without hesitation, she followed the arrow.

The next two signs along the road led to a narrow dirt path in between two small open fields surrounded by woods. As she strolled along it, Rosa came upon yet another open field. At the far end of it was the lake. Just beyond a patch of trees, there were hundreds of people scattered about. Most had formed a line long enough to stretch across a football field and appeared to be waiting to get into some sort of event. Many small tents were set up close by. Some folks were sitting in chairs near them, and lots of young kids were running around the field. It looked like they all had been there for days, maybe more.

Rosa couldn't believe all the folks she had stumbled upon and noted that the line wasn't moving, so she wasn't sure what to do. After several minutes of watching everyone, she decided to find out what was going on. She had a sense that something big was about to happen. Standing at the back of the line was a tall, older woman who appeared to be in her mid-50s. Nearby was a man about her age, sitting in a lawn chair near a tent, talking to a couple of young boys. Rosa gathered up her courage to ask her what was going on.

"Excuse me, I was wondering if you could tell me what this all about? There are so many people here. What are you all waiting for? What's happening here?" she shyly asked, stepping closer to the lady.

The lady's face was covered with a cotton teal scarf, revealing only her hazel blue eyes that quickly checked Rosa over as she answered, "We're just waiting our turn to hopefully get into the beach shelters where we can stay for the summer. Only a limited number of folks can get in. They should be letting folks down there soon, so we were told about two hours ago when one of them announced it through the speakers. I really hope we will get in."

She paused for a moment with her eyes sternly on Rosa, then said, "One rule to gain entrance is that we have to be in a group of four or we will be turned away."

She glanced behind Rosa as if looking for more people. Rosa had no idea what she was talking about. As she stayed focus on the lady, she couldn't help noticing her graying hair, pulled back in a lopsided bun, flop about when she spoke. Loose strands kept falling over her eyes that she constantly pushed aside.

"I don't understand. What do you mean? What's a beach shelter, and why does there have to be four in a group?" Rosa inquisitively asked.

"Well, dear, from what they've told us, there are about 20 lean-tos and room for about 40 tents along this particular beach line. That's about 240 of us that will get access today. Although there's a rumor running around saying there's more space down there. But who knows. Anyone who has less than four with them or more than four will get turned away, so they say. Where's the rest of your group, dear?" she asked, as she again looked past her to see if anyone else was coming down the path.

"It's just me, I'm afraid," Rosa replied, feeling a bit uneasy with the new information, still not quite understanding what was happening.

"Oh my, how old are you, child, and why are you alone?" The woman asked in a soft tone.

"I'm 15," Rosa answered, then added, "Both my parents died from the virus a while ago, and I just left a horrible living situation that wasn't good for me. So, yeah, just me." She felt her eyes temporarily welt up and tried to quickly blink back the tears.

"Oh, I'm so sorry, dear," the woman concerningly replied as she gently rubbed Rosa's arm for a few seconds before she continued, "Would you like some water? You surely must be thirsty."

Rosa nodded no, then quickly asked, "This is all rather odd. Why is everyone gathering here and not in their own homes, or hotels, or other places? Why would anyone want to live on the beach in tents?"

The lady quickly glanced over at the man sitting close by as he cleared his throat and shrugged his shoulders, then she answered, "My dear, don't you know? Most of these families lost their homes as they were all evacuated and burned. And most of them lost family members like you did. They have nowhere else to go except places like this or stay on the streets."

Rosa knew there was a lot she didn't know. It was quite obvious when she left the Chuso condo, shocked to see that so many places had been burned. She had no idea, or even knew about the extent of damage the pandemic had caused. Suddenly she got it, and fear crept in as she looked at the lady and the line in front of her, trying to put it all together in her head.

She slowly shook her head as she looked around then said to the lady, "I couldn't believe all the burned buildings I passed by just coming here. I guess I didn't connect the dots until now. My mom really kept me sheltered the last few years, so I'm having a hard time wrapping my head around the fact that there's nowhere else for all these people to go because I just came from a condo and an area that is still standing. This is awful."

The lady sensed Rosa's fear and confusion as she replied, "I know dear, it is how it is, and it is sad. So many people died in their own homes and other buildings because of the virus, but when the new strain came, it could live in those structures without the people. Even in some vehicles, so that's why the order is out to burn down as many as they can. Some of the larger buildings are just boarded up, waiting to be burned, and may never be, but the vagrants and others still seem to take residence in them. It's very scary!" She was getting herself a bit riled up over the subject, then asked, "It's hard to believe that your mother kept all this from you at your age. How did you manage to not see any of it?"

"I did know, well, sort of. Like I said, my mother kept me pretty sheltered from all of this. I wish she had shared more,'' Rosa answered and as her eyes once again teared up, asked, "I have nowhere else to go, and it's only me. What should I do now? I can't go back where I was."

"Well," the lady softly said as she lightly put her arm around Rosa, "you'll have to find a group of people in this line that need an extra person so you can get in here. There are already four of us. My husband and our two teen boys." They all waved as she pointed at them, then continued, "So, I can't help you out dear, as much as I'd love to. But I do know there are some groups ahead of us that need an extra head. Occasionally they drift back here to see if anyone new has joined the line."

She paused for a moment to wipe away one of Rosa's tears that had escaped, then added, "I'm sure you'd be welcomed. All you have to do is find them." Then she pointed toward the front of the line and said, "And try to get upfront, as close as you can."

Rosa wiped another tear off her cheek as she looked forward and calmly asked, "Just walk up and ask if I can join them?"

The lady nodded then removed her arm only to rest both hands on Rosa's shoulders as she instructed, "Most importantly, we'll all get tested before we can gain access. Any signs of the virus within any group of four will disqualify all of them, possibly even other groups that have been standing next to them. There are so many here who aren't covering their faces and could be carriers. I know we don't need to anymore, but we're all so close together here and one never really knows."

She stared at Rosa's exposed face, unintentionally making her feel uncomfortable. Rosa didn't think to grab anything of the sort to cover it when she had rushed out of Mr. Chuso's home. She realized it once she breathed in the polluted air and wished she had. The next thing she knew, the lady handed her a semi-tattered cotton blend, tan scarf.

"Here, dear, take my extra one. You should wear it now."

"Thanks so much. I wasn't thinking when I left this morning," Rosa said as she wrapped it loosely around her neck, adjusting it over her nose and mouth.

Rosa couldn't believe the chaos the silent killer had cast upon everyone. To be in the midst of it all was heart-wrenching as she looked at the line of people. Now she knew they all were there because they had nowhere else to go, yet they all seemed excited for even the chance to get into the beach shelter. It appeared nobody was letting the situation impact their spirits or determination to survive in the new environment. It was a lot for Rosa to grasp, but it gave her hope and a new sense of willpower. She wanted to be a part of it all and maybe, in a small way, make some kind of difference.

"No worries, dear. It's a lot to remember. We're not even sure we'll get in, as you see how big the line is. Lots of people have already come and gone, at least from the line in the back here, so we'll see. My family and I have been here a little over a week, just waiting for this day," the lady paused for a moment and then said, "I'm sorry, I didn't even get your name, dear. I'm Carmen."

"Rosa," she replied, now feeling the heat of her breath bounce off the scarf, back onto her face.

Carmen continued, "Okay. So, the plan is that you get to the front of the line. Start there. Look for the folks that need another head. Most likely, they'll spot you walking alone and approach you. Don't take any offers until you check out the front first. Got it?"

Rosa nodded, still uneasy with the idea, then asked, "How did this all come about anyways?"

"Well briefly, let me fill you in," Carmen said as her husband jumped up from his chair to join them, "The plan to create these beach communities with lean-tos and tent spaces along the lakeshore started several months ago and was led by a local advocacy group. The group of about 25 conducted research on and about the different projected waterfront sites, then they put a proposal together for the city council to approve."

"Hey Rosa, I'm Ed," her husband said as he interrupted and extended his hand to her, "This has been a pretty complex project. I'm surprised you hadn't heard about it."

"No I haven't, but again my mother kept me away from all this stuff. I think she thought it would just all go away and wanted to save me the worry, but please, tell me more," Rosa responded as she shook his hand.

Ed nodded at Carmen, then said, "Well, even though it was just a temporary, seasonal solution, the group saw it as a way to keep some of the people sheltered in a safer spot then the streets, away from abandoned structures that house the virus. The one thing that seems to be consistent is that those living outside, appear to be less vulnerable to catching the damn thing. And so far, none of us out here have gotten sick."

"Interesting," Rosa commented.

"Yeah, so a lot of these type of safe shelters, not just here but all over the country, are located close to distribution hubs where essentials come in weekly via boats," Ed said as he cleared his throat, then continued, "Burlington's hub is at the old ferry docks, just down the street from the floating restaurant. These particular tent communities are opening on 16 state beaches throughout Vermont on Lake Champlain. There's others too, but this is the biggest, most organized one. There's also a winter plan in place to get folks out of the cold and move into nearby safe shelters when the time comes."

"Where are those again?" Carmen asked.

Ed looked over at her then back at Rosa as he replied, "The local YMCA, the Memorial Auditorium, and I believe the middle school across the street from them."

"So why is there even a limit on the amount of people that can live on the beach? I mean the shoreline is endless around the lake, right?" Rosa asked, "And why just four in a group? Surely there's enough lakefront for anyone who wants to live there regardless if it's a family of one or ten."

Ed again responded, "Well, those are fair questions. There are many other communities along the shoreline, but again, this is the most organized one. This particular plan is something the city and state put together for just the 16 state-run beach sites. From what we heard, each site includes 20 or more wooden lean-tos with doors, I might add. The number is solely based on the size of each of the sites, and then 40 or more platforms are available for folks to pitch tents on. You know, keep them off the wet sand and all. The individual living areas were only designed to have enough space for four. I think the reason why four became the magic number was to ensure that there are no vacant spots or overflow in each area, and the smaller the number, the easier it will be on the community."

Rosa looked around at all the people hanging out in the field then replied, "I suppose that makes sense. But how can everyone just live on a beach?"

"Well," Ed replied, "it's liveable, believe me. Some of the amenities included are outhouses or porta potties, if you will."

"Ugh," Rosa commented, trying to imagine having to live full time with those type of amenities.

Ed laughed as he responded, "The public restrooms don't always work because of the unreliability of the power grid. Same with the showers. A good thing is there are lots of woods surrounding each site, so firewood will be plentiful to use for heat, cooking, and hot water. Every individual living area also has its own fire pit and picnic table."

Carmen excitedly added, "Yeah and I heard that cooking utensils, batteries, kerosene lanterns, candles, torches and all that good stuff should initially be provided. After that we'll just have to get our own, but at least to start, we'll have it."

"This is all so much to take in," Rosa said, thinking none of it sounded inviting and couldn't understand why they were so excited.

Ed saw the discomfort in her face and replied, "Well, it's darn better than hanging out in the middle of nowhere. It has more advantages than not." He chuckled then said, "You'll get used to it. We all will."

Carmen piped in, "Yeah, you were lucky enough to have a roof over your head, until today. Why did you decide to leave it or was it under an evacuation order?"

Rosa didn't know how to answer and wasn't sure she wanted to so she hesitantly replied, "It's a long story for another time."

Before outside shelters were established, thousands of homeless people wandered the city streets and its outskirts. The unburned structures housed trespassers that illegally took possession of them. Thievery, property destruction, and uncleanliness made conditions even worse with trash scattered about, urine and feces left behind in alleyways, and people unable to take care of themselves. Most had no choice. They were angry, frustrated, and scared. Tempers raged as physical and verbal fights among strangers eradicated the once peaceful area.

Transients continued to migrate into Burlington since it had the largest distribution hub in the state, which only added to the already unsettled population. Restrictions became tighter for the distribution of essentials with more people in need; some shipments were on a first-come, first-serve basis, which caused more chaos. The police force disintegrated and lost control of the city so pandemonium took over. The beach communities promised to alleviate some of the city's growing burden.

Carmen looked over at her family, then back at Rosa as she quietly said, "It's time Rosa. You can't linger here as much as I'd love to have you stay with us. You must get to the front of the line before the gates open. I'm sure you'll be someone's miracle and will be warmly welcome. If not for you, they'll be turned away, or so they say."

Rosa grabbed her hand and said, "I'm still not sure about all this but I trust you and thank you both. I wouldn't have known how all this worked without you. I can't believe everything that's happened and where things are now at. I hope I can find a group too, and I hope you all get in as well. I'll be watching for you."

Carmen pulled Rosa close and hugged her tightly, detecting her fear as she whispered in her ear, "You'll be okay, my dear, and God be with us both. If we get in this time around, I'll see you soon." She let go and pointed Rosa toward the lake, nudging her on her way.

Rosa felt her face flush as she was once again on her own, walking down the jagged line of people. She felt curious eyes upon her and didn't want to stare back. It was impossible to figure out which groups needed an extra person as people were scattered everywhere. Nobody approached her as she moved forward. Many were hanging out in large groups, while others were off by themselves, wandering about the field.

As she got closer to what seemed to be the front of it all, she heard a small, meek, yet anxious voice call out from just behind her, "Hey, you in the tan scarf. Are you alone?"

When Rosa turned around, she saw a young girl standing close enough that she almost bumped into her. She was about Rosa's height, appearing to be slightly older. Standing next to her, holding her hand, was a little boy no older than ten. His big brown eyes peeked over his Aquaman mask, blinking as their eyes met. On the girl's other side, stood a tall thin guy in his mid-20s. The three pairs of eyes intently locked on her, waiting for an answer.

Rosa's heart beat wildly with feelings of excitement and nervousness that flooded through her body. She knew at that moment, once again, her life was about to switch gears. The last few years had bombarded her with so many changes to a point it no longer was how much more she could take; it was just going with the flow and seeing where things took her. And at that very moment, she knew the three people standing in front of her needed her, and that was all that mattered. She was about to become part of the new community. She was in.

She quickly answered, "Yes, yes I'm alone."

The girl pulled down her flowered mask and made introductions, "Well, then. We hope you'll join us. I'm Sandy, and this is my little brother, Georgie, and my cousin, Larry! We're so happy that you came along! And just in the nick of time. You have no idea! Please, join us, please!"

Rosa watched tears roll down Sandy's cheeks while Larry and Georgie blinked back theirs. Then Sandy pulled her mask back up and grabbed Rosa's hand, pulling her closer to them.

"They're about to open the beachfront, and we would've been turned away if you didn't show up!" Larry exclaimed as he extended his hand out to Rosa.

"You have no idea how stressed we were! Where in the world did you come from, and more importantly, how long have you been here?" Sandy asked, talking a mile a minute as she continued to wipe her eyes, leaving behind some dirt streaks from her hands.

"Are you going to say yes?" Georgie's tiny voice interrupted, as he tapped Rosa's arm.

Rosa giggled then answered, "Yes, Georgie, I'm saying yes."

"Excellent," Larry replied.

"You have no idea," Sandy said as she gave Rosa a quick hug.

Through a brief introduction, Rosa found out that the three of them had been camping in that spot for almost four weeks, finding it quite by accident, just as the waitlist opened and the line started to form. It certainly explained why they were right up front. They hadn't traveled too far, coming from Charlotte, a rural town just south of Burlington. Sandy, 17, and her little brother Georgie, 10, had lost both of their parents six months earlier. They stayed at the family farmhouse until evacuation orders were in effect and it was targeted to be burned down.

Larry had lived farther south in Vergennes,Vermont's smallest town. Shortly after his parents and fiancé died from the deadly virus, Larry packed up and headed to Charlotte, only to find his two cousins left on their own. Once they no longer could stay at the house, they packed up and headed to Burlington to find better shelter. By luck, like Rosa, they landed on the community beach doorstep. All that time, they could not find a fourth person to join their group…until Rosa.

"Attention folks, listen up! Can everyone hear me?" a loud voice blurted out across the field.

Rosa spotted a short, plump, balding middle-aged man standing on a stage in front of them. He had a red bandana over his face and was dressed in a bright red t-shirt that hung over his jiggly belly, barely covering up the waistline of his jeans. He was accompanied by 25 other large men that looked like bodybuilders along with eight younger women, all uniformly masked with red bandanas and the same t-shirts. The man's deep, raspy voice blasted through the battery-operated microphone into the many speakers set up on the stage and throughout the field. A few high-pitched squeals escaped as his finger tapped the mic a few times to make sure it was working.

Upon hearing the man's voice, the crowd went completely silent and within seconds, acknowledged his presence as they hooted and hollered with excitement, knowing what was coming. It was the moment they had been waiting for. Kids scurried back to families; chairs folded up, tents were quickly disassembled, and the line began to form.

The man watched as everyone moved about and started to settle down, then he addressed them, "Okay, everyone! It's time! I'm Al and I'll be walking you through this process. Welcome to the North Beach community! We're the first of many and I now declare that we're officially open!"

Al stopped as the crowd went wild, breaking out in thunderous cheers. For a few moments he and his crew joined them, jumping about on the stage. Then he put his hands in the air, signaling for the masses to calm down, and continued with his announcement.

"First and foremost, as you all know, you must be in groups of four. This shouldn't come as a surprise. There will be no rule bending here, no matter what age or condition you're in. If you need an additional person or two this is your time right now, to find them, or you'll need to move on."

He paused and watched everyone as they looked around, but nobody moved so he continued in a softer, more sympathetic tone, "We're sorry if this does affect any of you, but you all knew the rules when you got here, and again, we can't make any exceptions."

"We really dodged a bullet," Sandy whispered to Larry as he put his arm around her shoulders and nodded in agreement.

The crowd grew a bit restless as desperate shout-outs shot out among the crowd, asking for available bodies to join their groups. Some were demanding, others desperate, while some sobbed loudly when nobody rose to their pleas. Others left without incident, knowing they had no chance of getting in. Twenty of the bodyguards had already disbursed themselves among the large group, prepared for any problematic situations that might emerge.

Rosa stepped out of line, just enough to see what was going on behind her, and watched as many folks reluctantly walked away. She was a bit puzzled as to why none of them called out to her when she strolled by earlier, but she was thankful to have joined Sandy's family. There were enough unmatched groups that could have gotten together and formed sets of four, but for whatever reason, chose not to.

Al knew folks were getting more anxious, even enraged, so he shouted into the mic, "Okay, folks, no need to panic or be upset. Rules are rules. And you need to know, there's some good news here as 60 groups of four will get entrance into the community today. I know there are many of you that won't, so for all of you, we'll provide information with some other resources you can look into. Just know, all the other beach communities will require four in a group to get in as well. So please be prepared if you go there."

A few cheers could be heard as others shouted out, "Let's get moving!"

"Let's do this!"

"Get on with it!"

Al continued, "Now, these eight young ladies standing next to me will come by shortly and give each person in your group a quick test to make sure you're not a carrier of the virus. It only takes 15 seconds for you to clear, and then you'll be handed a yellow plastic arm band to tie to your upper right arm and wear at all times. Even when you leave the community to head downtown or wherever, you need to have it on. This identifies you to this North Beach community. You can't get back in without it or get other privileges it provides, so again, don't leave home without it!"

One of the guys, upset hearing about the yellow bands, shouted, "What do you mean wear an arm band? What is this? Some kind of concentration camp?"

He got others riled up who then shouted out their concerns, and a burst of uncertainty flooded the unsettled crowd.

"Whoa, hang on now, everyone!" Al exclaimed, trying to get control of the situation.

Another angry shout blasted from the middle of the dismantling line, "Everyone, shut the fuck up and listen to Al and if you don't like what you hear, then fucking leave! We all want to get in there!"

The crowd shuffled about, not sure what to make of the curt demand, but Al finally gained control back as he shouted, "Let's all calm down now, or none of us will be going anywhere other than the streets! Of course we are not a concentration camp! Come on, people! This is 2023! We're all in a crisis, and without a way to identify folks to these beach communities, they'll become overrun and non-existent!"

He paused for a moment as most everyone quieted down, then continued, "Look it, people, I know you all know that this is a privilege to get you off the streets and somewhere safe while we wait this pandemic out. Nobody's controlling anyone. There just isn't room for everyone here and we have to live, at least for now, by the guidelines that have been set for our own safety. Just like living in the real world as we once knew it. We have rules to play by. If you don't want to play, then, by all means, nobody is making you stay."

At that, the mixed crowd of supporters cheered and booed but eventually settled down letting Al continue. "Once you've cleared your test results, your group will receive a number, 1 to 60, then you'll step over here to the right of the stage and form another line." He pointed to a spot about six yards away from him then said, "And when your number's called, you'll gather all your stuff, and I'll escort you to your new beach home. We're doing this one group at a time. There will be 60 groups, folks, so I'll need you to be patient and be ready so that we can move this along as quickly as possible. If all goes smoothly, I'll have you settled in before the dinner hour! Promise!"

Someone shouted out, "What happens if one of our group members tests positive?"

Al paused for a moment as he wiped some sweat from his forehead, took a drink of water then answered, "If you do not receive a clean test result, both you and your group will need to leave. No exceptions. And please, just keep your dignity and exit peacefully. I hope you all test negative!"

"Well, if he keeps talking, we're never going to get this ball rolling," Larry snidely said, half to Sandy and half to himself.

"No kidding," Sandy chuckled, "but we're so close now! I can't wait!"

Rosa was only half-listening, as her thoughts drifted between Mr. Chuso's threats and all the devastation she discovered once she walked away from his home. She wondered if he had noticed the gun was missing and was out looking for her. The new beach community seemed far enough off the beaten path that she was sure she was safe among the new chaos. Her body momentarily trembled with the thought of what would happen if he did find her; then, she heard Al's voice get a bit louder and tried to focus.

"I need you all to pay close attention. Again, there are obviously more than 240 of you here. So, let's be civil about this. If you do not get a number, you have to move on to some of the other locations that will be opening soon."

Rosa could feel the tension growing among the anxious crowd. Those in the mid-to-back section already had their exit papers, since they had no chance to get in. She knew that Carmen and her family were one of them so her heart sank, knowing she may never see them again. She watched the people continue to dwindle away.

"Alright, are you ready, folks?" Al screamed into the mic, like an excited sports announcer.

Once again the crowd burst into enthusiastic cheers as he yelled out, "Let's get this ball rolling!"

At that, he lowered his mic, and the eight women approached the line of people, counting off groups of four, then giving them each a quick finger prick. By all good graces, nobody tested positive. Rosa and her new beachmates were issued their yellow bands along with the number three.

Suddenly, from somewhere in the middle of the crowd, a lady hysterically yelled, "No, please, please! My baby won't take up any room at all, please!"

The terrifying screams rang through the air shortly after one of the test ladies discovered a single mom holding an eight-month-old baby in her arms while three small kids clung to her legs.

"I'm sorry, ma'am, like Al said, rules are rules, and we can't bend them and let five of you through," The test lady sympathetically said as the kids started to cry.

"She's just a baby," the lady pleadingly sobbed, "please, she won't take up any extra space, I promise."

The test lady, as bad as she felt, told her, "I'm really sorry, it is what it is. Here is a list of other places where you can hopefully find safe shelter for your family."

The mother ignored the handout, so the test lady gave it to one of the little kids, then unsuccessfully continued to try to get them to leave. All eyes were on them and Rosa watched as the mother became more frantic, dropping to her knees and begging to stay. All her children were frightened and confused by the scene she created, frantically screaming as they clung tighter to her. Six of the bodyguards and two other test ladies rushed over to help get the situation under control and move the family along as quickly as possible. It took about ten minutes, but the family was finally escorted out of the area. Their cries and pleads eventually faded off into the cool, evening air.

Rosa felt a pit form in her stomach and thought she was going to throw up. She was afraid for them and couldn't believe things had reached a point of such extreme measures. The kids were helpless victims in it all, kind of like how she felt hours earlier. But Rosa was beginning to understand the new rules driven by the pandemic, even as confusing and unfair as they were. All she could do was look ahead of what was to come, and hopefully, it would lead to better days.

The North Beach Community

A few weeks had passed, and the new North Beach community settled in without much controversy, despite the close quarters the 240 folks had to adjust to. As promised, the first couple of weeks' essentials were brought in by some volunteers and divided up between the 60 groups. Thereafter the community assigned some of their own to continue to gather supplies.

Rosa and her shelter mates were lucky enough to get into one of the lean-tos that offered a bit more room than being in a tent. They all got along well. Larry spent almost every day with Georgie, especially fishing, catching buckets full of them. Any extra fish were shared among the community. The boys were responsible for keeping the wood stacked that they used for their nightly campfires and also helped out some of the other families.

Rosa and Sandy spent some time together, mainly preparing most of the dinners. Sandy was good about keeping things in order as well as a watchful eye on their belongings. Not that folks were stealing from each other, but on occasion, some haphazardly wandered into their spaces and disrupted them.

Initially, Rosa spent a lot of her free time by herself, away from the community, just sitting on the rocks by the water, listening to the waves gently lap against the sandy shore. Many times she got lost in the familiar sounds that brought her back to happier times. She loved it when she and her dad spent hours on their beachfront in Barbados, building sandcastles while her mother sat close by, coaching and soaking in the sun's rays. Rosa cried every time the waves snuck up and washed away their masterpieces. The sense of losing something she deemed so valuable at that time took a while for her to get over. Little did she know at that time that much greater possessions would later be washed from her life.

As the weeks moved on within the beach community, Rosa spent a great deal of time visiting with the other members. She'd check in on how they were doing and offered to help out as needed. There were times she'd sit for hours and just visit with them. Despite the fact she was only 15, Rosa had a sincere, mature kindness about her that attracted many who began to lean on her for advice and share their continued frustrations and fears of the future. On occasion, she'd help sort out some conflicts that arose between the groups, working out peaceful resolutions.

A couple months after the North Beach community settled in and others had opened, food and other supplies became harder to get as the distribution hub tightened up on rations. The transport boats became less reliable, and when they did arrive, brought fewer supplies. It added to the tension among all the communities, a pressure to fill the void. Since there was no viable plan to deal with the shortages, or leaders among them to initiate one, a lot of disputes erupted, leaving many fending for themselves, not sharing when they found supplies.

Rosa saw her community start to unravel and knew something had to be figured out so that everyone would get equal shares of any supplies coming in the community. At that point, even though harmony among them was dissolving, nobody stepped up to take charge and eliminate the intense conflict that was brewing within them. Rosa was sure there was a happy medium and wanted to find it, quickly.

She recalled how her dad effectively managed over 350 employees, keeping the peace between them all. He gave them a sense of direction and security so they all played an equal part in the success of his company. If there was a way to apply anything he had shared with her to change their current course of self-destruction, she was determined to figure it out and make it happen before it was too late.

Once she formulated a practical plan, Rosa decided to present it to the community. One evening as everyone was hanging around their campfires, she strolled down to the shoreline, took a deep breath, and hollered out to them.

"Hey everyone! How are you all doing tonight?"

The chatter quickly subsided as they all turned to see what she was up to.

"So, I just wanted to run something by all of you. Could you all gather around over here, so I don't have to shout so loud? Please?"

Within a few minutes, most everyone meandered over, all curious to hear what she had to say.

"Look, as you know, we're all in a bit of a predicament that I believe we can easily get out of if we all work together," Rosa started, feeling the palms of her hands begin to sweat as her heart pounded hard against her chest.

Even though she had talked to most of the community on a one-to-one basis or in smaller groups, she had yet to address such a sizable crowd. It made her nervous and uncertain as she was worried about how they would respond to her taking on such a bold role.

"We know things have become extremely difficult, and some of us have decided to do things on our own, which I understand. But we need to keep in mind that we all are here for the same reason; first for survival and second to figure out what's next for us. In the course of doing this, we need to look out for each other!"

For a moment, nobody said anything. They all stood, eyes on her waiting to hear what she would say next until someone from the crowd broke the silence.

"Makes sense, Rosa!"

Then another hollered out, "I agree! We need to take care of each other."

The next thing Rosa heard was a disgruntled loud voice yell out, "Who made you the boss?"

"Let her talk!" another hollered.

The shout-outs made Rosa even more nervous, but she took a deep breath and continued, "Well, I have an idea that I think will help us all work together better as a team. As a community. And if you all approve, we can put it into action right away."

"What is this? A town hall meeting? Now we're going to have to decide what's best for everyone. Fuck this! I ain't looking out for anyone else!" one guy obnoxiously shouted as he sat by a nearby campfire, quite irritated his evening had been interrupted.

Rosa ignored him the best she could as she continued to face the group gathered in front of her, "It seems since the distribution hub has less to give us, we've all been drifting apart. It's also led to some of us only fending for ourselves and not caring about anyone else. There's definitely enough of everything to go around if we do it right, and we really should be sharing."

"Bullshit!" shouted another voice further back on the beachfront. "You're lecturing us like we're in grade school and news flash, you're just a kid yourself! If we don't look out for ourselves, ain't nobody else gonna do it for us! Especially you!"

"Shut up, Frank!" a man screamed from the crowd.

"Yeah, let her talk!" shouted another.

Rosa felt a bit intimidated by the remark but as she looked around at all the anxious eyes planted upon her, there was a sudden sense of empowerment that came over her. They all wanted to hear what she had to say, so she cleared her throat, ready to address them again.

"My goal is to help all of us make this a true community, and with all your help, we won't let anyone fall by the wayside. There's already too much turmoil going on for each of us. We need to be able to depend on each other, it will help make things better. We have no idea what the future holds, and we have nobody else but each other right now."

Rosa paused as someone yelled out, "Amen to that!"

Followed by, "You're spot on. Tell us more!"

"How do you see it working?" another asked.

"What's your idea?"

"You go, girl!"

Rosa watched as most everyone inched a bit closer, then responded, "I believe if we divide up certain responsibilities like finding food and essentials, gathering campfire wood, cooking community meals, along with other duties, as long as everyone participates, this will fix itself. This sets us on the path to equally share and create a true sense of comradery."

"Great idea, Rosa!" a lady in the front of the crowd shouted.

"Not a bad one!" another agreed.

"That will never happen!" barked another disgruntled guy as he walked away from the gathering.

"Yeah, never! I don't see it!" another yelled, following him.

Rosa felt the tension build and quickly continued before more negativity could surface, "Hold on, everyone. Think about this. We have nothing to lose by giving it a shot! We already have a group of guys that go to the distribution hub and others helping out in some other areas. You know that has worked well for all of us, so why not just expand the concept? And we all get involved as a team instead of just for ourselves. Something has to change, and I know deep down every one of you agrees. We're all we have. Right here, right now. We're family, no matter how you look at it. So, let's take care of each other," she paused for a moment, then asked, "Who's on board?"

For a short time, the crowd chattered among themselves until one man yelled out, "That is a damn good idea! Why didn't we think of this earlier? Count me in!"

Within seconds others followed with, "Great idea, I'm in!"; "Let's do it, I'm in"; "A brilliant concept!"

"Count me out!" one guy gruffly shouted over the crowds' growing enthusiasm, then walked away, followed by a handful of others.

It didn't stop the positive vibes from flowing as the group started praising Rosa, jumping up and down, clapping and chanting, "Go Rosa! Go Rosa! Go Rosa!"

Early the next morning, per Rosa's request, the supporters of the plan got together to establish the community's new teams. Rosa wanted everyone to take part, but there were several who refused even though they liked the concept, so she let them be. By an unexpected unanimous vote, Rosa was chosen to be at the helm of it all. As days went on, the plan had proved to be a gold mine as food became more plentiful, spirits were higher, folks watched out for each other more, and the tension level lowered.

The Street Thugs

Even though the community was in a better place and things were running smoothly, unrest was just around the corner and involuntarily invited itself into the community a couple of weeks later.

Just a few months earlier, a small street gang had moved into the Burlington area and took stake in some territory near the center of the city. There were only four of them, but they quickly became an extreme nuisance and threat to those trying to gather essentials. Everyone did the best they could to avoid contact, but it was inevitable. Since the street thugs thought that their 'claimed turf' was unrightfully invaded when others passed through it, they harassed, followed, and stole from them. They particularly took an interest in the beach communities, knowing their main purpose in town was to gather goods.

The burly thugs were a force to be reckoned with, ranging from mid-30's to 50s and standing well over six-foot-two. Despite any coolness or humidity in the air, each wore leather vests over filthy white t-shirts displaying armfuls of bulging muscles covered with prison and street-made tattoos. Unified blue bandanas held their straggly, long greasy hair out of their faces, and each forehead sported a small, black skull tattoo. Unmanicured beards hung down past their neckline, and thick silver chains jingled from their belt loops with every step they took. The sight of them together made many avoid them at all costs, even if it meant no goods for that day.

The street thugs had once been members of the Sons of Arches, a motorcycle club out of Montreal, and had rolled into Burlington just as the second wave of the pandemic settled in. When they first arrived in Vermont, they permanently parked their motorcycles due to a gas shortage, then marked their new territory within walking distance to the distribution hub and the center of the city. There they patrolled around and quickly made a name for themselves as they terrorized helpless victims that crossed their path. Trouble wasn't foreign to them, and each had their share of bouts with the law, serving prison time on several occasions. They vandalized occupied homes, sneaking into them in the middle of the night and snatching any valuables they could find. They took what they wanted when they wanted, and if the victims didn't cooperate, they paid the price of getting beaten up, some raped, and even killed for denying them goods.

They had no sense of morals or sympathy for the young, old, women, or children. The abusive behavior, sexual acts, and fatal fights they bestowed upon the city were almost an everyday occurrence. Even the small amount of law enforcement that was left, did their best to avoid the thugs.

Any alcohol, drugs, jewelry, or essentials the thugs stole were considered hot commodities in the ever growing black market. They would sell the stolen goods to it and get money for drugs and other various things. Then the black market sold the items back to the public at ridiculously high prices. It was an endless circle of untouchable crime.

It wasn't long before the thugs decided they had enough of the newly formed yellow banded groups who had recently heavily invaded their territory. In their eyes, the banders were taking money out of their pockets, and the thugs agreed it was time to put a stop to it. For a few days, they kept their eye on five of the yellow banders who, almost daily, came to town and gathered up supplies. The thugs watched as they'd rejoin a larger group of banders on Church Street before they headed back to their community.

The thugs had decided it was time to teach them a lesson. The five yellow banders had finished their daily task and were heading through an alleyway to Church Street, where they planned to meet up with the rest of their group as usual. The boys knew about the thugs and had been warned, but they had been pretty carefree with their ventures, not thinking anything was going to happen to them, especially in broad daylight. That was until they heard the jangle of small chains getting louder behind them. They were all too familiar with the horrible stories people told about the thugs but shrugged them off since they had never laid eyes on them. For the most part, none of the yellow banders had either. But that day, when the boys turned around to see what the noise was, was a day they would never forget, the day they laid eyes on the four oversized thugs quickly moving toward them.

One of the boys mustered up a scream while another yelled, "Run! Run now!"

"Shit," another screamed, as they started racing down the alley.

They weren't quick enough. Two of the banders dodged the thugs as they tried to grab their backpacks, and raced to the end of the alleyway, then quickly darted out of sight. The other three weren't so lucky. It was as if they hit a brick wall when the thugs stopped them dead in their tracks, slammed them down to the ground, and pushed their faces into the loose stone pavement. They were terrified and helpless as the thugs stood over them and yanked off their backpacks.

"Who the hell do you think you all are? Coming in here every day or so, and stealing from us, trespassing on our territory. You wimpy, no good punk asses!" Jeremy shouted as the other thugs kicked the boys' ribs with their thick, heavy boots.

Jeremy's six-foot-five frame and 300 pound body made the boys tremble. Jeremy had spent many years as a club member with the Sons of Arches and was kicked out due to his physically aggressive nature with civilians. After forming his own group with five others, they eventually decided to head across the border into the Laconia, New Hampshire area. They had been there several times before the virus invaded, to attend major motorcycle rallies held along the lakeshore. The thugs were surprised that so many folks were still there despite the pandemic warnings to stay out. They mingled and partied hearty with them for a few weeks. But then two of the thugs came down with high fevers, headaches, and slight coughs. Just a few days later one of them died, and the other was too weak to travel. At that point, Jeremy and the remaining three thugs decided to take off to Burlington, Vermont, where they heard a major distribution hub was. It was there that Jeremy, Blitz, Chug, and Bunyan's reign of terror, deceit, thievery, and violence took hold of the area.

The boys were ill-prepared for such an attack and certainly no match to defend themselves against the big burly guys or the pure terror that they encountered over those several minutes. All they could do was beg the thugs to stop but were only kicked harder in their sides for doing so.

"You're all about to learn a hard lesson, and make sure you send it back to all the other pieces of shit in your group. I don't want to see your grungy punk ass faces in this area again, and the same goes with the punk ass friends that you rolled in here with, or things will be much worse next time," Jeremy yelled as he bent down close enough to their heads that they felt his spit flying upon their faces.

All three were curled up in a fetal position, protecting their chests and hoping to soften the several blows they continued to encounter. Eventually, the thugs backed off and stood, watching the boys sob in pain.

"Bunch of babies! Stay the fuck out of our way. Next time, you won't know what hit you, and I promise you all, there will be no crying, you bunch of punk asses!" Chug hollered as the thugs screamed a few more obscenities, loaded the backpacks on their backs, and headed out of the other side of the alleyway, high fiving each other over their success.

It took a few minutes after the thugs were gone for the boys to get themselves together enough to even verbally check in on each other.

"Holy shit, I can't believe that just happened to us," one of them weakly said.

"It could have been far worse," another replied, "I couldn't breathe there for a minute."

"Well, we're still breathing, so that is a start. Hopefully, none of us have any broken bones. But I know they beat the shit out of me, and I'm not sure I can move," the third one replied.

They laid there a bit longer, barely able to move when a large group of yellow banders raced to their side. They helped the boys to their feet and got them out of the alleyway, back into the daylight, where they saw how badly their chest and sides were battered. Miraculously, no bones were broken.

Once back at the North Beach Community, nobody could believe what had happened. Up until that day, they all had been lucky enough to ward off any type of attacks from the thugs. Even though there were other gangs out there, the street thugs had the most violent reputation, even with just four of them. Rosa called everyone together to talk about what happened and how to best handle it.

It was decided that the community needed to step up their awareness of the thugs as well as tighten security on the beach, knowing that the incident wasn't going to be the last with them. The thugs had been spotted invading some of the other beach communities, but had yet to strike theirs. Rosa felt after that encounter, they were most likely high on their target list. The last thing they needed was to let the thugs instill fear that would prevent gathering essentials from downtown. Business as usual would prevail, but with some slight modifications when they next went into town. The plan was simple in the banders' minds; keep their groups to a minimum of ten or even more at all times, especially if any threats lurked about. Staying away from shortcuts was mandatory.

The five teens that were involved with the attack were assigned to other tasks away from the city, so there'd be no chance to run into the thugs again. Several older, more muscular guys took their place and Rosa hoped that the new changes would be more intimidating and ward off any future attacks from the thugs as they moved through the city. Forty of them would travel together, then split up into a few smaller groups while gathering essentials, then would meet back up. A couple of days later, they headed downtown.

No sooner did the new team of yellow banders arrive on Church Street when they spotted the four street thugs sitting just a block away, on one of the large boulders. The banders knew they were being watched and most likely would be followed, so at that point, they decided not to take any chances and only split up into two groups. Then they took off in different directions, waiting to see which one the thugs would follow. But they didn't follow. Instead, they just sat patiently in the same spot, waiting for the group to reunite.

"Wow, I think this plan worked," Jimmy stated, the leader of the yellow bander group, "They haven't moved. I believe we showed them!"

James Richard Stark was in his mid-30s and stood a little over six-feet tall, was quite muscular, and had a personality that would easily entice people to follow his direction. Jimmy was of Jamaican descent, born and raised there until his late teens when he came to the states to attend the Harvard Business School on a scholarship. After he graduated, Jimmy got a job in Vermont, where he worked on some major projects for a large technology firm. In his free time, he traveled back to his home country to visit family and a girl that he had been sweet on. He had been working on getting her into the states until the virus put a halt to it. He had not seen any of them since.

Jimmy had been the leader of the original distribution hub gatherers and continued to be one of Rosa's right-hand persons. He also was involved with most of the decisions around the community and was well-liked by most, even though his aggressive personality came out to play when he wanted things to get done.

"I'm not so sure, Boss Man," one of the banders said as he pointed down the street.

The four street thugs were rapidly heading right toward them, as Jeremy yelled, "Listen, you no good punk asses, you were told to stay the hell out of our territory! We gave you fair warning!"

His loud baritone voice had everyone's undivided attention, both the yellow banders and the onlookers. The general instinct of the group was to get the hell out of there but knew the protocol, to stand firm and not move or shout anything back. They had numbers on their side. Forty of them versus four. So, they just watched as the thugs got closer, then abruptly stopped about ten feet away. The thugs stood in a line with their feet apart, and arms crossed, flexing their huge arm muscles. The message was clear. They were ready to fight, yet they didn't move any closer.

Blitz belted out, "If you know what's good for you right now, you best be dropping all those goods and getting your asses out of dodge!"

Nobody moved.

Claude Francis, known as Blitz, had always been the quieter one of the thugs, even when he was a member of the Sons of Arches motorcycle club. For the most part, his 34-year-old six-foot-three frame was way more intimidating than his actions. Blitz stayed in the background and out of sight during any major incidents the gang got involved with. But since they had shrunk to only four of them, he had to take more responsibility, or Jeremy told him he would be cut loose to fend for himself. Blitz had nowhere else to go, so he sucked it up and followed his demands.

Again, Jeremy screamed at the top of his lungs as he moved a couple steps closer, "Did you not hear him? Drop the damn goods and all your backpacks, or else you'll be sorry, and there will be a much higher price to pay! Now!"

Still, the yellow banders made no effort to move, respond or hand over their belongings. The thugs stood there, waiting to see what was going to happen next. Despite their intimidation tactics, they knew they were outnumbered not only by the group but by other curious folks that had since gathered around. For the moment, they were defeated and could only watch as the yellow banders flipped the bird, then turned and calmly walked away, around the corner, and out of sight.

Jeremy was fuming as he screamed after them, "You'll be sorry, and make no mistake, you'll pay, you fucking punk asses!"

Payback

A lot of the other beach communities weren't as lucky as the yellow banders, having been burglarized, even physically terrorized by the street thugs in the middle of the night. Up until that point, the thugs had no qualms with the North Beach community. Their site was just far enough off the main street, surrounded by rocks on either side of the shore that the thugs deemed it not worth their efforts when others were much easier to access and invade.

Initially, the yellow banders had a few safety procedures in place just in case they were raided, but they seemingly only concerned the few wild animals that occasionally ransacked their supplies.

The street thugs were hot to get payback from the yellow banders for not staying out of their territory and disrespecting them, especially in front of others. They weren't used to losing control of any situation and planned to make sure it wasn't going to happen again. They knew all too well they were outnumbered and for the time being, confronting the banders on the streets wasn't an option. Even though the North Beach site was more difficult to get to, the thugs knew a couple of shortcuts without being seen, and knew it was time to make their entrance.

It was shortly after midnight, just a couple days after the banders ignored their demands on Church Street, when the thugs arrived on the North Beach shore. Everyone was already asleep in their respective shelters as the quarter moon dimly lit the little community resting peacefully on the sand. The street thugs planned to swiftly grab as much stuff from a few of the tents then get out of there without too much ruckus. They wanted the message to be loud and clear that more invasions would follow if they didn't conform to the thugs' downtown rules. The risk was already against them being in unfamiliar territory, not knowing what kind of weapons or manpower the yellow banders would lash out with. Regardless, the thugs felt there was no other choice but to make good on their threat and put the yellow banders in their place. They were ready to take back and protect what they considered was theirs … and so it began.

The street thugs had lots of experience with quick raids. They knew how to get in and out without any mishaps. The four of them picked a separate tent to invade, ones that were closer to the shoreline for easier in and out access. From experience with the other communities, they knew that most essentials were generally stored in the middle of the tents to keep them safe from animal theft. It also made it convenient to quickly unzip the tent door, slowly crawl part way in, grab the goods, and briskly escape. They had a high success rate with their process and had no reason to believe it would be any different with the yellow banders.

Despite a few challenges along the lakeshore with the terrain and having to wade through some water, the thugs made it to the yellow banded community. Just off to the side of the sleeping banders, they paused for a few moments within the tree shadows and listened for any movements across the sandy beach. Most of the campfire coals had died down, and the only noise was the gentle caress of the waves against the shore. All suggested their plan was good to go.

"This is it. Let's stick to the plan that works. No funny business, idiots," Jeremy loudly whispered as they stood in a small circle firming up their attack.

"Got it, Boss," Blitz agreed, as the others all nodded.

Jeremy got in a little closer to his gang and gruffly said, "Get the shit and get out as soon as you have it. Don't hang around for anything else, and that especially means you, Bunyan, keep it in your pants! And make sure as you leave to do as we discussed and pull the tents down on top of them. I want them all to get a clear message that we're the ones that took their shit. I'm done messing around. Just make sure you don't wake them up before you get out! You all got it?" he paused, then slapped Bunyan upside his head and gave a thumbs up signal to move forward as he huffed at Bunyan, "and I mean it."

They quietly moved out into the open along the shoreline toward their prey and waited until Jeremy threw his arms forward, giving them the go ahead to pounce. The plan had to be perfectly executed with the timing coordinated as all four approached the tents, unzipped the doors, and grabbed their possessions. Then they'd knock it over. Jeremy anticipated the screams from underneath it would wake the others just in time to catch sight of the thugs running off the beachfront. He wanted the banders to know it was them and instill a fear that would entice them to conform to his territory rules.

But the plan backfired as some of the victims woke up confused and scared during the raid; some even tried to grab back their valuables.

"Shut up, you little bitch!" Jeremy yelled as a woman's uncontrollable cries filled the air, begging him not to hurt her family.

"Don't even try it, you punk ass!" Chug hollered from another tent.

Within a few minutes, more of the community had woken and quickly came out of their living spaces as terrifying screams filled the air. Pleas for help were heard as the thugs had no other choice but to throw their weight around, roughing up a few of the victims who tried to stand in their way.

"Hey, what's going on out here?" one of the yellow banders hollered.

"Help us!" someone screamed from a nearby victimized tent.

The thugs realized that the community was on alert, and they needed to get off the beach sooner than later. One by one, they fled the tents, some without any goods, as they escaped up the sandy lakeshore toward the rocks before the rest of the community realized what had happened. But for those that were awakened and outside trying to figure out what was going on, witnessed three of the thugs' silhouettes dash off down the beach.

Jeremy was still there, eerily standing in the moon's light near the trees, delighting in the chaos they just created. He watched the crowd as they frightfully scampered about. Even though he managed to instill fear among them, he wasn't sure it was enough since his plan had failed.

As he got ready to exit, he decided to make his presence known and hollered out, "I told you all that you'd pay! You better watch your backs, you bunch of pansy-ass yellow banders, and stay out of our sight! Next time it won't be so pretty! You're ours now!"

Then he darted off into the woods and was gone.

Go Rosa! Go Rosa!

It was the first day of August; the summer sun was already throwing out heat in the early morning hours. A lot of folks at the North Beach community were up and tending to their assigned tasks. It had been a few weeks since the thugs had invaded their territory, and everyone was beginning to finally feel more relaxed. It had been decided that all but one group was to stay clear of the downtown area for a while so as to avoid the street thugs. They hoped their reign of terror was over and didn't want to give them any reason to come back.

The day after the attack, Rosa had assigned a team to find some knives, pepper spray, and other items for each group to have for protection, especially at night. She was opposed to having any type of firearms onsite, even though she still had Chuso's Beretta M9 in her backpack, but nobody knew, and she never planned to use it. The biggest fear with having others carry guns around was having them end up in the wrong hands. There were occasional check-ins to make sure people didn't bring them on-site, and for the most part, they didn't. Occasionally someone was caught trying to sneak them in, but they were quickly discarded.

Later that morning, as folks scurried about the beach community, Rosa sat on one of the rocks near the water, taking in the sun's warmth as it fell upon her shoulders. She was going over some notes she had taken when she was at the library, about some of the rumored virus-free places that were out there. It corresponded with the information she had heard from some transients who claimed they had traveled through those areas. The concept still seemed a little far fetched as the virus was invading most parts of the world, finding hiding places to survive in. How some territories were able to dodge it, didn't make sense to her.

From the news articles she pulled up, the places were referred to as *better lands* and new hope. The areas were remote ones, mainly south and further west of New England. They all appeared to be by water, had originally been evacuated during the beginning of the first round of the pandemic, and remained vacant from that point on. The editorials described that the vacancy somehow allowed mother nature time to regenerate the air and refresh the grounds, building up immunities against it. Some researchers insisted that it meant the better lands were also immune to any future attacks and wouldn't support the life of any new virus droplets.

Rosa felt excited yet skeptical as she continued to browse her notes. Although she could not find any supporting documentation on any of the claims or statements and no information about what would happen if an affected person or object were to go there, she was intrigued. She wanted to know more and if there was some truth behind the stories. She also found some information and even a few pictures of new settlers who moved into some parts of the better lands. Their venture was described as complicated and risky. Even though they found nirvana away from the virus, it was clear that many of the settlements were contentiously protective and not willing to share the lands once they claimed territories.

The better lands were few and far between, found in just four states: Kentucky, Missouri, Montana, and Wyoming. It was hard to believe that the country's original population of 330 million just three years earlier, had drastically declined to under 100 million. Although the 2023 census wasn't entirely accurate, it also predicted the numbers would continue to drastically decline once the third virus strain arrived. She thought by that time, those states would house the brunt of the population, if there was any truth behind it.

Rosa spent some time mapping out the distance of a couple of the places, trying to figure out which destination made the most sense to go to if she decided to make the trek. Since travel would only be on foot, Kentucky made the top of her list. There the better lands were located on an inland peninsula, surrounded by two lakes. She decided the best route would be through New York State then follow Lake Erie south. It provided the most distribution centers along the way, where she could seek some inside shelter and replenish supplies. Rosa calculated it would take a little over a month to get there without any foreseen mishaps.

Through her continued research, she found out that the inland peninsula was the largest in the country and had about 170,000 virus-free acres. The surrounding lakes, Kentucky Lake and Lake Barkley, had about 300 miles of untouched shoreline. Pre-pandemic days attracted a million-plus folks a year to the over 1,400 campsites on the land. Because it remained mainly untouched, wooden camps, RVs, boats, and other structures most likely had not been burned to rubble. She planned to research it a bit more.

Just as she started to make some more notes in her book, a frantic voice shouted from behind her, "Rosa, I need you to come over to the main tent and quickly!"

She turned around and greeted Ryan's distraught face. He was one of the youngest members on the team that was assigned to still gather essentials from the downtown area. He was clearly shaken up.

"What's the matter, Ryan?" she asked as she closed her notebook, hopped off the rock, and rushed over toward him.

"You've got to come with me, like now!" he exclaimed as he turned and started heading back to the main part of the community.

Ryan had been handpicked by Jimmy to work with him on the team. He had just turned 18 when he, his two younger sisters, and his uncle arrived at the beachfront. Prior to his new life, he had lost both his parents to a home burglary that went bad just before the evacuation notice arrived to burn their home. Ryan was timid but loyal, and Jimmy kept him close by his side.

"Over here," Ryan said as he motioned Rosa to the other side of one of the food tents where nine anxious and distraught members of the solo team were standing.

"What's up guys," she asked as her eyes fell upon four of the guys standing in the back of the group, who looked pretty roughed up, "What in the world happened to you all?"

"We saw them, rather….er…they saw us first," Jimmy answered, quite distraught himself.

One of Jimmy's shortcomings was caving into fear and frustration in certain situations. From time to time, it held him captive from taking control when he needed to step up to the plate. Instead of doing so, his inner child came out and preferred to shy away from the harsher circumstances. Rosa had asked him to be a team lead because she was initially impressed by his background, his kindness, and how dependable he was. It was shortly afterward that she noticed it was hard for Jimmy to make the tougher decisions necessary to run the team. But she liked and believed in him enough that she made it one of her missions to work with him on doing better.

At that moment, Rosa looked at Jimmy as he paused and waited for her response. She felt a sudden rush of fear come over her as she asked the next question, "Who saw you?"

Without hesitation, one of the other team members exclaimed, "The street thugs! The street thugs saw us and charged at us without any warning. They came out of nowhere, ran right up to us, and grabbed them." He turned and pointed at the four guys Rosa's eyes were focused on.

The boys weren't any older than Ryan and were the designated runners in the group. Their job was to go ahead of the rest of them to scout out places for the essentials they couldn't get at the distribution hub. Then the boys would take the leads back to the team, and they'd all go together to gather the goods.

One of them had a bloody lip; the others had some nasty bruising on their faces and arms. Their shirts were tattered. Rosa shuttered at the thought that the street thugs weren't done with them and knew much more was coming. It was apparent to her that they picked on the weaker links in the group as the boys had no recourse or strength to fight against them.

Rosa cleared her throat as she kept her eyes on the wounded, then harshly asked, "How did this happen? You all were instructed to not go anywhere near downtown!"

Nobody answered. She quickly moved closer to the boys to check them out and again, in a more forceful tone, asked, "How did this happen?"

Jimmy hesitantly responded, "Those damn street thugs! And that's just it, Rosa, we weren't anywhere near their supposed turf. We were down off Pine Street, checking out a lead the boys got us at the old chocolate plant, and poof, there they were! We were all together, the boys weren't alone, but we barely had time for eye contact when they suddenly ran toward us and jumped us. We panicked, and all of us, except them," he pointed to the injured boys as he continued, "were able to run from them. But Rosa, we had no idea that they were there or would even be that aggressive outside of their supposed turf. We really were ambushed!"

Rosa continued to check the boys out, then addressed the rest of the team, "I don't understand how all of you ran and didn't make sure these boys were with you. We will talk more about that later, but right now, we have to get a few of these guys some medical attention."

Rosa directed some of the team to take them to the medical tent then asked to speak privately with Jimmy.

"Hey Doc, we need your help," Ryan anxiously blurted out as he barged into the tent with the boys right behind him.

Dr. Parker looked up as several of the group entered.

"What in the world happened?" one of the nurses asked as she and a couple of others rushed to their side.

"The street thugs beat the shit out of us!" one guy answered.

"You're kidding!" Dr. Parker replied as she got up from a table full of paperwork and went over to check them out, "It certainly could have been worse, but how in the world did you run into them? You boys weren't down on Church Street, were you?"

"No, ma'am," another responded.

Dr. Lauren Parker was a tall, thin woman in her early 40s who had been a practicing pediatrician at the local hospital before the pandemic. The first wave of the virus took her two young children and her husband from her. She was grief-stricken, but she still had her job, and managed to get through the year, semi-healing until the second wave hit. This time the pandemic took her job and home. She was devastated and for a few weeks just wandered aimlessly around the city, blending into the homeless world, no longer caring about anything.

Eventually, Dr. Parker stumbled upon the North Beach community, and luck had it, there was a group looking for an extra person to share their space. Shortly after she settled in, her much needed healthcare skills came into play and, along with some other medical professionals, opened up the community medical tent. She was able to find some solace being around others in the same situation.

"Well, I think you boys will be fine. A few stitches are needed here and there but for the most part, consider yourselves lucky. Those are some vicious fellows for sure, and if I were you, I'd stay clear. Next time might not be so pretty," Dr. Parker lectured them all as the nurses continued to patch them up.

After the rest of the group dispersed, Rosa took a few moments with Jimmy and asked, "So Jimmy, you of all people, how could you leave those boys behind and not help defend them?"

He slightly shook his head and apologetically responded, "I don't know. It was completely stupid and uncalled for. I know I should've gone back for them, but it all happened so fast. None of us even knew the thugs grabbed those boys until they screamed. And we honestly thought they were right behind us, so we just ran and didn't think about it."

Rosa could tell in his voice how bad he felt. She knew the thugs were prone to such attacks, and in the end, they all took the chance to even be outside of their beachfront. It wasn't her job to reprimand him; she only had wanted to hear what took place and then focused on what they needed to do next.

"Okay, Jimmy, what's done is done, so now what we need to do is better prepare everyone. And I mean everyone. I hate to say this, but I know that these guys will come back here now. I have no doubt because they're pissed off. But, Jimmy, this time, we need to be ready for them, or things could get really bad."

He shook his head in agreement then worriedly asked, "What do you mean be ready for them?"

"Really, Jimmy, you already know. We need to defend our community. That's what I mean," she said, knowing he probably just wanted to hear her say it. "Those thugs are snakes in the grass, and from everything I've heard from other communities is that once they get in, they don't go away. Their pattern is unpredictable, but they basically attack in the middle of the night. Like they did here when they thought everyone was asleep. And they generally only go after the tents closest to the lake so they can easily escape with whatever they steal."

Jimmy shuttered at the thought as he said, "I can't believe they'd come back here, but if they do, it will be awful. They shook everyone up pretty good the first time around. And what do you mean other shelters? They were attacked too?"

"Sure, Jimmy, you don't think ours is the only one they ever preyed upon, do you?" Rosa asked but didn't give him time to respond, "Certainly not! I've spoken to some of the other communities; some felt their wrath way more than we have even begun to. I know they're capable of way more than what we saw here, and I fear we might just get a taste of it real soon. So we have to come up with a plan."

"This is unbelievable. How do just four street punks instill so much fear into so many?" Jimmy asked, getting a little testy.

Rosa just looked at him for a moment as she shook her head then responded, "I have no idea, but when they come back here, as I'm sure they will, they most likely won't be after just our supplies. They're going to want to make a bigger impact than before."

Jimmy quickly interrupted, "So what exactly are you saying? They will come after us, personally?"

"Yes, Jimmy. Exactly," she responded, a little irritated with his lack of foresight. "So, here's what I think we should do for the next few nights. We need the bigger, stronger guys to stay in the front line tents. All women, children and supplies will be moved to tents and lean-tos furthest away from the lake."

"This is crazy, Rosa! This disrupts a lot of folks' living conditions that are hard enough already!" he exclaimed. "You can't even be certain they will come back here."

"You're right; I'm not sure. But I'm more sure than not and don't want to take that chance of not being ready. Besides, Jimmy, this is only temporary. Folks will adjust."

"I suppose and guess that makes sense," he said reluctantly, nodding his head in agreement.

"Oh, one more thing, Jimmy," Rosa said as she lightly grabbed his hand, "I'd like you to be one of those guys in those tents."

Jimmy shuffled about, kicking around some sand, not happy to hear Rosa wanted him to be a front liner. He would do almost anything for her and the community, but the thought of possibly going face-to-face with the thugs again and in such close quarters wasn't one of them. He blankly stared at her, feeling his nerves pulse within him, and at that moment wished he never agreed to be a team lead or her right-hand person. She wanted him to step into an explosive situation that he knew he couldn't handle, nor wanted to.

Jimmy noted how the sun's rays intertwined with her blonde hair and how her blue eyes sparkled in it when she looked at him. He thought she was beautiful and admired her maturity and ability to help others wade through tough times and still come out on top. She had not failed anyone yet.

"Jimmy, are you listening to me?" she asked and continued, "I need you to get the other team leaders together and get this organized immediately! I want to meet with all these guys as soon as it's decided who will be in those tents. Can I count on you, Jimmy?"

He took a moment and looked across the lake, watching some small white caps form, then quickly disappear, then repeat. He felt her hand squeeze his then looked back into her eyes. He knew what he had to do.

"Yes. You can count on me," he nodded in agreement, then started to head toward the main part of the community where folks were busy taking care of their daily tasks.

Before he got too far away, Rosa added, "Thanks, Jimmy, I knew I could."

That same night, under Rosa's direction, the 12 front row tents filled up with the planned mixture of the older, more muscular guys, Jimmy included. They were all equipped and ready to defend the community if the intruders showed up. There was a sense of fear and anxiety lurking about as nobody knew when the street thugs would even show up, if they'd bring backup with them, or what the outcome would be. The only thing there was no doubt about was they were as ready as they could be. If they won the battle, then maybe the thugs would leave them alone for good.

A couple of evenings went by with no incident, so people started to question if the thugs might not be coming after all. Even though most of the guys were committed to staying on the front line, some of them felt it was unnecessary and wanted to go back to sleep with their families. At that point, Rosa wasn't inclined to have anyone drop their guard, even though she understood how they were feeling. She agreed to re-evaluate the situation in a few days but was sure they weren't out of the woods yet. The thugs were streetwise and letting things subside, laying low and waiting until their prey once again became vulnerable. That was something Rosa was sure they were doing and refused to surrender to.

A couple more nights went by with no sign of them. Rosa began to rethink her strategy, as promised, knowing everyone was frustrated and patience was low. She knew there needed to be another plan to keep the community protected without continuing to keep the families separated. She decided she'd call a meeting the next day, to discuss other alternatives.

Despite the underlying threat of the thugs and the frustrations it placed within the community; they still enjoyed fun evenings together by the campfires. They played guitars, sang songs, toasted marshmallows, and enjoyed the coolness of the summer evening air after the long hot days. That evening was no different. As a few of the kids ran around the beach, their laughter was occasionally drowned out by the sounds of the waves rolling across the water. The full moon cast its light across the lake and upon the community. For that moment, all was peaceful for the yellow banders.

It had been a long day; Rosa turned in a bit early. She planned to hit the library in the morning to do some more research on the better lands, if the internet cooperated. The team leads were looking forward to getting together with her afterward, to come up with a new safety plan for the community. She was just about to drift off to sleep when Sandy and Georgie came into the lean-to. She heard them get settled and hoped they'd go right to sleep. Georgie did. She heard his light snores almost as soon as his head hit the pillow.

"Rosa, you awake?" Sandy whispered as she got in the sleeping bag next to her.

Rosa thought about pretending to be asleep but took a deep breath, then turned toward her and whispered, "Just barely, Sandy. What's up?"

"Well, I was thinking about what we all are going to do next with summer soon winding down. Larry and I were chatting about it earlier. We know the winter shelter is available to all of us with the option to come back here in the spring, but I'm not sure that's what we really want to do. Larry knows a place just a bit north that we may head to. I just want to make sure we make the right choice. I really hope things will get back to normal, and life goes on, but at this point, what do you think the chances of that are?" she asked, seemingly a bit frazzled, looking for some reassurance and guidance.

"I don't know, Sandy," Rosa said, hesitating for a moment, contemplating how to respond to her. "I do know it is predicted the virus is going to hit again. I don't have all the facts on it yet and will look into it more tomorrow when I go to the library. I just don't see things ever getting better. In fact, I'm not sure next summer will be as good as this summer. I would advise you guys to come to the winter shelter with us and decide from there. There should be a better prediction on the virus at that point."

Sandy sat up and let out a bit of a sigh. Rosa knew she was upset; she also sat up and put her arm around her as she added, "But we can't worry about it. We have to just take each day as it comes and worry about getting through them, day by day. Just get some rest, Sandy. Right now, we're okay."

Rosa felt Sandy's body shake as she tried not to cry, then responded, "Okay, Rosa, thanks. I appreciate it. I'll talk to Larry in the morning. Good night." She laid back down and curled up in her sleeping bag.

"Night, Sandy," Rosa said as she laid down next to her, listening to her sniffle.

Rosa finally fell asleep, and into dreamland. And what a dream she had with chilling screams that pierced the silence of the night. She abruptly sat up and realized it wasn't a dream. The frantic screams and cries only got louder and were coming from somewhere outside their lean-to.

Then a voice yelled out, "Oh my God, no, no, please don't! Get away! Get out, kids! Run!"

Rosa heard little kids yelling off to the left of the lean-to, "No, leave me alone, no…get away! Mommy!"

Larry had gotten back to the tent just an hour earlier, and now he, Sandy, and Georgie were also awake, sitting up in their sleeping bags, staring at the lean-to door, trying to figure out what was going on outside their walls.

As Georgie jumped into Sandy's sleeping bag with her he asked in a high pitched, scared voice, "What's happening, Sandy? Are they coming in here?"

She hugged him tightly and answered, "No, Georgie, nobody is getting in here."

More screams came from the other side of their lean-to. Rosa heard tent doors unzipping and assumed folks were coming out of them to see what was going on.

Suddenly, a deep loud voice rang out into the air yelling, "Shut the fuck up," making Rosa shutter from the inside out.

She had no doubt it came from one of the thugs and they weren't near the frontline tents. They had made their way into the community, right next to her. As more people started yelling and screaming, Rosa felt her heart thumping against her chest. It was obvious something very bad was happening outside of the lean-to, and she had to find out what it was before it got worse.

"I'm going out there to see what's going on," she quickly announced to her three roommates as she got up and threw on some clothes, trying not to let panic take over.

"You can't go out there, Rosa!" Sandy exclaimed as she hopped up in front of her. "Larry, stop her!"

Rosa grabbed Sandy's arms, trying to calm her down a bit as she exclaimed, "I'm fine, don't worry! You guys just stay put. Too many of us roaming around out there right now is a recipe for a greater disaster. I just want to see what's happening, so please, just hang tight."

As she started to open the door, Larry forcefully grabbed her arm and tried to reason with her, "What are you doing, Rosa? Come on, you can't be serious. Listen to what is going on out there! It's some bad stuff. You can't go out there!"

"I'll be fine," she said, trying to break his tight grip.

He held on as he continued, "This is not the time and place to subject yourself to whatever it is! We need to stay right here until we know for sure what is happening."

Rosa wasn't happy or surprised with Larry's reaction. He had always avoided any type of conflict around the community by hiding away until it was resolved. At that moment, she wanted him to put on his big boy pants and demands to go out there instead of her, or at least with her. As the continual pleas and intense screams penetrated through the air, she knew it was time to get out there, but also knew she couldn't do it alone.

Rosa abruptly pulled her arm away from him and said, "You're right, Larry, I can't go out there!" She took a moment and stared into his eyes, watching them soften as he thought he had won. "At least not by myself!" she exclaimed as she grabbed her backpack.

The moon's rays sliced through the small ceiling vents just enough to provide some light to find Chuso's gun and the box of ammunition. Sandy gasped and grabbed Georgie closer as they watched Rosa put the bullets into the clip.

"What are you doing, Rosa? Where did you get that?" Sandy nervously asked over the continued screams.

Larry froze in his tracks, unable to say anything, shocked to see the little, friendly, sweet, caring Rosa he thought he knew, loading a gun.

As Rosa pushed the loaded clip into it, he timidly asked, "Where in the hell did you get that?"

"Don't worry about it. It's a long story, and right now, it's going to come in handy, trust me. All will be fine. Just please, stay put," she said as she looked at them one last time before she pushed the door open and disappeared into the night.

Once outside of the lean-to, she saw many folks already gathered not too far from the commotion. The desperate cries for help and muffled moans were much louder. Rosa spotted three little kids standing alone in front of a nearby tent, pleading for help. She couldn't comprehend why there were so many just standing around, not helping them. It had become obvious that their mother was still inside their tent being brutally attacked. Rosa could see the muted shadows of one of the street thugs moving within it.

Just a few tents from there were more screams, followed by another all too familiar boisterous voice from within, "You stupid bitch, shut the fuck up and just do what I tell you, or your kids won't see you walk out of here!"

Jeremy and his gang were ready to teach the community a lesson and have some fun doing it, but the lady wasn't cooperating. Rosa spotted his shadow within the tent, his hand raising above the woman and then the sound of contact that rang out for all the nearby ears to hear. Her kids were finally shuffled away by some neighbors but were still close enough to know what was happening to their mother. Everyone just stood and watched as the shadow began to roughly move up and down on the woman. Panic had most of them frozen in place.

Rosa took a deep breath and shouted out to some of them to take all the kids away from the area. It was then she spotted Sandy, who had already sprung into action, escorting several of them away. For that split second, Rosa was relieved Sandy didn't listen to her and didn't stay put.

Knowing things were going to get worse before they got better, Rosa tightened her grip on the gun and pulled the slide back to load a bullet into the chamber as she got closer to the tent door and a clearer vision of Jeremy. He got his way as he savagely raped the woman. Rosa's blood was boiling, and she couldn't hold back any longer.

"Get off her now, or I will shoot!" she exclaimed, surprised by her own stern demand, then barged into the tent with the gun pointed at Jeremy's head.

She could hear everyone around her gasp and some chatter about her boldness and the realization there was a gun among them.

"Get off her!" Rosa demanded again as she stepped a bit closer.

A momentary silence filled the air. Rosa's hands were sweaty, and her body trembled as she tried to hold the gun steady. She watched as

Jeremy turned his head, locking his eyes on hers while still inside the woman.

Rosa felt a lump in her throat as he grunted at her, "You ain't going to shoot me, you little bitch! Just get out! Mind your own damn business!"

Then he ignored her, roughly slamming himself in and out of the sobbing woman. Rosa took a deep breath then clicked off the safety.

"I said get off her! Now!" she screamed, getting his undivided attention.

It was clear Jeremy was agitated by the threat as he jumped up off the half-naked woman, yanked his pants up, and fidgeted to zip his fly as he moved toward Rosa with rage dashing from his eyes.

"Who are you to threaten me, you little punk ass bitch! I told you to get lost! Maybe you're just jealous I didn't go after your ass! I can fix that now, no problem!" he exclaimed as he put his hand over the bulge still in his pants, not taking her or the gun seriously.

Rosa was overwhelmed by the all too familiar aftermath of whisky reeking from him. She could not escape the wretched smell. For a brief moment, it brought her back to the day in the kitchen when Mr. Chuso's fat, sweaty body was pressed against hers.

Jeremy started to hysterically laugh at her before he continued, "This has got to be a joke, you fucking little twit! Like you are going to shoot me! Let's see if you even can. Come on, do it! I dare you!"

He pounded on his chest and shouted even louder for her to shoot as he moved a few steps closer. Rosa slowly backed out of the tent and was aware of everyone standing around, seemingly unwilling to step in and help out, but she stayed focused on the monster in front of her.

"Come on! What are you waiting for, you little chicken ass? You want to shoot me? Just do it! Otherwise, I'll show you how to use it!" he angrily screamed as his face became beet red.

Rosa remembered Mr. Chuso's threats as he had her pinned against the kitchen counter; his hot, whisky breath against her face, the smell of his body stench, and his sickening whispers in her ear of what he wanted to do to her. For a moment, she thought she was going to throw up. Then she heard the woman scream from inside the tent, frantically calling out for her kids.

"Come on bitch, let's see what you got!" Jeremy continued to bait her, keeping his eyes glued on the gun.

"Get out of here now and take your three bloody ass terrorists with you, or I promise, I will shoot you all!" Rosa screamed as loud as she could, hoping he would just walk away fearing the gun, but he wasn't taking her seriously, and she knew it.

He glared at her and didn't seem phased by the Beretta M9 pointed directly at his chest. He was sure she had no idea how to use it and was pretty sure it wasn't even loaded. The more he thought about it, the more irritated he got and had about enough of her threats. Suddenly he let out a gigantic roar as he lunged toward her to gain control of the situation.

For just a moment, one could have heard a pin drop in between the waves brushing against the shore as the sounds of three quick gunshots rang out in the cool, night air. It happened so fast, without a second thought, Rosa pulled the trigger as he plunged toward her. As the gun silenced, Jeremy laid on his back, in front of the tent. His open tattered leather vest revealed a white t-shirt quickly soaking up the blood coming from the left side of his chest. His eyes were wide open, staring straight at Rosa.

She felt her body quiver as she lowered the gun, knowing he was justifiably dead. The thug's reign of terror was finally over.

"No! Jeremy!" Bunyan screeched as he came racing out of a nearby tent that he had been terrorizing.

Out of the corner of her eye, she saw Bunyan briefly pause and look at his friend, who lay motionless in a pile of blood. Just as she turned toward him, Bunyan immediately charged at her with a knife in hand. The next thing she knew, the gun fired three more times, taking him down before he knew what hit him. He didn't survive. Again silence blanketed the community long enough to hear the other two thugs running across the sand. Everyone stood still as they watched them continue down the shoreline and out of sight.

A few minutes later, the silence was broken. Everyone was in shock as they started talking amongst themselves about the unbelievable acts that unfolded right in front of them. Not only were two dead men lying on their turf, Rosa had the gun that killed them. For the most part, a sense of relief fell over the community knowing the thugs could no longer torment them. As they tried to come to terms with it all, most of them realized how courageous Rosa was to stand up to the intruders, and help those that were being brutally attacked. That evening bore a life changing event for the beach community.

Rosa felt her body shake. She was upset and shocked by what had transpired yet couldn't believe how easy it had been to pull the trigger and eliminate two people, two human beasts that had spewed so much terror on everyone. For a brief moment, she wished Mr. Chuso was lying next to them. As she stood by many of the others looking at the bodies, she felt a small sense of peace and triumph. At last she had really made a difference and it was time to talk to everyone.

As she stood near the dead thugs, her trembling voice spoke out, "All I can say is this happened so fast. I really don't know what else to say except it's over now."

"It could have been way worse," a man standing near her said, watching as others comforted one of the victims.

One of the ladies worriedly asked, "Will the other two come back? Are we still not safe?"

"Yeah, will they? They know what happened here!" another concerningly stated.

Rosa replied, "No. They won't come back here. Too much has happened."

"Right, you don't think they will want revenge?" The man asked.

Jimmy approached Rosa as she continued to look at the dead bodies and asked, "What are we supposed to do with them?"

Rosa looked at him then back at the bodies as she authoritatively instructed, "I need some of you to get them out of here. Just move the bodies into the woods for now, and we will deal with them at the first sign of light. Get a blanket and cover them up," she paused as several men started moving toward the dead thugs, then continued in a softer tone, addressing everyone within earshot, "I'm very sure the two other thugs won't come back. There are only two of them. They can't get revenge. You all are safe to go back to your lean-tos and tents and get some sleep. Let's all regroup in the morning."

The shaken community just stood and watched as Jimmy, Ryan, and several other men picked up the bodies and carted them off into the woods. A couple brought over some blankets as Rosa watched the victimized mothers, reunited with their children. Once again she could hear the waves beating against the shore as she took the clip out of the gun, emptied the chamber, then headed into her lean-to.

Larry was all riled up as he followed her inside and started yelling at her, "Are you crazy, Rosa? Did you really just murder two people? And you had a gun in here the whole time? What the fuck were you thinking?"

As she put the gun safely in her backpack, she was angered by his frantic, unsympathetic behavior. He knew the situation was bad and knew what she was up against as he just stood by. He certainly didn't come to her aid or even ask how she was doing after the fact.

"Yes, I did, Larry. I shot them! Tell me, what choice did I have? They were raping women; both attempted to charge at me. It would've been me laying there if they got to me first and I'm sure you know that."

Larry just stood near the lean-to door, his hands on his hips as he sarcastically responded, "No matter how you swing, Rosa, you murdered them in cold blood!"

Rosa stood directly in front of him, angrily responding, "Again, what choice was there, and by the way, Larry, where were you in all this? You didn't stay in here like I asked you to do. None of you did. So you were out there watching all this unfold, and you didn't think to help. You're such a man! Get out of my way." She tried to move past him.

"What and let you go back out there? You've done enough damage, don't you think?" he asked as he continued to block the door.

At that moment, Rosa was more infuriated by his reaction than what had just happened and lashed out, "If you can't get behind this and understand it was the best outcome to protect the community, then feel free to pack up and leave!"

Not waiting for his response, she swiftly pushed past him and went outside to see how everyone was doing.

As she approached one of the victims and her kids, they embraced and praised her for being so brave and saving them. Others started gathering around, also expressing their gratitude.

Suddenly, a man shouted at the top of his lungs, "Thank you, Rosa! You saved us!"

Another shouted, "Thank you!"

After a few more shout outs, most of the community joined in unison for the next several minutes as they ranted, "Go Rosa! Go Rosa! Go Rosa!"

It wasn't until then that she allowed tears to escape down her cheeks. She had no regrets of the outcome of the evening and relished in the acknowledgment from her beach family. The world they all lived in would never be the same again, and challenging times were far from over. The need for protection for everyone was evident, and Rosa knew more work needed to be done sooner than later.

Moments later, Sandy and Georgie ran over, giving her a tight, warm hug. The three stood with arms locked around each other until the chanting died down and the air once again filled with the sounds of the waves hitting the shore. Folks made their way back to their sleep areas as the moonlight shined across the beach.

When the three got back to their lean-to, they found Larry in his sleeping bag, his back towards them. Rosa never bothered to see if he was awake or not, although she was sure he was. For the most part, she was glad he didn't leave. It was close to 4:00 a.m. when they all finally fell asleep, escaping a real-life nightmare that had found its way into their little community that evening.

The Decision

Just a few weeks later, life had once again settled down. It was time for the beach communities to prepare to move to the designated winter shelters as the colder months were just ahead. There were no more encounters with the street thugs, for any of the communities. Word had gotten out that the teenage gal was responsible for the peace. Nobody seemed to question the fact Rosa had killed them with a gun, nor did they ask where it came from or if she still had it. It didn't seem to matter as folks stopped and thanked her for being so brave, and sometimes shared their own horrific encounters they had with the thugs. Even at her young age, Rosa had gained a reputation of a leader, a confident, a protector, and a friend among not only her community but others as well.

Rosa had yet to share with anyone what she discovered about the better lands. She wasn't even sure it was a good idea, thinking nobody would take her seriously and possibly feel she was acting irresponsibly. There was more thinking to do on it as to whether it was worth trying to convince anyone to take the journey with her or just go on her own. With so much going on in their day-to-day survival procedures, there never seemed to be a right time to bring it up. What she did know was at that moment, everyone certainly was in a better place than they were before joining the community.

It was hard to believe that the summer had passed so quickly, and the last night of sleeping on the beach was upon them. Folks had pretty much packed up and were ready to leave the next morning. There were little signs of excitement as anxiety levels were high, not knowing what to expect once they hit the winter shelters. They had just really settled in, and things were working. Not all the yellow banders were heading to the shelter, some decided to move on to other places. Rumors were running rampant about the third wave of the virus creeping closer, making its way down from the north, adding additional stress to most.

But despite everyones' apprehensions and their different destinations, that night they all gathered around a few big bonfires sharing drinks, singing songs, and just enjoying each other, as if, just for that moment in time, all was back to normal.

Rosa had her own challenges after she made the decision to find the better lands on her own and knew she had to tell everyone that night. She knew not going to the winter shelter with them would be a letdown, and felt a bit nervous about making the announcement. She took a deep breath, stood among them, and began.

"Hey everyone, there's something that I'd like to share with you, if I could just have your attention for a moment."

The music, laughter and chatter eventually stopped as everyone shuffled around to face her, then listened as she said, "Some of you already know this, but most of you don't. I've been doing some research in the library over the last couple months about some land that might be virus free. I don't know for sure, but I feel confident enough in the decision that I've made. So what I wanted to tell you all is that I won't be going to the winter shelter tomorrow."

For a moment nobody said anything, then someone asked, "What do you mean, Rosa, you're not coming with us?"

"Yeah, what are you talking about?" another shouted.

She looked around at all the puzzled eyes planted firmly on her, then answered, "I'm going to head to the better lands on my own to check it out."

"We don't understand What better lands?" another person loudly questioned followed by more from others.

"What are better lands?"

"Traitor!"

"What about all of us?"

"This is a joke, right?"

"Are you crazy?" Jimmy piped in, knowing a bit about her research, and had been intrigued enough to go with her, but never expected her announcement and felt a bit jilted.

Rosa quickly focused on him as she softly said, "No, Jimmy, I'm not," then turned back to address the crowd, "Listen, everyone, I hear your concerns, but I promise that I'm not going to forget about you here, especially if there is really something out there that is safer than here."

"This is absurd," one person shouted as many more yelled out in agreement.

"You can't be serious?"

"What is really going on here?"

Just as she anticipated, the questions fluently flowed. Yet, so many more concerned and scared faces sat silently in front of her. The last thing she wanted to do was create any type of panic among them.

"I knew you all would have questions, and I'm sorry I didn't mention it earlier but so much has been going on. Besides, I just made my final decision today. Shortly after talking to some transients who shared there are some places out there that are virus free, I decided to do some research of my own, and it appears there are some. Places that the virus can no longer live. But who really knows what the extent of the truth is. Like I said, if they really are safe places, I will come back for you all."

"That's a true leader, leave us all behind," someone angrily lashed out.

Rosa's enthusiasm quickly faded, hearing that nobody else seemed excited for her. The questions died down and they all sat in silence, not knowing what to say next.

"Where is this place?" a voice asked, finally breaking the silence.

"You can't leave us, Rosa, not now!" someone else quickly screamed out. "We've been through so much and we need you at the winter shelter!"

Rosa wasn't sure how to respond and didn't want to make the last night all about her but knew she owed them more of an explanation so she responded, "Okay, the place I'm heading to is in Kentucky, a long way from here. It will take me well over a month to get there. It's like a small island surrounded by two lakes. And for reasons I don't know, the virus supposedly can't survive on it. With the third round ready to attack us, I decided to check it out. This has nothing to do with me wanting to leave you all. I promise I'll be back if it's a safe spot!"

Just as Rosa finished, someone yelled out, "You're a true leader, Rosa!"

"Why can't we all go?" Jimmy curiously asked, still irritated by her news.

"Yeah, why can't we?" several others asked.

Rosa answered, "It wouldn't be fair to bring you all along on my own whims, not even knowing what I will find. It could be far worse than here, I can't do that to any of you.

"But by yourself makes no sense," Ryan chimed in.

"He's right, you are a high risk traveler on your own," Dr. Parker agreed.

Jimmy moved closer to her and asked "Why leave now then? Why not wait until spring, at least when the weather will be better?"

"I want to come!" someone shouted out as many others simultaneously responded, "Me too!"

Rosa couldn't believe the positive responses and suggestions, but replied, "I just think now is a good time for me to go."

"You are not making sense but it sounds like there is no changing your mind," Dr. Parker responded.

Rosa slowly shook her head no, feeling a sadness take over the enthusiasm she had earlier, "This is just something I feel I need to do on my own. If I could take you all, I would, but I just can't. Not now."

"This is not a good idea," Dr. Parker replied.

After another lapse of silence, Ryan stood up, held his beer can above his head, and yelled out, "We'll miss you, Rosa! Here's to Rosa!"

At that point most everyone stood up and cheered her on. The rest of the evening Rosa spent her time sharing the plan with those that wanted hear to more, which were mainly everyone. Eventually, the fires died down and folks headed back to their shelters for the last time, not knowing if any of them would return in the Spring or ever see Rosa again.

Jimmy and Rosa were last to retire for the evening. They sat together for a bit, watching the last of one of the campfires fizzle out.

"You know, you don't have to do this by yourself, Rosa. I can just go with you. In fact, I'd prefer to go with you."

"You're really a good friend, Jimmy, but I really think I have to do this by myself. I would feel so bad to drag anyone along on this venture, especially you, and it's not what I thought. Besides, someone needs to stay and watch over the community and I believe you're the best one to do that."

Jimmy picked up a small stick that was laying in the sand and moved around some of the hot coals as he replied, "I think you're wrong, Rosa. You have way more support here than you think you do. At least just think about it a bit more before you run off by yourself. It ain't safe out here for someone like you and you will eventually wish me and some of the others came with you."

"Thank you, Jimmy. It is tempting, but I saw it in their eyes as I sprung this news on them. I'm sure they're all thinking that I'm young and irresponsible, and when push came to shove, believe me, none of them would have taken the plunge with me, well other than you. But it's okay, that is why I want to do it by myself, and it's the right decision and in my opinion, the right time. If it all works out, I'll be back, I promise."

"And if it doesn't?" Jimmy coyly asked.

"It will," she answered.

"I don't agree with this, Rosa," Jimmy replied as they both stood up, ready to head back to their shelters.

"You don't have to," Rosa softly said as she gave him a tight hug, "I appreciate you more than you know, and I'll be okay, Jimmy. I'll see you in the morning," then she headed off to her lean-to.

When Rosa woke the next morning, she was alone in the lean-to. Sandy, Larry, Georgie, and all their belongings were already gone. For a second, her heart sank, and she felt crushed that they left without even saying goodbye, but she knew why. They weren't very happy with her decision and had accused her of abandoning them, thinking only of herself. They, along with some others, barely spoke to her after the announcement the night before. She slowly packed up all her stuff and stepped out onto the beach to a sight that momentarily took her breath away.

The air was brisk, and a blanket of light dew covered the sand as the sun's rays danced upon it, causing it to glitter like a sea of diamonds. Fall was in the air. To her surprise, the tents were already disassembled and nobody was in sight. The living area that once was so lively, was vacant. But as she looked off to her right, along the beach shore, she saw most of the yellow banders grouped together with all eyes focused on her, so she slowly approached them. There was an unexplainable exhilaration that excelled from the group.

Just a couple of hours beforehand, Jimmy had woken the yellow banders up and called a meeting to further discuss Rosa's plans. At the end of it, they had made a serious decision.

Rosa knew something was going on and inquisitively asked the happy onlookers, "Hey guys, you're all up early and packed. I certainly didn't expect to see you all sitting here together. What's up?"

"We're waiting for you, Rosa," Jimmy stood up and moved toward her as he giddily announced, "We wanted to tell you that all of us here, well, we want to go to the better lands with you! We've decided you have two choices. You can either take us all with you today, or stay with us through the winter months so together, we can properly prepare for the travel to the better lands in early Spring. Either way, we're going with you!"

Some of the others chimed in, "We're with you, Rosa!"

"We're in this together!"

"We're going with you!"

"Let's do this together, Rosa," Jimmy excitedly said as he took her hands in his, as if he was going to propose.

Rosa was overwhelmed as she looked at Jimmy's tearful eyes then at the rest of the group standing behind him. Her eyes swelled up with tears as she realized everyone was serious and really wanted to take the risk with her.

"We won't take no for an answer!" Dr. Parker yelled out.

"Wow," Rosa replied, "This is truly amazing guys, I don't know what to say. I'm speechless. Do you all really want to go with me? For real?"

Sandy moved closer to her and responded, "You can't go without your family, Rosa. We all love you and trust you," then gave her a quick hug.

"We're all in this together, you're no longer alone, Rosa!" Jimmy exclaimed, still holding her sweaty hands.

She had not felt that wanted since living with her parents on Shelburne Bay. She had loved every minute they were in each other's presence. Never did she feel alone, pushed aside or that she was in the way. She missed them every day.

As she looked around at all the excited faces, their eyes begging her to stay with them, she didn't know how to say no, and at that point, didn't want to. Rosa squeezed Jimmy's hands before she let go, then slowly took her backpack off and set it down on the damp sand. She took a deep breath and responded to her community.

"Thank you. I can't tell you all what this means to me. I feel so honored that you all care this much and trust me enough to be willing to put all aside, and come with me. I'm not going to sugar coat it, it's a risky venture but, if this is what you all want, I mean truly want, to go with me to the better lands," she paused for a moment, then flung her arms up in the air as she excitedly screamed, "Okay! Yes! Let's do this!"

Everyone jumped around, cheering with enthusiasm as they moved closer to her, all seemingly talking at once. The celebration continued into the next hour, and it was decided they'd wait until Spring to migrate to the better lands.

Finally, after all settled down, Rosa said, "Okay, everyone, let's get our stuff and go to our winter home! I'll see you all over at the Memorial Auditorium!" She paused for a moment then shouted out, "Let's do this, family!"

Georgie ran over and grabbed her hand. After one last look around, Sandy and Larry also joined them. Even though they had decided to go to the auditorium for the winter months, they had no plans to follow Rosa to the better lands.

Just a couple of weeks later, Jean-Pierre Berger & Darcy Couture strolled into Rosa's life.

The Connection

From the moment Rosa and Jean-Pierre's eyes met, there was an undeniable connection between them. They both were taken back by a momentary feeling of Déjà vu and believed somewhere in a past life, their paths had crossed. Initially meeting the boys and listening to their story, Rosa wasn't sure why they landed in the Burlington area, or if they could be trusted, or why her heart thumped about in her chest when she stood next to Jean-Pierre. She was surprised and almost embarrassed by her reaction to him and hoped he didn't pick up on it. Little did she know, he felt the same.

Most of her young, pre-virus life was spent at an all girls' private school. Any outside activities were supervised by her mother or other girlfriends' moms and excluded little, if any, boy company. However, at one point, there was a boy who made her heart pitter-patter. They went to the same church and attended Sunday school classes together and exchanged flirty glances and smiles during those lone two hours per week. Rosa looked forward to those interactions despite the fact it didn't progress further. She recalled they abruptly stopped soon after he had a girlfriend. Rosa was heartbroken for months and dreaded attending the Sunday classes, knowing he totally ignored her. Just a year later, the pandemic hit, and everyone stopped going to church, so they never saw each other again.

Jean-Pierre felt the same pull towards Rosa, a feeling from inside, a tingle, like butterflies fluttering about. A feeling that he had once experienced but never acted on it. He never had a girlfriend nor had the time to really devote to one. Most of his free time had been spent hanging out with friends, playing basketball, volunteering at community events, and helping out within the family as things deteriorated. In the evenings, Jean-Pierre stayed in his room and played video games, did homework, and wrote in his secret journal. Even though, at the time, he had other siblings, he sometimes felt alone, with nobody to talk to so he'd write in the journal to help offset those feelings.

At one point, there was a girl he secretly admired. Danielle lived in the same neighborhood and they had known each other since being toddlers. They were best friends up until they turned 11 and he started spending more with his buddies. Then the pandemic hit.

Jean-Pierre found himself periodically thinking about Danielle and missed her company, wishing they still hung out. She vividly danced around in his memory and the times he used to love watching the breeze blow her long blonde hair across her delicate facial features as they'd sit by the river. He always wanted to gently move it away from her eyes, but never did. There were many times they were close enough that he just wanted to kiss her, but never did.

Danielle was one of the more popular girls at school and head cheerleader for the basketball team he was on. At times, Jean-Pierre felt she was an unwelcome distraction, especially during the games when he'd miss some plays because he was to busy keeping an eye on her. Group gatherings brought them together, which only stirred up more romantic feelings toward her. There were times he felt himself fill up with spurts of jealousy when she flirted with other guys. He got angry at himself, and didn't understand why he couldn't control those feelings.

Just as he decided it was time to make a move and let her know how he felt, the second wave of the virus strolled in, shutting down the town and she and her family quickly moved out of the area. Jean-Pierre continued to journal about her, forever wondering what it would've been like if they had gotten together. He never saw her again, but never forgot her.

Without a doubt, Rosa stirred up something inside him that he thought he'd never feel again. The cool, fall breeze blew her long blonde hair over her delicate facial features, and her sea-blue eyes smiled at him when their eyes locked. Jean-Pierre was intrigued by her and the leadership role she had assumed. He was smitten from the time their eyes first met. Maybe she just reminded him of Danielle, but this time, he hoped to explore his feelings.

The Winter Shelter

The boys gladly accepted the invitation to go back to the winter shelter with Rosa, at least until they decided what their next moves were. The new living arrangements in the Memorial Auditorium, had 1,000 spots available, giving priority to the beach community members. The auditorium was part of Burlington's history, built-in 1927 to honor World War I veterans and had seated over 2,000 people, pre-pandemic. Over the years, it has hosted events such as music concerts, wrestling mania, comedians, plays, and public events.

Among some of the new residents, besides Rosa's yellow band community, were the Leddy Beach red banders, the Oakledge Beach green banders, and some individual public and private beach members that had formed smaller communities who didn't have bands. Initially, those who had them, wore them.

Half walls were installed to keep each community together, making it easier to identify the groups. Many other survivors were housed in the nearby YMCA, and middle school. When the shelters filled up and were at overflow capacity, the homeless had to find other places to stay.

Some rooms on the lower level of the auditorium were used for healthcare, food and essential storage, and on occasion, to house an overflow of transients. Other rooms were available to use as a quiet escape from the masses; book reading, board games or mediating. Everyone stayed pretty much in their assigned sleep areas and occasionally intermingled with others outside of the building. For safety precautions, nobody was allowed to visit other shelters.

Because of the close quarters, everyone was tested for the virus once a day, around the breakfast hour and when coming back from outside of the building. Security was assigned the responsibility and if there were any positives, those people would be escorted off the property without their belongings, but able to collect them in a nearby alleyway later that day. Anyone that had been in contact with the infected was to be quarantined in a designated room for 24 hours, then retested. Luck once again was on everyone's side, as the auditorium remained virus free.

At that point, most everyone had heard of Rosa, the young girl who put a stop to the thugs' brutality. It was as if she was a celebrity among them. Nobody questioned or even spoke about how she did it, but many assumed, since the two thugs were never seen again. And the other two thugs, even though they were still around, didn't create any more trouble.

Rosa started hosting weekly rallies on the middle school grounds and in Battery Park, for all those interested in joining the Spring migration to the better lands. The attendees had grown from a mere few hundred to close to a thousand per gathering. It was far more than Rosa had ever expected. She felt a sense of responsibility to give them all they wanted, but wasn't sure she could safely move that big of a group. She had a few months to figure it out.

Rosa & Jean-Pierre

Over the next few weeks after Jean-Pierre's arrival, he and Rosa spent a lot of time together. Many late nights they stayed up chatting and getting to know each other. It became clearer, as time went on, that the platonic yet flirty friendship was headed in a different direction. The butterflies that fluttered between them were about to land.

One late afternoon Jean-Pierre and Rosa were hanging around in the yellow band section when he mustered up the courage to ask her out on a real date. She was delighted and quickly accepted the invite. Feelings were growing and she was excited to see what might be in store for them.

It was the first week of November and Fall was on the downside. Most of the trees had shed their once vibrant colored leaves, leaving the ground blanketed in the crispy brown leftovers. There were still a couple of hours before the sun started to set, so the couple packed up some munchies, grabbed a blanket and headed down to a desolate place along the lakeshore, one they had already spent some time exploring.

They picked a spot, laid the blanket over the damp sand and sat to watch as the sun's orange ball of fire disappeared slowly over the horizon, dimly casting its colors onto the lake.

"This is picture perfect," Rosa softly said, resting her head against Jean-Pierre's shoulder.

"That it is," he replied, putting his arm around her, gazing at her beauty he so admired.

As the waves continued to rub up against the shore, they sporadically talked about their day, the different groups they lived among, and what the future may hold for them. Rosa felt safe next to Jean-Pierre. There was a presence about him that made her feel like nothing else mattered and felt that he would defend her with his own life, if things ever came to that.

"Jean-Pierre, I have to ask you something," she said with a bit of hesitance in her voice.

He gazed into her eyes and softly touched her cheek as he said, "I'm listening."

"When the migration happens, we're going to have to split up in groups. There's no way that all the folks that want to join this migration can all leave at once. You see how the crowds are growing at each of the meetings. It's crazy. On top of that, I have no idea what to expect once we get there. Too many people traveling at one time could work against us. We also don't know how easy or hard the journey will be and in this case more is not merrier," she stopped for a moment and looked away from him, then continued.

"Darcy and I've been talking about it, and it seems to make more sense if we break up into teams of a hundred or less and have those teams travel about a week apart from each other. I've shared that there are some distribution hubs along the way that we can stop at, five to be exact. They may not like it or even provide for us if hundreds of people show up at a time. It makes sense, doesn't it?" She looked over at him to gauge his reaction.

Jean-Pierre caught sight of the sun just as the last of its color disappeared behind the horizon, then answered, "It does make sense. I was wondering how it would work out with so many people leaving at once. I think you guys are right. Having a team or even up to four or five teams of about a hundred or so trailing behind the other, will give us a better shot to move more people. But who knows, maybe the safety is in the numbers. Who would mess with a thousand or more people tromping down the street."

They both laughed, then nodded in agreement as Rosa continued, "Yeah, that would be a sight for sure. Well, we still have time to think about it and put a plan together. Spring is really just around the corner. But there's something else I wanted to say."

Jean-Pierre held her closer as she continued, "Well, if you don't know it by now, I like you, Jean-Pierre, alot. I'm pretty sure you feel the same. It's so crazy. You just came out of nowhere and now you never leave my thoughts when we're apart, and I can't wait to be with you when we aren't together."

Jean-Pierre felt his heart pound harder in his chest as he again softly touched her cheek, then gently took her hand in his and responded, "You don't know what that means to me, Rosa. And I'll be honest with you, I've fallen in love with you. I just can't keep it in any longer. I've wanted to tell you this for a while now."

Rosa felt her eyes tear up and was overjoyed hearing his words, and softly replied, "I love you too, Jean-Pierre. I've been waiting to tell you too."

Their lips softly touched as they drew each other closer, their eyes locked as tears of joy rolled down both their cheeks. For all they had been through in their young lives, that moment fused all that was, and all that will be, together for them.

"Oh, and just one more thing," Rosa whispered, after their long passionate kiss, "I want you to travel with me so we're not apart from one another. I can't even imagine doing this without you. Is that okay with you?"

Jean-Pierre quickly responded, "Of course, my sweet Rosa, I wouldn't have it any other way. Wherever you go, I will follow," then he softly kissed her.

"Thank you," she responded.

"Oh, and just for the record," Jean-Pierre chuckled, " I bet you're more than glad you didn't leave on your own."

"You have no idea," she responded as he leaned in to kiss her again, and from that moment on, they were inseparable.

Darcy & Trap

Shortly after they met, Rosa and Darcy developed a close bond over the better lands' migration plans as Darcy became heavily involved with it. He had always been one for adventure, although Kentucky was a far cry from NYC. Rosa welcomed his input and willingness to work beside her, and the communities welcomed him into the winter shelter with open arms. He was knowledgeable, personable, caring and along with Rosa, helped guide them through the continual challenging situations of living amongst each other.

When he wasn't helping Rosa out, and to pass time, he hung out in the auditorium reading books that he had borrowed from the library. He spent lots of time researching The Land Between the Lakes, as well as the overnight distribution hubs they planned to stop at. The peninsula had a history that caught Darcy's attention. It had been named as a national recreational area by President Kennedy back in 1963. He was fascinated with the inordinate number of moonshine stills that popped up over the years throughout the 170,000 acres.

Rosa had already done a vast amount of the research before the boys had arrived in town. After looking over her original plans, Darcy had no doubt the migration plan was viable, even necessary, as the third virus strain was getting closer. He wanted to be involved in as much of the ongoing planning as he could, and Rosa embraced his help.

Darcy also had another motive to hang out in the yellow band area, other than just reading. He wanted to keep close tabs on the unsupervised folks who ran freely about the auditorium, interjecting when he detected anything out of the ordinary like arguments, fights, or thievery. Initially, people were warned to not leave their personal belongings alone when they left their assigned areas. It wasn't enforceable and as time went on more people ignored it, even when stuff came up missing.

For the most part, the general population within the winter shelter was trustworthy. But some of them, due to the frustrating challenges the new normal living corralled them into, found themselves doing unthinkable acts. Some stole from neighbors they hung out with; others stole from those they didn't know. It was too easy to cross those boundaries, blurring right from wrong.

One particular morning, while Darcy was waiting for Rosa to shower before they headed over to the library, he noticed one of the red banders roaming about in the green band section. Darcy pretended to continue reading but kept his eyeballs locked in on the scroungy-looking man who appeared to be in his mid-forties. It wasn't the first time he saw him sneaking around and suspected he was one of the thieves responsible for missing items.

Trap, aka Larry Fielding, got his nickname from his reputation when he first entered the green banded community at Leddy Park. He was distraught from the recent loss of his job, his home, his wife, and three children. Four years before the virus hit, they lived comfortably in a four-bedroom home just north of Burlington. For most of his career he worked as a Program Manager at a major technology company which provided a nice income for all of their creature comforts, like a boat, travel, and a hefty savings account. They were happy; he was happy.

But after losing everything, he became bitter and didn't care about himself or anything around him. He'd sneer at any rules or plans that he didn't come up with, or others who got in his way, lashing out with verbal obscentities just to piss everyone off around him. Most told him to shut his 'trap' which only irritated him more and eventually became his nickname.

Since living at the winter shelter in such close quarters, Trap wandered about others' living spaces when they weren't around and spitefully went through their stuff, especially those he had disputes with. He didn't take things because he wanted or needed them; it was to rile the victims up and watch them try to figure out who the thief was. It was a game and purely done for his personal entertainment. He had nothing to lose, and for the most part, nobody paid that close attention to him. That morning he thought the coast was clear other than Darcy, who had been laying on his makeshift bed reading. Trap figured he was far enough away not to see his shenanigans.

Darcy felt his heart race as he watched Trap leave his area and roam about. He knew what he was up to, but couldn't seem to ever catch him in the act. He watched as Trap stopped and kicked some piles of blankets around in the green band section. It was obvious that he was checking to see if there was anything stowed away under. Others had also suspected Trap had sticky fingers but never found any items after they were taken. There was no way Trap could've hid them in his sleep area. He knew that and got rid of the unwanted stolen goods shortly after he took them, mainly in trash cans outside of the auditorium. Despite any concrete evidence, many outwardly accused him, which only made him more determined to continue his petty heists. Darcy felt certain at that moment, he was going to finally catch him.

Trap had stumbled upon his prize, a lone backpack laying under a pile of blankets. Darcy watched Trap shrewdly look around to see if anyone was watching and even looked straight at him. Once satisfied nobody was, Trap squatted down and opened the backpack. Darcy saw him pull something out of it then stuff it in his shirt. At that point he knew what he needed to do.

Trap looked around again to make sure he wasn't spotted, then as he tried to stand up, he felt a huge blow in the middle of his back that threw him down on his knees.

Before he even had time to figure what happened, Darcy's deep, loud voice exclaimed, "I saw what you did, old man!," as he lowered his foot that had pushed him over.

Trap didn't move, so Darcy moved in front of him and yelled, "If I were you, I'd put back whatever is under your shirt or so help me God, Trap, I will get you banned from here for good."

Trap just looked up at him and quietly said, "I don't know what you're talking about, son."

Darcy felt himself get angrier as he replied, "Come on, Trap, really? Enough is enough. Hand it over and just stop this shit that you have been pulling around here. Let's call a truce and I won't say anything to the others."

It was a little late to keep the secret as a few of the community members had heard the commotion and made their way over to see what was going on. Trap wasn't happy with Darcy or the onlookers. His back hurt, so for the moment he stayed on his knees, keeping his head down, wanting to tell them all to mind their own damn business, but didn't.

As he looked up at Darcy, he sarcastically replied, "I don't know what the hell you think you saw, kid, but I don't have anything."

"Bullshit, Trap!" Darcy exclaimed, a bit agitated that someone almost three times his age, someone he should look up to, was lying to him.

Darcy took his foot and pushed it against Trap's chest, taking him by surprise as he fell onto his butt. Before he knew what was happening, Darcy tugged on his shirt and a tan leather wallet dropped to the floor.

He swiftly grabbed it and loudly replied, "Oh, you call this nothing? I'm warning you, old man, you better get a grip on this crap you keep pulling. We all knew it was you taking stuff, and now you're caught red-handed. I have the proof right here and witnesses," then he pointed to the larger crowd of people that had gathered around as he raised his voice, "I should report you and have you thrown out!"

"You should've kept that no good nose buried in your book and minded your own goddamn business. But go ahead, you little jerk, do what you gotta do," Trap hastily replied, suddenly feeling quite angry and somewhat vulnerable that he was discovered.

"Don't worry. I will!," he paused for a moment and watched as more folks gathered then said, "So call this your lucky day, Trap! Kind of like a last chance warning. Just leave other people's shit alone! You should be ashamed of yourself!"

At that, Darcy put the wallet back in the backpack, then stood, along with the others and watched as Trap got up and slowly meandered across the auditorium and out the main door. Without saying a word to anyone, Darcy went back to his area and continued to wait for Rosa so he could fill her in. As he sat down and grabbed his book, he knew he was too worked up to continue reading. Then he heard a few of the folks who had witnessed the scene, holler out to him.

"Thanks, man! You caught him red-handed!"

"You did good!"

"We knew it was him!"

"You're a hero!"

Their claps echoed throughout the auditorium and Darcy raised his hand up in the air in acknowledgment. He didn't think of himself as a hero nor did he want to be recognized as such. He just hoped the embarrassment of being caught would make Trap think twice about what he did, and not do it again. Darcy knew he should make more of a fuss over it all, but wanted to give Trap a second chance. Times were already tough enough, and he felt it was worth a shot. Whether or not he would take it would be up to him.

The Other Street Thugs

One night, as Rosa and Jean-Pierre were sitting around talking, she decided to share what happened with the street thugs that one night on North Beach. Rosa described the thugs right down to the matching skulls they all had etched on their forehead. She told the boys about the terror the thugs had caused around town and their fateful night they invaded her community. It was the first time they learned that she had a gun; even more shocking, that she had used it to kill two of the thugs.

Darcy was more affected by the news, not so much that she had killed others, but the fact he almost was, by thugs that resembled her description. He broke out in a sweat, thinking back to the terror he experienced that night in the barn, from six of the ex Sons of Arches club thugs. He thought there was too much similarity to not be the same group, but hoped he was wrong.

"Yeah, the leader and his sidekick met their demise after they brutally victimized two of the women," Jean-Pierre added to Rosa's story, having been privy to a part of it a few weeks earlier.

"Do you happen to know their names?" Darcy reluctantly asked, still not quite sure it was the same bunch that had attacked him.

"Yes, they were pretty well-known in the area for their reign of terror. Still mind boggling, since there were only four of them. One was Chug, and there were Bunyan and Blitz. The leader was Jeremy," Rosa replied, "Blitz and Chug were the lucky ones that night. They got away, and haven't bothered anyone since. I'm sure we're done with them."

Darcy took a deep breath as he felt his heart pound in his head. He thought he was going to throw up. The names hit him like a ton of bricks. He had no doubt that they were the same thugs who had terrorized him. There wasn't a day that went by that he didn't count his lucky blessings that he got away, unscathed by them. The thought that the two could still be in the close vicinity made him sick, so he hoped

Rosa was right, and they had faded into the shadows. He wasn't ready to share his story, and continued to listen to her tell how the gun ended up in her possession. She had been through so much in such a short time. He admired how she had come out on top of it all.

It was shortly after the New Year, and for the most part, things were running smoothly at the auditorium. Trap stayed to himself and didn't touch things that didn't belong to him; Rosa celebrated her sixteenth birthday, and the migration plan was falling into place. Darcy and Rosa were at the library preparing for a rally they were holding later that morning in Battery Park. While she put together the final notes, Darcy decided to take a stroll down by the lake to meet up with some others before heading over to the gathering.

There wasn't a cloud in the sky as the sun beamed down on the newly fallen snow, almost blinding Darcy's eyes with its brightness. He put on his shades, then spotted his friends hanging down the street. The next thing he knew, an hour had gone by, and realized Rosa might already be at the park waiting for him. They were anxious to finally share the full migration plans with everyone, so he decided to hurry along and take a shortcut down one of the side streets to the park.

The findings they found were encouraging and felt that the better lands were large enough to house everyone who wanted to go. The only catch was they weren't sure how many folks were already settled on the unique peninsula. They had looked into the different campgrounds that were part of the national park region, and discovered there were over 1400 they could choose from. Darcy favored the Fenton Campground that rested right on the Kentucky Lake shoreline as the area seemed more secluded then others. It also was the closest to the main distribution hub located on the Kentucky mainland, via a bridge. Fenton was also very near the once thriving Elk and Bison territory, an undeveloped grassland that could be good for planting various seeds.

The 118 acres of shorelines along Lake Barkley bordered the other side of the peninsula, closer to the Tennessee state line. Both the Kentucky and Barkley Lakes connected at the northern end of the peninsula, which made it the world's largest man-made body of water. Darcy was ecstatic Rosa was on board with Fenton Campground and they planned to announce their choice at the meeting.

As Darcy strolled down the side street, his thoughts were quickly interrupted when out of nowhere, he heard a deep, raspy voice loudly yell out, "Hey, you, punk ass! Where do you think you're headed?"

Darcy's heart accelerated as he heard a familiar jingle quickly approaching from behind. He knew two of the street thugs were still out there, but never in his wildest dreams, expected to run into them. His first instinct was to run, but knew if he weren't quick enough, they would be all over him. As much as he didn't want to, there was no other choice but to confront. Darcy took a deep breath, stopped dead in his tracks, then abruptly turned around to face them. He felt faint as he recognized the two faces standing in front of him, and at that moment, knew he should have ran.

Darcy couldn't believe that two of the six thugs who had relentlessly stomped on him with their big heavy leather boots that night in the barn, were there. He noted the familiar weathered leather jackets, their holey jeans, the long, greasy hair that intermingled with their out-of-control beards and their black leather ankle boots. Lastly, and most disturbingly; the skull tattoos on their foreheads. His worst nightmare had come true.

Darcy often thought about what he'd do if he ever ran into any of them again, but all plans disappeared as he stood there, frozen in his tracks, scared to death. His body broke out in a hot sweat despite the frigid temperature as he looked straight at Blitz and Chug smuggling smiling at him.

As nervous as he was, he spoke first, but pissed at himself once the questions rolled out, "You guys? What the fuck?"

The thugs looked at each other, not quite making the connection with who the young kid was standing in front of them. All they knew was he had trespassed on the turf they had claimed for the last few months after Jeremy and Bunyan's murder. That night on the beach had been a game changer for them, and their survival depended upon them staying under the radar, since there were only two of them left.

That night, when they heard the gunshots coming from the other side of the yellow banded community, they both rushed out of the tents they were victimizing to see what had happened. Before they could get their bearings, they heard the second round of shots. They knew Jeremy and Bunyan were on the other side of the community, but it was too risky to find them. They didn't carry guns, so the two thugs knew their friends were the victims.

They waited for a few minutes then heard someone holler out, "They're dead! Rosa saved us!"

That fateful day, like dogs with tails between their legs, they beelined it out of there, hiding in nearby woods until the crack of dawn, when they felt it was safe enough to make a full exit. Blitz and Chug vowed to never step foot in any of the beach communities again or anywhere they would encounter large groups, including Church Street. For the most part, their reign over the city was done. But they still found ways to dabble within the black market. Chug negotiated a smaller turf in the area that was easier to control and keep low profiles. At least until that moment.

"Do we know you?" Blitz curiously as he looked him up and down.

Chug immediately jumped in, not waiting for an answer as he asked, "What's your business here, boy? You know you are trespassing on our turf right now, don't you or are you just plain stupid?"

"Look, guys, I'm just passing through, heading to the park, man. I'm not after anything. Just heading to the end of this street and out of here. Didn't even know it was your turf. Sorry. I'll just be on my way," Darcy said, realizing they didn't recognize him even though they moved a bit closer.

His small frame was no match for even one of them, and he had a feeling his day was about to get really bad as Blitz folded his arms, rested his chin against his hand, as he blurted out, "Wait a minute, I recognize that punk ass voice," he paused for a moment then exclaimed, "Yes, I got it! You're that kid that was in the barn that night," then he slightly looked behind Darcy and laughed as he added, "Yeah, I recognize that backpack. No fucking way! You're a long way from home, boy!"

"Hot damn!" Chug exclaimed as he checked out the backpack, then excitedly said, "You are that punk ass! Long time no see!" then gave Blitz a high five for figuring it out.

Darcy listened to them roar with laughter for a few minutes then said, "I'm not sure what you're talking about. I don't recall being in any barn anywhere," he lied, knowing he had to deflect a potentially serious situation.

"Oh, come on, boy, how could you forget. You probably smelled for days after we threw you into that muddy shit pile!" Chug exclaimed; they continued laughing, keeping their eyes locked on him.

At that moment, Darcy knew he had to do something and it wasn't sticking around to acknowledge and reminisce about that night. He could smell the alcohol seeping from them and wondered if they were tipsy enough that he could outrun them. Even though the sidewalks and road were icy might work against his attempt to run, he had to take the chance.

He counted to five and started to take off, but his attempt to sprint past them failed when his sneakers were unable to get a good grip on the icy ground. He was lucky enough to stop himself from falling, but knew the rest of his luck was about to run out.

"Whoa, boy, where do you think you're going?" Chug asked as he and Blitz moved together to block any more attempts to get away, "We were just getting reacquainted and having some fun. Why would you want to leave so quickly? Is that how you treat old friends?"

Again, they both cracked up, then each grabbed one of Darcy's arms with enough force that they almost lifted him off the ground. Even though through his heavy coat, he felt his skin pinched enough it made him wince.

"Answer him, boy!" Blitz aggressively demanded as they both relished in the harassment they were dishing out, "Is that how you treat old friends?"

Darcy didn't plan to answer the question. It seemed any words of sort were going to end in the same result, a less desirable one than his outcome could have been if he just ran from them when he had the chance.

So he replied, "Hey, come on guys, just let me go. I won't come down this street again. That's a promise. I have people waiting for me and I need to get to them, or they will come looking for me. I don't want any trouble with either of you, so please," Darcy felt himself frantically begging.

"I don't want any trouble with either of you, please…please," Chug mocked him in a frail wailing tone and made a pouty face.

"See what you made my partner do? Go get all sad on us!" Blitz sarcastically exclaimed.

At that point, both thugs broke out into hysterical laughter and tightened their grip around his arms. The pain made Darcy's eyes water, but he knew he couldn't show any type of weakness or vulnerability around them. They would have played even harder with it.

"So, Blitz, what do you propose we do with this little punk ass dweeb?" Chug asked as he let go of an arm then stood in front of Darcy.

"Well, for starters, let's see what's in that piece of shit backpack," Blitz replied.

"Probably nothing, like before," Chug replied.

They both nodded at each other seconds before Blitz turned Darcy around and ripped his backpack off of him, then handed it Chug. He held both of Darcy's arms tightly behind his back while Chug emptied out the contents into the snow. Just as they suspected, there wasn't anything of worth in it, so it got kicked aside as they continued to harass Darcy. Chug ripped off his sunglasses, threw them down, stomped on them, and then gut-punched him, causing him to keel over from the excruciating pain. Blitz let go of Darcy's arms, as he pushed Darcy down on his knees.

Before Darcy knew it, the all too familiar weight of a heavy boot pounding into his muscles landed him flat on his stomach. He quickly moved into a fetal position knowing there was no way to fight them off. All he could do was brace himself for more pain, and pain certainly was on their agenda. The next thing he felt was a tremendous blow to the side of his head as Chug threw a punch. He wasn't sure how long everything went silent or if he had permanently lost his hearing, but figured at that point he wouldn't live long enough to find out. His entire body trembled as Chug cast his second and third blows. The more Darcy begged him to stop, the harder the punches were.

Darcy's ears were ringing; his head was spinning. He was sure his mind was playing tricks on him when he heard a gunshot go off and a familiar voice scream, "Get away from him right now, or I will shoot you both!"

Darcy mustered up all his strength to slightly lift his head off the cold sidewalk, enough to catch a glimpse of Rosa standing there with the gun pointed directly at the thugs. He couldn't believe her timing and let his head fall back onto the snow, thankful he wasn't going to die, not that day anyway.

"I mean it, I will shoot!" she said, quite aware her hands were slightly shaking from both the cold and fear of what was going to happen next.

She had taken them by surprise. As Chug stood over Darcy not daring to move, he stayed focused on Rosa's gun pointed directly at him. Blitz watched as she moved it back and forth between them, steadily keeping it aimed at their chests. Although the thugs had never laid eyes on Rosa before, they knew she was the one who had pulled the trigger on Jeremy and Bunyan. They knew the gun was loaded, and she meant business. Chug knew he had to quickly defuse the situation before it got out of hand.

"Whoa, hang on, little missy," Chug said as softly as his raspy voice allowed, "we were just having a little fun, no harm, no foul." He looked down at Darcy and extended his hand out to him, "Come on now, boy, up you go," but Darcy just laid there, not accepting the offer.

"Yeah, right, some fun. You piece of shits!" Rosa shouted, still pointing the gun at them, then asked, "You okay, Darcy?"

"Yeah, I'm fine," he hoarsely grimaced as he mustered up some strength to sit up. His head was pounding, but realized his hearing was intact. He suddenly felt some warm liquid run over his lips. He tried to rub it away only to get blood all over his hand, then saw blood on Chug's fistful of rings and knew they were the culprit that ripped through his skin.

"Oh, looks like we got ourselves a bigger reunion here, Blitz. So, girl, you know this boy?" Chug coyly asked as she just stared at him, so he continued, "And do we have the honor of knowing who you are? I mean, we ought to get all proper here. I'm pretty sure you're the infamous Rosa, right? Well, I'm Chug, and this is my partner, Blitz. Oh, and of course, you know the boy. Darcy, right?"

Rosa was unnerved knowing Chug was sizing her up, trying to figure out what her next moves were. She didn't answer and certainly wasn't going to let her guard down. She had left the library a few minutes early, and was headed toward the park when she heard all the commotion coming from the side street, then she heard Darcy's voice. She knew something wasn't right and decided to explore. As she got closer, she saw the thugs terrorizing her friend, so she quickly got her gun ready. Since the incident at the beach, she kept it with her at all times. The thugs were too busy beating on Darcy to hear her footsteps as she walked up behind them and fired the gun into the air, getting their attention.

"Now, where are your manners? We're just being friendly, nobody needs to get hurt here," Chug softly said, realizing she wasn't going to respond to his bantor.

Rosa kept the gun pointed at them, and Blitz cowered behind Chug as she harshly demanded, "Get away from him now!"

Chug knew she wasn't going to co-operate and he sure as hell wasn't going to just hand Darcy over to her. It was time for her to pay for what she had done and he couldn't believe his luck, that she was all alone standing in front of him; Jeremy and Bunyan's murderer. He had a chance to finally get rid of her and decided to take full advantage..

He took a step closer to Rosa as he angrily yelled "Enough is enough! I'm not going to have a two-bit prissy ass killer bitch threaten me any longer!" His beet red face tightened up as he lunged at Rosa.

Without hesitation, she pulled the trigger and watched as he fell to the ground on his back, staring into the sky. She didn't take the time to see if he was dead or not before she aimed the gun directly at Blitz.

"Make one move toward me, and you will meet the same fate, you bastard!"

Blitz wearily looked at the blood gurgling out of Chug's mouth then back at Rosa, and slowly put his hands up above his head as fear took over his once barbaric attitude.

"Please don't shoot me. Please, I beg you to spare me my life, and I promise you won't see me again. I'll leave the area right now. Please," Blitz begged as his tired eyes welled up with tears.

He had always been the weak link in the group. There were some occasions, despite all the horrific things he had done, where he played peacemaker among them. His sporadic sobriety dictated which role he assumed during any conflict; good Blitz or bad Blitz. Either one still couldn't shake his embedded thug qualities, even when he tried.

Born 34 years earlier into a destitute family who had lived in the poorer section of Quebec City, Claude Francois' life seemingly never had a fair shot. His mother had no idea who fathered him and had kept company with a local biker gang, mainly for the free street drugs she got in return for the various favors she did for them. She was high on heroin when Claude was born, so, no fault of his, he entered the world as a drug addict. Eventually, by the age of thirteen, he dove into the drug scene.

Claude dropped out of school at 15 and found some refuge in hanging out with a local biker gang. The leader, who had known his family through drug related transactions, took him under his wing and eventually got him involved in some of their businesses. Claude had a new kind of roof over his head and drugs readily available that helped continue his longtime addiction, but eventually was told he had to clean up. After many failed attempts to get it under control along with his constant involvement in street fights caused the gang to finally toss him out.

Not long after that, Claude ran into Jeremy, who was already a club member with the Sons of Arches. The club was hunting for new prospects, and Claude's resume fit the bill with his huge physique, quick temperament, and tainted, streetwise background. It was Jeremy who came up with his nickname, Blitz, mainly because Claude was rarely in a sober state. And it was Jeremy that had helped him fight the deadly addiction through many detoxes and setbacks until he finally won the battle. Blitz remained clean and sober for several years but eventually found occasional comfort in the bottle. He never did touch drugs again.

Rosa's finger was still on the trigger, gripping the gun tightly. She watched fear take over the big tough thug that everyone was afraid of. She knew, at that moment, it was up to her whether he lived or died and thought about what his miserable life even meant. Quite sure that it was far worse than Mr. Chuso's, and it would only make sense to end it all with one quick click. Rosa didn't trust Blitz's word that he'd just disappear or cease with his reign of terror among the innocent. She watched as a couple of tears rolled down his cheeks. He looked lost, alone, and afraid. She momentarily felt sad for him, and if he had been anyone else, she would have offered him a warm hug. But she reminded herself he was pure evil.

"I should kill you just like the rest of them," she started, her voice a bit shaky, "You all have done nothing but reign terror on this city and its good people. Even the cops won't deal with you. I'm sure there are more of you somewhere, and if I end your life now, you can't bring them here. Our world would be much safer and better off without a bunch of nasty, evil thugs in it like you. Especially in these times."

Blitz stood there feeling completely vulnerable as more tears rolled down his cheeks, knowing in just moments it could be over. He would die alone. He wondered what more his life had to offer anyways. He had no place to go, nobody left to hang with, and no protector. His mere survival had always depended on some sort of leader to follow, and without that guidance, good or bad, he was lost.

He often laid awake at night and thought about what it would have been like to have lived a different life. A peaceful one. One with family, friends, and even companionship by his side. To have a real job, a real home, even kids, to just to feel loved just one time. He feared death as it stared him in the eyes, as it had done so many times before. He felt the end near but wasn't ready to die.

Rosa watched his demeanor crumble before her as he begged one more time, "Please, I don't want to die. I promise you I will disappear, please," then he got down on his knees praying, looked into her eyes and said, "I'm sorry. I'm so sorry."

It threw Rosa off to hear his pleas, his apology. She told herself it was a decoy, but yet for a second, her heart melted. Darcy's battered body finally managed to get up, and stood next to her as she again addressed Blitz.

"I have no idea how the four of you thugs ever pulled it off to begin with, and even when it was just the two of you, you still managed to instill fear in innocent people! For what? Why? You all are despicable. Take a good look at my friend here. You did this to him. Why? What is wrong with you?"

Rosa felt her blood boil and her sweaty hands squeeze the gun a little tighter. As Darcy continued to glare at Blitz, he held onto his badly bruised side. He still couldn't believe their paths had crossed again, and that he took another beating. But he felt in the end, they got what was coming to them and paid the ultimate price. He leaned closer to Rosa as he muttered, "Maybe you just need to pull the trigger, Rosa, so we can get out of here."

Blitz could not contain his emotions as he sobbed louder, still pleading, "Rosa, please. I beg you. I'm truly sorry. Please just let me go."

There was something about hearing him say her name that let a sudden sense of sadness engulf her. As she watched him fall apart, she felt sympathy and compassion intruding on her anger. She hated the fact that she had now killed four people, even though it was in self-defense. Initially it had been so easy to just pull the trigger and walk away from the other three lifeless bodies; they all deserved it. Even Chug laying dead in front of her. But she sensed Blitz was a bit different. He asked her to save him. He even addressed her by name. For the next couple minutes, nobody spoke.

Then Rosa broke the silence and surprised them all, including herself, as she said, “Okay, Blitz, get yourself together. I’ve decided that I’m not going to kill you today if you promise you will leave this town immediately. No exceptions, and if I see you again, there will be no conversation. I will kill you. If I hear that anyone else has seen you, I will hunt you down, and I will kill you. Do you understand?”

Rosa’s voice had accelerated to an angry scream by the time she was done. She wasn’t sure who she was more irritated with, Blitz or herself. Still on his knees, Blitz vigorously shook his head in agreement, thanking her over and over.

“This is your lucky day, if you can call it that. Now, get the fuck out of our sight!” Darcy piped in with as much gusto as he could while Rosa kept the gun still aimed at Blitz.

At that point, all Blitz wanted to do was get away from the gun and out of her sight as quickly as possible before she changed her mind. He couldn’t believe that she was letting him go. He looked over at Chug, the last of his family, and hated leaving him there, even though it no longer mattered. Blitz knew his hands were tied and just needed to move on.

As he got up, he looked Rosa straight in her eyes and quietly said, “Thank you so much, Rosa. You won’t regret it,” Then he looked over at Darcy and continued, “Hey man, I’m sorry,” then quickly turned and clumsily ran up the street, out of sight.

As she watched him stomp away, Rosa reflected on the sadness his eyes had revealed and the despondency in his voice. She felt sorry for him, despite the trail of chaos he left behind, and believed she had done the right thing.

"What the hell, Rosa! I get you have a big heart and all, but something tells me you should've shot him and then we'd all be done with the thugs. Why didn't you shoot him?" Darcy asked as he tried to hold back tears, clutching his stomach and trying to control his cold shaking body.

"Believe me," she stated as she put the gun away then grabbed some clean snow to wipe the blood from his face, "Big 'ole Blitzy won't be bothering us again. He is really gone this time and who knows what is in store for him if he can't keep his word. But I think he will."

Rosa looked over at Chug's cold, limp body as it laid on the frozen ground. She knew it would slowly cool off but stay slightly preserved until someone else found it and disposed of it. That wasn't in her job jar.

"Yeah, but didn't you tell everyone that night on the beach when those two thugs got away that they would be next if you ever came face-to-face with them? Yet you let one go," he winced with a bit of sarcasm as the snow's coldness against his skin stung more than the couple facial wounds did.

Darcy knew he was putting her on the spot, but up until then, she had always made good on her word. Rosa was a bit taken back by his sharpness, and as she moved her hand away from his head, she replied, "You're right. I did say that. But Blitz didn't threaten me as the other three thugs did. I couldn't kill him for no real reason. And I'm sorry that you paid the price of their madness, not once but twice. But you know as well as me, I had to let Blitz go. I'm also sure he won't make trouble again, at least not around here."

“Maybe you’re right,” Darcy said as she put more snow against his skin.

Rosa’s tone reflected more compassion as she responded, “I’m really sorry this happened to you, Darcy, but I couldn’t pull the trigger on him. You saw him, he was really sorry,” she paused for a moment, putting a finger over his lips to stop him from replying, then continued, “I truly believe this isn’t a life he chose, and maybe now he’s really free from all that crap and will just disappear like he promised. I don’t know why I feel this way. By all accounts, I should want him as dead as the others. But it’s a gut feeling, I suppose. Believe me. I’ll keep my word if I see him again. Now, let’s get you back to the auditorium and get this patched up properly.”

For a moment, they stood staring at the bright redness of Chug’s blood, as it started to meshed into the snow then Darcy responded, “No, I’m fine, really. We can’t keep people waiting. This is an important day for all of us.”

After a brief hug of assurance that all would be okay, they headed over to Battery Park only to be surprised by the larger than expected crowd that had gathered there, patiently waiting for them.

The Announcement

As the hundreds of folks spotted them, sounds of clapping and cheers filled the air. Jimmy, Ryan, and many of the community bodyguards had already surrounded the stage as Rosa and Darcy jumped up on it. Once the crowd quieted down, the two were ready to reveal more details about the migration plans and the groups that were chosen to take the initial journey.

Rosa's followers had grown from just their yellow band community to others, along with locals and transients. They all were curious about the better lands and what it meant for their futures. Very few of them didn't know who Rosa was, and those that did, had come to respect, trust, and even idolize her over the last several months.

The crowd listened intently as Rosa got into the heart of the migration plan. She went over how the first groups leaving would be filled with the strongest community members, ranging mainly from their late teens to mid-thirties. It had been decided that no young children should join the initial travel, mainly because nobody knew what to expect along the way.

"So based on that plan, we have chosen a total of 400 folks to take the initial trek," Rosa excitedly announced, then continued, "and they will be broken up into four groups of 100 each who will trail approximately a week behind each other. A couple of team leads will be assigned to each group, which has yet to be determined. Jean-Pierre and I will lead the first one."

The crowd got a bit louder as they talked among themselves, most worried they might not be the ones chosen to make the first trip. Rosa continued over the chatter and knew there would be push back, no matter who was chosen.

"Most of the overnights along the predicted 35 to 40 day journey will be in tents along the route. However, as you may have heard already, we found five major indoor distribution hubs that we should be able to spend a night or two at and replenish our supplies."

Some of the crowd still couldn't get over the fact that only a select few were initially going and one angry person opened up the floodgates that Rosa had hoped to avoid.

"What about the rest of us?" he angrily hollered.

"Yeah, what about us?" another yelled.

"It ain't fair to limit the number of folks going!" another blurted out.

The atmosphere continued to get tenser as several more expressed their disagreement, some shouting obscenities to show their disapproval. Both Rosa and Darcy knew they should have pulled the plug on the meeting, but didn't. She had worked so hard for that day's announcement and felt she owed it to the people to not delay it any further, despite the few disgruntled ones.

"Look, I hear your concerns," she started but was quickly interrupted.

"Why make the groups so small? You surely can make room for more!" a man close to the stage yelled.

Darcy felt he had to chime in even though his head was throbbing, "First of all, limiting the first migration to just 400 folks instead of hundreds or even thousands of us, is way safer."

"Safer for who," he yelled back.

Darcy held his hand up to the restless crowd, hoping they would let him finish before his head burst, "Hold on, everyone, please let me explain this. First of all, splitting us up into smaller, limited groups will help in terms of finding enough food to feed everyone along the journey and secondly, it won't attract too much attention on us as we pass through all the different towns. Don't forget, we have no idea what to expect out there. We can't say that enough. And thirdly, the distribution hubs might not be able to accommodate larger groups and I'm not even sure if they will accommodate the 100 at a time."

"So where are these distribution hubs, and if they don't take in a group of 100, then what?" someone hollered out.

"Great question," Rosa started, "So, there are five of them, all large enough that they should be able to accommodate a group of 100. They're spaced out enough between each that we shouldn't run out of supplies before we get to the better lands."

"But where are they?" another yelled before Rosa could finish.

Rosa looked at all the concerned faces, then took a deep breath before she answered, "The first stop is at the Fort Drum Army Base in New York; then the next three are stadiums in Ohio, spread out several days from each other."

Darcy added, " They're in Cleveland, Ashton, and Cincinnati."

Rosa continued, "The final hub stop is at the Fort Knox Army base in Kentucky. Five days later, we'll arrive in the better lands. The nearest hub there is on the Kentucky mainland, so we are looking to settle as close as we can to it."

"How do you know they will even be there or be safe for us to go into?" someone asked.

"What about the rest of us? When do we go?" another yelled.

Darcy responded, "They will be there. As for the rest of you that still want to go to the better lands, well, you will stay here with me until we get word it is safe to go. We'll head back to the beach communities in the Spring then prepare to leave sometime in the Fall. That gives the initial folks time to settle in and get word back to us."

Many folks were growing angrier and yelled out at Rosa.

"Fucking Fall?" "

"Are you crazy?"

"It won't take that long to get word back to us!"

"I'm not waiting that long!"

Rosa was a bit worried that the unrest of the crowd was growing more forceful so she attempted to calm it, “Listen, everyone. It is a well-known fact that our world has stepped back in time in so many ways. You all know that. We have no reliable use of cell phones or any other modes of communication, as well as no consistent power to keep us in the creature comforts we all once were used to. We have no other transportation, other than ourselves. The third wave is coming, and we hope that we all get to the better lands before it does. But we have to make sure it is the right place and it’s better for some of us then all of us to go at once.”

“That’s all you got. That’s your reason to leave so many behind?” an angry guy hollered, stirring up discontent.

“This is bullshit!”

“We should all go!”

“Who are the supposed lucky ones?”

“Hey! Let’s all calm down and let Rosa talk!” exclaimed Jimmy as he hopped up on the stage, hoping his voice would help settle the crowd, “One way or another, we all will get there but not at the same time. Look, I’m staying behind too, so just listen up. Nobody will be left behind!”

“Thanks, Jimmy!” exclaimed Darcy, then added, “Come on, folks, this should be no surprise. Rosa made it clear from the beginning what to expect. And most of you have been to all her meetings, so let’s all just take it easy. Jimmy is right, everyone one of you that wants to migrate will get to, but we have to do it strategically. We don’t know what is on the other end, just like you don’t!” Darcy felt his face burn as his open wounds screamed for more ice.

To his relief, the crowd semi-settled down, so Darcy waved for Rosa to continue.

“Yes, everyone, that’s right. We all will get there but let us do the hard part first. We’re paving the way for you, so when it is your turn, it will be easier, and the expectations will be known. Look, as we already said, the plan for the rest of you to start migrating will happen about three to four months after the last group leaves. That's sometime in September."

Suddenly several guys demanded to have new leaders; older with more experience. Others insisted they were going regardless. Rosa realized not everyone was on board as they originally had professed to be. She wasn't quite sure how to handle the toxic negativity and just wanted to avoid confrontations that could lead to a vicious outbreak among the crowd.

She tried to reason with them again, "Look, I get where you're all coming from, and I appreciate your concerns, but it is better to have a few of us take the initial risk than the whole community. It's for your own protection, really."

Many supporters cheered her on but were quickly drowned out with more damaging slander.

"You know this ain't right!" a young man screamed, throwing his fists up in the air.

"You can't dictate what we can and can't do," another yelled.

The final straw came when an irate protester provoked a rant that spread like wildfire, "I say we all go, or nobody goes."

"We go or nobody goes! We go or nobody goes! We go or nobody goes!"

Rumbles of "yeah, that's right, man," and "you can't stop us" rang through the divided group. Suddenly the crowd came unglued and started pushing and pulling on each other, kids wailed, and people screamed as fistfights broke out. Some folks ran away from it, while others piled into it. Things continued to disintegrate rapidly, so Jimmy grabbed both Rosa and Darcy then rushed them off the stage and away from the mob scene. They quickly scurried out of the park, unnoticed by anyone.

Blitz

A week after the Battery Park incident, Rosa and Jean-Pierre took a stroll down by the waterfront, planning to check out a different place to hold the next meeting. They had decided it needed to be in a more private setting to avoid larger, unwelcomed peace breakers, so there would be no interruptions when they announced who would be assigned to each of the migration teams.

The sun peeked through a couple white, fluffy clouds, not able to provide strong enough rays to ward off the afternoon's cold, crisp air. As they got closer to the floating restaurant, Rosa noticed a familiar looking big, burly man sitting on one of the wooden benches nearby. He was slumped over with his head resting in his exposed, bare hands. She felt her heart skip a couple beats as her hands became cold and clammy. There was little doubt who he was and her mind raced as she stopped dead in her tracks.

"What's up, Rosa?" Jean-Pierre asked, detecting something was wrong.

Rosa didn't say a word as they stood several feet from the bench, staring at the man who was oblivious to their presence.

Jean-Pierre grabbed her arm as he realized who was sitting on it and quietly asked "Is that who I think it is?"

She didn't answer. Instead dropped her backpack in front of them, reached into it, and pulled out Chuso's gun. So much rattled through her thoughts as to what she should do or, rather, what she had to do. Fear started to take over, but Rosa knew she had to stand her ground and keep her word. If she didn't, he would win and eventually terrorize her and many others. Why else was he still there?

"What are you going to do?" Jean-Pierre asked, wanting to turn her around and leave the area.

Rosa started to move closer then yelled out in a murky tone, "You've got to be kidding! What the fuck are you doing here?"

Blitz immediately knew whose voice it belonged to before he even looked up to see Rosa standing directly in front of him. He knew they'd eventually meet up since he had decided not to follow through with his plan to leave the city. It was the dead of winter, and he had no other place to go until the weather warmed up, then he planned to head back to Montreal. He had been lucky enough to find some temporary shelter here and there, at least to get out of the cold at night. During the day he was left to wander about the city, trying to keep a low profile. He was tired, cold and hungry.

As Rosa stared at him, she noted how red his face looked from the cold even though it was covered with streaks of dirt. She was disturbed by how hollow his eyes looked, with little life shining through them as they rested on puffy welts just under his long black lashes. Rosa felt goosebumps form on her skin as their eyes stayed locked onto each other, feeling as though, for that brief moment, his lost soul touched hers. She slowly pulled the gun up from her side and pointed it directly at his head, then watched his eyes well up. The afternoon sun continued to dance in and out of the clouds; dead silence was all around. No traffic, people, or birds attempted to break it.

Rosa surrendered to it, annoyed with the situation at hand and demanded an answer, "Why are you still here? I told you if I saw you again, I would kill you! Why are you here?"

She watched as a tear escaped and left a path down his dirty cheek, then put his hands up in the air in response to the gun. He didn't answer her. She wasn't sure what to do and certainly didn't expect him to react in that manner. It was as though he was just sitting there waiting for her.

Rosa asked herself if she should just hurry up and shoot him, but she felt a tug from within, as part of her wondered if she should just walk away. His face begged for the latter. As Rosa stood for a few moments trying to decide, empathy crept in. Again, surprised by her own reaction, she stared at him for a few more moments then lowered the gun. Sitting there completely exposed and vulnerable, Blitz loudly sobbed, relieved it wasn't pointing at him but still didn't utter a word.

Rosa wasn't sure what was happening but suddenly felt the gun was overkill based on Blitz's reaction, so she quickly shoved it back inside her bag then calmly said, "Look, I know what I said to you the last time and I'm good on my word. Anyone will tell you that. I asked you to leave over a week ago, but here you sit. You broke your promise."

Blitz shifted about on the bench as he lowered his hands, then she continued, "But the truth is, I really don't want to shoot you or anyone else for that matter. That is not who I am, but you gotta know I don't trust you because of all the horrific stuff you and the other thugs put us and this city through. You created so much havoc, and I just wanted it all to stop."

Blitz tried to gain some sense of composure then quietly responded, "I know. Me too. Thank you."

For a moment, both Rosa and Jean-Pierre stared at his sad yet empty expression. Their eyes remained locked for several seconds as she tried to decide what to do next. All she knew was the grisly, pathetic human sitting in front of them had somehow reached rock bottom, and she suddenly felt sorry for him. To all their surprise, Rosa set her backpack down and took a seat next to Blitz on the rickety bench, not sure it would even hold them both. Jean-Pierre huffed in disapproval as she reached out and gently touched Blitz's cold, dirty hand.

She looked at him as he bowed his head then softly said, "I'm sorry, Blitz. I really am, for everything that you've gone through. I can't even imagine what kind of life you were living or have lived even before this pandemic. I'm sure it wasn't easy. And now, here you sit all alone."

Blitz closed his eyes as tears once again rolled down his cheeks. Rosa continued, "I think somewhere in there you're a good person; you've just made some very bad choices. And now, here you are, no place to go, no food, nothing. Don't you have any family anywhere that you can go to?" At that point, she felt her tears form as he once again looked at her.

He gently reciprocated and held her warm hand as he finally spoke in a low, sullen voice, "No, I have nobody. They are all dead or ran off somewhere." Rosa squeezed his hand a little tighter as he continued, "It ain't easy, that's a certain. And yeah, life certainly has sucked for me. You have no idea, but that doesn't make anything right. I know that."

He paused for a moment as he wiped his face with his other arm, streaking it more, then added, "I hate to admit that I'm scared shitless, and it's so out of character for me to be sitting here fucking telling this to you. Hell, you're young enough to be my kid," he paused then quietly said, "But I don't know where to go or what to do. All I've done in this last week since you killed Chug, was to try to figure out where the hell to go. I was going to head back to Montreal, but the weather is way too cold to travel that far so I'll be damned if I can figure it out." Then he took his hand back and buried his face in them both.

"Ah, Rosa, come on. What are you doing?" Jean-Pierre sternly asked, and when she ignored him, he cleared his throat, raised his voice, and said, "We need to get going, like now!" then reached out to grab her arm to nudge her along.

Rosa immediately pulled her arm away, and her glare signaled him to stay put while she continued to focus on Blitz, patiently waiting for him to gain back his composure. Jean-Pierre wasn't happy but decided not to make a fuss, afraid he would wake up the monster in Blitz, only to have worse to deal with.

Blitz knew how close he was to having his life just end. All it would have taken was a minor disagreement or a 'fuck you' for Rosa to have pulled the trigger and, it all would have been over. He knew she'd do it. She did it before. Three times that he knew of. It wasn't the first time he experienced his life flash before him, not knowing what the next minute would lead to. His thoughts momentarily drifted back to the night in the Montreal bar.

It had already been a decade since he had walked in that bar and spotted her in the corner, by the jukebox, with another man all over her. He had one of his hands up her midrift tank top, fondling her braless chest as her long, bare leg was wrapped around one of his.

Their lips were locked. Immediate jealousy provoked Blitz as his rage took hold. He and his ex-girlfriend had recently broken up, and he suspected she had been carrying on with someone else for a few months beforehand. He had just come from the bar next door, having several whisky shots with some of his cronies. At that point, he couldn't control his emotions and ran over to the romantically engrossed couple, grabbed the skinny, older man by the back of his neck, threw him to the floor, and stomped on his face. His ex screamed for him to stop then the next thing he knew, three of his drinking buddies pulled him off of the man and pinned him down on the floor.

"Calm down, Blitz," Chug shouted, trying to tame his flailing arms.

"Jesus man, you dumb fuck, you almost smashed his face in!" Bunyan screamed, pushing his boot against one of his thighs.

"Fuck you!" Blitz hollered back, spitting at their faces as he tried to fight them off.

"Listen, you dumb ass, stop while you're ahead. She's moved on, and you need to too," Chug responded as Blitz started to give in.

It took a few minutes but he finally calmed down, up until he watched his ex-girlfriend help her new lover to his feet and head to the bar. Shortly after Blitz got up, he charged at the guy, forcefully attacking him again. Chug and Bunyan intercepted, then dragged him outside so he could cool off. Blitz relentlessly kept fighting them and kicked Bunyan so hard in his balls that he laid yelping on the pavement. Then Blitz belted Chug upside the head. Within seconds several other club members arrived on the scene to help out but only ended up beating him to a pulp. Blitz was pretty sure it was the end when everything went black.

Hours later, long after the bar had closed, he managed to drag himself home, somewhat thankful to still be alive, although wasn't sure he would have been if he didn't black out. It was the closest he felt he ever came to death at the hands of his own club members and wasn't sure they wouldn't finish what they had started.

Rosa caringly smiled at Blitz as she said, "You're right, Blitz. I have no idea. I can't even imagine what your life was like for you, especially now. Believe me, everyone has something they wish they hadn't done, but that is life."

She saw a glimmer of hope in his eyes as he shyly smiled back then continued, "Look, maybe there is something I can help out with, short-term," she paused for a moment, briefly glanced at Jean-Pierre, then said, "How about this, Blitz. You come back with us to the auditorium, which is our winter shelter. You can get cleaned up and have some food and a warm place to sleep. It will keep you out of the cold until you figure out where it is you can go without being on the cold streets. You'll need to keep to yourself and don't cause any trouble for anyone. I'm going way out on a limb here."

Rosa wasn't sure if she was doing the right thing and knew she could be setting herself and others up for a shit storm. But she couldn't shoot him, nor could she just leave him in the cold or take a chance he'd show up somewhere else with a different agenda. She felt compelled to take the chance.

"Rosa!" Jean-Pierre exclaimed, his blood boiling as he paced around in front of them after hearing her offer to Blitz, "What are you doing? We can't bring this thug back to the auditorium! If you don't kill him, they surely will! What the fuck, Rosa?"

Immediately Rosa snapped back, "Stop it, Jean-Pierre! I know what I'm doing! Nobody is going to kill Blitz today!" Then she turned and waited for Blitz to answer.

Jean-Pierre could feel his blood boil, he was so mad and wanted to scream at her and him, but felt he still shouldn't rock the boat. For a few moments, Blitz stared at them both, waiting to see if the outcome changed, but it didn't so he responded, "Rosa, he's right. This is not a good idea at all."

Jean-Pierre quickly agreed and saw an opportunity to plead with Rosa to renege on the offer. Once again, she ignored him. He was furious and couldn't comprehend how she even considered such an invite after past conversations agreeing that all four thugs deserved to be dead, even Blitz. Up until that afternoon, it had been clear there was only one choice. Jean-Pierre knew Rosa had a big heart but never imagined it would stretch that big.

"Blitz, I'm serious. Please consider my offer," Rosa said again.

After pondering over the generous invitation and both pair of eyes intensely focused on him, Blitz responded, "Truth is, I'm not sure how you can sit there and offer this to me," his head slowly shaking back and forth as he continued in a softer tone, "You took all my buddies lives without a second thought. You played judge and jury. They were all I had," his voice cracked a bit as his eyes welled up again, "but what we did was wrong. I admit it and there ain't no good excuse for it. But it's confusing that now you want to help me and just a few minutes ago you wanted to kill me," he briefly paused, "I don't know what to think. But I don't have anywhere else to go."

He looked over at Jean-Pierre and added, "and I know this is going to be a fucking ordeal for you and many others," then turned to Rosa, "but I have nowhere else so … okay, I'll take you up on it and won't stay long, that I promise."

The New Guest

One could've heard a pin drop on the auditorium's tile floor as Rosa and Jean-Pierre walked in that afternoon. Blitz's crusty presence alone was enough to shake up the community. Those who saw him coming ran off to anxiously spread the news of the new guest. Rosa knew there would be a long bridge to gap and hadn't thought about how she was going to do it, but knew she'd find a way. She had no other choice.

Darcy was sitting in his usual spot on his sleeping bag, reading a book. He heard the room suddenly quiet down and sensed something was off. As he glanced toward the door and laid eyes on Blitz, he thought he'd have to pinch himself to make sure he wasn't dreaming. Immediately, he felt his head start to pound as anxiety pumped through him. He threw the book down, stood up, and stared directly at his nightmare. For a brief moment, he felt his whole body go numb and couldn't catch his breath. He felt as though he was suffocating.

Rosa knew she had to get to Darcy before he decided to make a scene, so before she headed over she quickly said to both Jean-Pierre and Blitz, "Okay, guys, first I have to go talk to Darcy and then let everyone know what's going on here. As you see Blitz, your presence already has an impact here, which just means we have some work ahead of us. But don't worry, I have a plan." She lightly patted his arm then instructed Jean-Pierre, "You need to stay close to him. I mean, right here next to him. I'm going to go fill Darcy in and hopefully get this settled without too much push back."

Jean-Pierre reluctantly nodded in agreement even though he felt her task at hand wouldn't be greeted with the support she hoped for. A part of him just wanted to shove Blitz out the door to avoid the fall out.

Rosa caught Darcy's eye and immediately headed toward him. She knew it was going to take a lot for him to understand why she brought Blitz there.

Darcy was more then frazzled as he started yelling when she approached, "What the fuck is he doing here, Rosa? Tell me he's our captive, and we're going to lock him away in a room downstairs and you will find the right time to shoot his sorry ass! That's what's happening, right?"

He watched her eyes water up from his abruptness then meekly respond, "Darcy, please, let me explain."

At that point he didn't want to hear any type of reasoning and forcefully grabbed her arms, yelling, "Rosa! What in hell are you thinking? The guy is a murderer, and you brought him here? Oh my God, what is wrong with you? The guy was ready to kill me and would have if you didn't show up! What the fuck, Rosa! Get him out of here!"

Rosa tried to diffuse his growing anger as she grabbed onto him and hastily responded, "Stop Darcy, please. Hear me out. Blitz is not a threat to any of us. Not at this moment, and I don't believe ever again. He never once threatened to kill any of us, only to scare us with his barbaric ways. He is not a murderer, Darcy! I probably killed more people than him! So, stop it and listen to me for a minute!"

By then, several small groups were gathering around, taking in their conversation. Darcy couldn't believe what he was hearing and wanted to shake Rosa hard enough to get her senses back, but didn't. Instead, he let go of her arms and crossed his.

"Do tell, Rosa! You have really gone off the deep end this time! The guy almost killed me! Does that mean anything to you? Jesus! What the hell!" he screamed as he rubbed his head for a moment, then raised his voice another octave, "You think we have problems at our meetings? Christ, girl, what the hell have you just done."

At that point, they both were aware most of the room's focus was on their public dispute. Some of them started to speak out.

"What's going on here?"

"Why is that street thug here?"

"We will take care of him, Rosa," another hollered.

"No!" Rosa quickly exclaimed and addressed the crowd, "We got this! Please, everyone, give us a few moments."

Darcy knew she was desperate for a resolution and for him to back her up. He shook his head in disgust, not sure what to make of what was happening, but she was his friend and had taken him in at a time when he didn't know where to go. As the crowd got a bit more persistent, he decided to hear her out, but first needed to address the angry mob who were not listening to Rosa at that moment.

"Hang on, everyone! Everything is okay. I trust Rosa, and you should too. I don't think that guy is a threat to any of us, and we both will personally make sure of it before giving the final okay for him to stay here. Trust me. Just give us a minute to get this figured out."

It took a few moments, but the majority of the folks backed away, some only by several feet, hoping to hear more specifics on the new guest. Jean-Pierre and Blitz were still near the entranceway leaning up against the wall, not speaking a word to each other. They watched as people skirted around them, careful not to get too close, their glares sending messages of disapproval. Jean-Pierre felt trouble brewing and hoped that Rosa could fix the bizarre situation she had put them all in, sooner than later.

Rosa tried to get Darcy to understand why she didn't shoot Blitz as promised but instead brought him back to the shelter. He felt her compassion and wished he could share it but strongly felt her decision was reckless. After conversing more and despite his feelings, Darcy hesitantly agreed to temporarily support Rosa's decision with the stipulation that Blitz stayed away from the general population and was monitored at all times. Rosa agreed and promised to throw Blitz out at the sign of even an ounce of trouble.

"Only for you, Rosa. I hope I'm not signing up for a disaster waiting to happen. And believe me, the rest of the folks here most likely won't be as tolerant to this crazy notion of yours," he said as he gave her a tight hug.

Rosa hesisitantly responded, "That's where you come in, Darcy. You had the last encounter with him, and everyone knows what happened. Now that you agreed with me to let him stay for a while, that alone will convince everyone to eventually accept or at least tolerate him for a short period of time. So I need you to talk to the folks, please. Otherwise, you're right. We will have a disaster on our hands before he even moves from that wall."

Together, over the next couple of hours, they both met with various groups within the community and convinced them it was safe to let Blitz stay for the time being. They were surprised to get as little resistance as they did as everyone reluctantly backed off. It wasn't because they wanted to or necessarily agreed, but because Darcy asked them to and assured them that all would be okay, just like Rosa had assumed.

Rosa's next task was to get Jimmy on board to help keep an eye on Blitz. She was met with some reluctance but finally managed to get him to agree to help out along with a couple others in his team. His first task was to get Blitz cleaned up and get him placed safely within the yellow band section.

"Only for you, Rosa," Jimmy said even though he wasn't comfortable with the whole idea.

"I appreciate it, Jimmy. I wouldn't have asked you if there was someone else I felt I could trust to do this," she responded, thankful for his loyalty, then gave him a big hug.

"Just know I'm not a happy camper right now," he added, half chuckling, as he went off to round up Blitz.

"Okay, you're coming with me now," Jimmy timidly said as he approached Jean-Pierre and Blitz, sitting against the wall near the entranceway.

"About damn time! He's all yours!" Jean-Pierre exclaimed as he immediately darted off to find Rosa.

Blitz stood up, didn't say a word, and followed Jimmy over to the yellow band section. He was aware that everyone watched his every step, so he kept his eyes down. Jimmy brought him to a spot in the far corner of their area.

"This is where you'll be staying. It's as private as you'll get in here. Just keep your stuff nearby, although I see you didn't come with anything," Jimmy's voice softened, feeling a bit bad for the big guy and less threatened by his presence, "and I sleep right next to ya so no funny business, okay?"

"Thanks, and don't worry," Blitz responded as he immediately sat down on the sleeping bag laying on top of an air mattress. "Man, this is like a fucking luxury hotel here compared to where I've slept recently," he kind of chuckled, as he looked up at Jimmy and smiled.

For a moment Jimmy watched him just lay there, then said, "Well, don't make yourself too comfortable. We're going to get you cleaned up. I know we have some extra clothes downstairs that you can have. So, get up. Let's go."

Without any reluctance, Blitz got up and followed him downstairs, first to the barber, who shaved off his beard and chopped his hair only to shoulder length, at Blitz's request. He wanted it just long enough to pull back in a ponytail. Then Jimmy escorted him to the showers where some fresh clothes were waiting for him.

When Blitz surfaced from the shower room Jimmy exclaimed, "Wow, dude, I didn't even recognize you! You clean up real damn nice and don't even look like one of those nasty thugs anymore, well except the leather jacket and boots but hell, nobody's going to recognize you! We should've done this before you walked in the building!" They both chuckled.

Blitz's new appearance seemed to have a calming effect among the community members as well as his own attitude. As promised, he stayed to himself as much as he could, out of the way. Jimmy got a few books from Darcy for him to read, and even though reading wasn't one of his strong points, it passed the time. It had been years since he even looked through one. Rosa constantly checked in on him and gradually introduced other yellow banders. Blitz was both amazed and thankful that she saw some good in him worth saving. He hoped he didn't disappoint, and as time went on, he started to see a glimmer of hope grow within himself that change was possible.

Three uneventful days passed, and Blitz was settling in. Darcy had yet to make eye contact with him and kept his distance as much as he could. Some of the other folks started acknowledging Blitz a bit more, engaging in small talk when they were nearby. Others still wanted him gone as soon as possible but became less vocal about it as they watched his peaceful interactions among the community. And there were a handful that cursed at him if in range.

Trap was one of them and became an annoyance, shouting vulgarity at him every chance he got, whether he was close by or on the other side of the auditorium. He had several warnings from Rosa to keep his trap shut, but for the most part, he failed to listen.

Blitz & Trap

The street thugs were familiar with Trap as they had attacked the red band beach community several times, including his lean-to. They heard him spiel off obscenities every time they escaped from the community. When Blitz first heard his voice, he wanted to haul off and belt him, something he felt was long overdue but had to contain himself, for Rosa's sake.

Trap couldn't believe that she brought Blitz into the winter shelter after all he had heard she went through with the other thugs. He was ecstatic knowing three of them were dead but when Blitz showed up at the auditorium, he was beside himself. Trap would never forgive or live peacefully with Blitz. Every chance he got, he tried to egg him on, hoping he'd show his true colors and attack him. He knew that would've got him kicked out but Blitz didn't jump to the bait as hard as Trap tried.

In fact, all Trap's torment eventually backfired on him. Darcy and Jean-Pierre reprimanded him for his constant probing, but as soon as they were out of sight, he would be onto his next scheme.

"Come on, Trap, give it a rest," Jean-Pierre told him as they caught him trying to throw some garbage in Blitz's sleeping bag while he was out with Jimmy.

"Fuck you two clowns. Back the fuck off from me. You know as well as I do, that piece of shit doesn't deserve to be here!" he screamed at them, then mumbled under his breath as he walked away.

All they could do was stay on top of his antics and hoped they could keep everything under control or knew they'd be dealing with way more than they bargained for. Rosa realized the extent of Trap's childish behavior and decided she would give him a clear ultimatum. Trap wasn't happy that she assigned him to help Jimmy watch over

Blitz, or he could pack his bags and leave. He hated the choices and would have left, but had nowhere else to go.

"And Trap, you need to keep it under wraps and change your attitude around Blitz real quick, and others while you're at it. I'm over the top with listening to your filthy mouth. And so are others. There are kids here! I know there is a time and place for that behavior, but not here, not now. I want to be able to count on you," Rosa lectured him, then he mumbled a few choice words under his breath and walked away.

The task was simple. To keep an eye on Blitz when Jimmy had other assignments to take care of. The hardest part for Trap was to keep his own mouth shut. Rosa contributed a lot of his foulness from the messed up life the pandemic left him, unable to face the new reality so he masked it with crudeness. She knew it was a matter of relearning a new behavior and asked Jimmy to help out with that part, since they had to spend a lot of time together. Jimmy reluctantly agreed.

Trap's progress went in waves and, for the most part, revealed his calmer, cheerier side. When he was in a bad mood, it all went out the door. He mainly took his aggression out on Blitz, still spewing his vile language all over him. Blitz never once flinched at Trap's verbal abuse, after all, he had grown up and lived around it all his life. Blitz's patience with Trap won over some of the community members who began to stick up for him when Trap started his tirades.

But there was one point those confrontations got physical, taking Trap by surprise.

"You're a damn loud mouthed thief! We've all heard enough! Grow up, will ya!" exclaimed one of the green banded guys, as he stood nose to nose with Trap. "It's bad enough you intruded in our areas, and were lucky your ass didn't get thrown out. Now nobody wants to hear your piece of shit mouth running anymore! Just give it a rest!"

"Who the hell are you?" Trap barely got the question out when the angry guy shoved him to the floor then pounced on top of him.

"Who cares who I am! Just know lots of us are sick and tired of listening to your crappy ass voice!" he screamed as he threw a couple of punches at Trap's face, shortly joined by another.

The two guys had it out for Trap since they had arrived at the winter shelter. Almost immediately, they had supplies missing and suspected it was him. They saw him roaming around in other places he wasn't supposed to be and the next thing everyone knew, stuff was missing. From that point, the guys verbally abused and tormented Trap every chance they got, like Trap had tormented Blitz. They wanted payback for themselves as well as others, and started going into his sleep area raising havoc on it when he wasn't there. Eventually, Trap caught them, and from that day forward, they became mortal enemies.

The next thing the guys knew, the two guys were yanked away from Trap and heard Blitz's loud stern voice scream out, "Enough!"

It was loud enough that most of the room went silent as everyone's heads swung around to check out the commotion. The young men, even though fearful of Blitz, demanded him to let go as he tightly held them by the back of their necks. Meanwhile Trap laid in front of them with a bloody face.

"Hey!" Darcy yelled as he pushed through the growing crowd to see what was going on.

He couldn't believe the scene he came upon and was sure that Blitz was the root cause of the bloody mess. Darcy was afraid things were going to get worse.

As he got closer, he was even more shocked, watching as Blitz yelled at the green banders, "You no good punk asses! This is the last time you'll ever talk to him again! And if I catch you near him, well," he chuckled, "you know my potential, so get the fuck out of here now!"

Then he let go of the two men, who quickly ran towards the outside door. Still not knowing what to think, Darcy watched Blitz whip off his t-shirt, bend down, and gently wipe Trap's bleeding nose as he lay sprawled out on the floor.

Once Blitz was sure he was able to move, he helped Trap to his feet, then quickly addressed the growing crowd, "Don't worry everyone, he'll be fine. I'm going to bring him over to the doc."

Trap grabbed Blitz's arm and, in a low, unsteady voice, said, "Thanks, man, appreciate it," then they shuffled off to find Dr. Parker.

Darcy just shook his head as he walked back to his area, wondering if there really was such a thing as miracles after all.

From that point on, Trap and Blitz, bullheaded enough not to publicly display it, formed a truce and a friendly bond with each other. As time went on, they discovered they had more in common than expected. Blitz was sympathetic that Trap was a recovering alcoholic and experienced occasional slip-ups, just like him. They shared their pasts: the good, bad, and ugly, and eventually came to respect each other.

The community took notice as Trap's personality transformed from the vulgar, impossible man they constantly had dealt with, to a more jubilant one. He even offered, with a smile, to help folks out when needed, something they weren't used to, but appreciated. It also didn't go unnoticed how the monstrous street thug the community once despised, came into his own, making himself more available and started supporting Rosa at the migration meetings. He even made time to play with the kids.

The atmosphere within the winter shelter had become more positive and many started hanging out with the two misfits, listening to their stories, laughing with them, and getting them both involved in more community decisions. An unexplainable calm had finally fallen within the walls, maybe miracles were happening after all. But there were still a few who weren't onboard with the community's newest changes and weren't ready to let the chaos rest.

The Red Bander 'Thugs'

Scott Minor and Jeff Gottlieb were among the red bander members who moved into the winter shelter the same day as Trap. They kept their distance from him due to several unresolvable disputes they had while living at the Leddy Park beach community. The two tent-mates had been at the beach community for a few weeks when there was a vacancy in a neighboring lean-to. Trap happened to be in the right place at the right time and moved in. Since he had his own issues to work out, he chose not to mingle, and his gruffness prevented him from making any friends. Jeff was just as big a bully. Scott, being his tent-mate, was along for the ride.

Scott was in his mid-twenties and, for the most part, pretty laid back. He had an average body build, was slightly balding, and a personality that melded within any type of situation. He rarely defended his own beliefs, standing behind those that were more vocal and intimidating to others. He believed his silence and ill-fated followings shielded him from his worst fears, confrontations. He knew it was a serious flaw he carried around.

Scott grew up in the lower income section of the Burlington, Vermont area. He lived in a small apartment with his two brothers and father. They lost their mother when he was in seventh grade. It all had happened so quickly. She wasn't there one day when he came home from school and was told she had been rushed to the hospital, where she died shortly afterward due to complications with cancer. It never made sense to him that nobody told him she was sick until she died.

The brothers, even their mother, were all afraid of the dad. Many times, they experienced his drunken rages that lead to everyone in the household taking harsh beatings for no reason. Scott learned to counteract some of the anger by offering more alcohol to him that he secretly stashed away for such reasons. It helped to divert his dad's attention so the others could run and hide, to avoid any type of beating for that day.

Scott always regretted that he didn't better defend his younger brothers and his mom, but his small, young body was no match against his dad. Deep down, Scott knew his mom most likely died of a severe beating, not cancer. The night before she passed, his dad was overly enraged that there was no extra alcohol in the house and some dishes were left in the sink. He took it out on their mother and started hitting on her. She told the boys to run from the house and not to come back that night. They ran and never saw her again.

For a while, he and his brothers continued to live at home, but he eventually found some solace on the streets, hanging out with some kids that he knew he shouldn't be with. He tried to do well in school and wanted so badly to be the first in his family to attend college. Due to some of the bad choices he made that lead to skipping classes, sometimes days on end, his GPA failed him. Eventually, he dropped out of high school and got a job at a local pizza shop. His dad became even more unbearable during that time, so Scott finally moved in with some of his buddies.

Once the virus made its second sweep through, Scott's job and living situation disappeared. Eventually, he ended up at the red bander beach community. It was there he met up with Jeff, who was the first to befriend him. Then he met Trap and was one of the few that was able to engage in small, civil conversations with him.

Jeff had been the main instigator for most vicious quarrels around the beach community, especially with Trap. At 31, his mannerisms were childish at best, but his muscular body and outlandish remarks kept people at bay. Most times, he appeared to look more serious than he was, and many were intimidated by his narcissistic personality. Since graduating high school, Jeff had been a bouncer at different local bars and dance clubs, until the pandemic shut them down. He took his work seriously but also liked his booze, his women, and getting the last word in no matter what the situation was. Jeff knew how to throw his weight around to get what he wanted. That was until he and Trap started bucking up against each other. Trap was a challenge, who brought out the worst in him.

Their brief initial introduction upon first meeting, was the only time they experienced any civil conversation. After that, Trap and Jeff verbally attacked each other anytime they could, and nobody knew why. It appeared to have started the night Trap joined some folks who were sitting around the community campfire. Initially things were fine as he listened in on all the chatter, some singing, and watched the remnants of the sun's rays fall off of the horizon. The night seemed peaceful.

"Oh, come on, guys, you don't believe that story about the vigilante who single-handedly killed off two of the street thugs? It's bullshit. You know it, and I know it. And really, some teen bitch pulling the trigger on them? They would've pounced all over her before it got to that point. What is wrong with all of you believing such shit! You need to stop talking about it! It's just some damn myth that has gone viral. There's no bodies, and no guns. Those thugs more than likely ran the fuck off somewhere, maybe back to hell where they belong!" Jeff, already half lit, boisterously chimed in as he joined the group, catching the conversation about the yellow band teenager.

Trap had been listening to Jeff throw around verbal abuse within the community for a few days and had enough so he sarcastically barked out, "Who the hell are you to say it ain't true. I doubt it's any fucking myth invented for some dumbass campfire story."

"What the fuck did you just say, old man?" Jeff loudly questioned as he moved closer to Trap, puffing his chest out at him.

Jeff didn't like Trap from the beginning. He labeled him as a gruff old troublemaker who wasn't going to conform to any of Jeff's rules he had laid down within the community. He made himself the boss and wasn't going to have Trap challenge it. He felt his blood begin to boil and was ready to pick a fight with him after Trap dared to question his words. Most of the folks knew what was coming as they had seen Jeff's wrath many times before, so they stepped away from the once peaceful gathering.

"You heard me loud and clear, or are you fucking deaf," Trap shrewdly yelled, standing with his arms folded across his chest, not intimidated by Jeff's growing anger.

"Listen, you old fuck. I don't like your attitude. You don't know what the fuck you're talking about, and I would strongly suggest you crawl back under the hole you came out of, you piece of horse shit."

At that, others scampered away while Jeff and Trap engaged in a short stare down until Trap threw his hands up in the air and walked back to his lean-to without saying a word. He knew Jeff's type and really didn't want to get involved at his level, especially with families running about, trying to enjoy the evening. Trap wasn't going to stand by to be bullied by Jeff. Not that night.

"That's right old man, get the fuck out of my face and stay out of it," Jeff hollered after him, irritated that Trap had the nerve to challenge him in front of everyone.

From that point on, when their paths crossed, it was far from peaceful as they'd sputter obscenities to each other, but luckily had no physical encounters. Once they all moved to the auditorium and were in closer quarters, Jeff kept an eye on Trap, continually taunting him whenever he could. He knew Trap had been caught stealing from several of the members and wanted to exploit him so he would get kicked out.

Shortly after Blitz arrived at the winter shelter, Trap and Jeff got into a heated confrontation that changed everything. Jeff had just gotten his dinner and was bringing it back to eat in his area when he spotted

Trap roaming around in the yellow band community, checking out someone's stuff. He knew Darcy had recently caught him in the act and was enraged that his behavior was continuing. Now he had proof Trap didn't reform, and wasn't going to let him get away with it. Jeff quickly set his tray down, then rushed over stopping Trap dead in his tracks.

He firmly latched onto Trap's arm and yelled, "You just don't learn you fucking no good thief! You were given one undeserved chance to keep your dirty paws to yourself, but I caught you again, old man! Your ass will finally get tossed out of here, and I will have front row seats to the show!" Jeff squeezed Trap's arm even harder as he looked around to see if Darcy or Rosa were anywhere in sight.

"Get your fucking hands off me!" Trap demanded, trying not to wince as Jeff's nails dug into his skin, "I haven't touched jack shit!" Trap tried to pull his arm away, but Jeff's grip tightened even more.

"Bullshit! I just caught you in the act, you fucking liar!" Jeff hollered, getting more agitated.

Jeff saw his moment where he could finally haul off and belt Trap, something he had been waiting to do for months. Just as he was about to punch him in the face, someone grabbed his shoulders from behind and forcefully pulled him away from Trap.

"Knock it off, you punk ass!" exclaimed Blitz, "You're the one that doesn't know jack shit and have no business getting your nose in where it doesn't belong. But just for your information, I asked Trap to come over here and get something for me! This is my area!" Blitz yelled right in Jeff's face as he watched him cower.

Blitz let go of him and for a few seconds Jeff just stood there rubbing his shoulders. He felt them sting. Nobody had touched him like that in years and couldn't believe the one person he most feared there, was pissed off at him. He never wanted to get on his bad side and wasn't sure what was going to happen next. Jeff glanced over at Trap as he babied his arm and at that moment, was glad he didn't snap it like he had intended doing.

At that point, Jeff was free to walk away and knew he should have, but he was riled up and decided to lie his way into getting Blitz to side with him, "Look Blitz, I saw that piece of shit. He was looking through a couple of others' stuff as well, not just yours and I'm sure he took something. You can't trust him! He needs to be thrown out of here! Once you tell Darcy, he will make sure of it!"

"Enough!" Blitz hollered back, "I've sat back and watched your punk ass throw your weight around and intimidate everyone near you. You fucking give the definition of bully a run for its money! But I'm telling you it stops now. Trap was doing what I asked him to. He didn't go through anyone else's stuff. Keep lying and bullying. It will be your dirty ass that will get thrown out!"

Then he turned to Trap and asked, "You okay, bud?"

Trap nodded as Blitz patted his back, then turned to Jeff and said, "Let's go, Jeff. I want to have a talk with you."

Jeff froze in his tracks as Blitz headed toward the main door and motioned for him to follow. He wasn't sure he would be able to defend himself from what he thought was going to happen next. Again, he looked around for Darcy, Rosa, and even Scott. Nobody was there to help him. Jeff was certain the onlookers would be pleased to see his battered body after Blitz was done with him. Jeff took another look over at Trap, who sneered at him, most likely anticipating his horrible fate. He had no other choice but to follow Blitz as nosey gatherers lined up to watch his exit.

Blitz was already sitting on the outside steps when Jeff got out there and told him to have a seat. Jeff reluctantly obeyed. The concrete was dry and warm from the late morning sun casting its heat upon it. It had snowed a few inches the night before, one of the first snow falls of the season. Some kids were already taking advantage of it as they played on the middle school grounds just across the street. Others were outside taking in its freshness.

"Listen, Jeff, I get it, man, things are so fucked up right now, and it's hard to know what or who to trust. I've lived that my whole life," Blitz started as he watched the kids toss snowballs at each other.

"He's a piece of shit, you know it, and I know it, man, come on, Blitz," Jeff looked at him with pleading eyes, not knowing what was going to happen next, "His ass needs to be tossed out of here! All we've got to do is tell Darcy, and then his ass will get thrown out!"

Blitz paused for a moment then quietly said, "That ain't so, man. What part of me saying he didn't do anything can't you understand? Maybe Trap was a piece of shit when he first got here and at your beachfront. I don't know and don't care. At this point, I've gotten to know him pretty well, and he's a good person, Jeff. The pandemic has fucked so many of us up that it's hard to say who we really are anymore. But I know Rosa and the rest of us have come to respect who he is. He's come a long way and has gotten us out of a few jams. People deserve more chances with their lives. Christ, look at me." Blitz shook his head.

Jeff sat silently for a few minutes, watching the snow sparkle in the sun, then replied, "Fuck man, I hear ya, but he's been nothing but shit to me."

Blitz turned to look at him then responded, "Yeah, I hear ya. I know what that's like, to do others wrong, but in Trap's case, well, you play a big role in that too, brother. You need to calm your ass down. You're fucking bullying and intimidating everyone around you really needs to stop, or I hate to say it, you will get yourself tossed out. And there is no better place to be right now especially with the migration coming up. It's a lot to lose; besides, once you make some changes, you'll be pleasantly surprised. That I promise."

Jeff just nodded in agreement, not daring to get into any type of confrontation with Blitz, even though he didn't agree.

As Blitz started to get up, he added, "So my friend, just go back in there and make amends with him. Start fresh like the rest of us. We can't have this shit continue. Not here, not now. Rosa wants these disturbances to cease before the migration. All of us do. Don't make it any harder." At that, Blitz got up, patted him on the back, and went back inside.

Jeff sat there for a few moments thinking how relieved he was that he didn't get his ass handed to him and beat to a pulp, but was fuming with the thought he had to bow down to Trap. It was apparent there was no other option. He didn't want to be thrown out. So, he took a few deep breaths of the cool, wintery air, then went inside to look for Trap.

Trap was already back in his area, sitting on his bed, watching as Jeff approached. He wasn't sure what was going to happen, so he quickly stood up, ready for a confrontation as Jeff continued to meander over. Neither could explain or expected what happened next.

As Jeff stood in front of him, he took another deep breath then half heartedly said, "Okay, Trap, let's call a truce. Neither of us want to get kicked out, and even though I'm not doing this of my own free will, I apologize. I'll do what I can to stay out of your way and won't get in your business, and I expect the same in return."

Trap watched as Jeff extended his hand out to shake it. He was taken off guard by the apology and knew it was most likely under pressure. He had no intent to reciprocate, especially still feeling the sting in his arm from Jeff's grip earlier.

But Trap surprised himself blurting out, "Okay, man, let's do that, call a truce," then grabbed his hand.

They smiled at each other as they shook. Blitz was nearby and smiled to himself as he watched them peacefully walk away from each other. He was sure things were on the mend.

Rosa was pleased with Blitz's growth within the community and even more pleased after finding out about him resolving some bad blood between Trap and Jeff. She asked him to help out at more migration gatherings due to the increasing numbers of uninvited protesters. The fact that most everyone in the city knew who Blitz was tamed some of the angry crowds. His sense to spot street-worthy trouble and escort them away from the meetings without incidents was warmly welcomed by everyone.

At one of the smaller migration meetings, when Blitz was on the rally stage with Darcy, he spotted a familiar gang he and his street thugs had encountered in the past. They continued to pull a lot of disruptive shenanigans around the city but generally ran if they spotted Blitz. It wasn't long before they began spewing out angry threats that their civil rights were being violated by not being part of the initial migration, and were there to make people pay for their oversight.

Trap was also at that rally and heard the commotion. He could tell from Blitz's reaction that something wasn't right. Then he watched Blitz jump off the stage and dart toward the disruptive group. Trap didn't think twice and was right on his heels. By the time they both reached the gang, some had already run, knowing Blitz was coming after them, but a few tried to stand firm and continued to demand their rights. Blitz, Trap, and a few others eventually escorted the derelicts away from the scene, gave them a hardcore scare as they roughed them up, and promised more if they came back. It was enough to keep them away from all future rallies. Word spread on how Blitz and Trap handled the gang together, and a new respect for them both grew within the communities.

The Necklace

After getting settled into their new routine at the winter shelter, Rosa had befriended a green bander girl from the Oakledge community. Holly French was just a couple months younger than she was and initially joined the beach community with her grandparents and younger sister. Just a few months earlier, she had lost her parents and baby brother to the virus. Holly had approached Rosa shortly after they all got settled in and asked if she'd help her find a necklace she lost on the beachfront.

Holly had worn the necklace ever since her mother gave it to her, but the night that the beach community moved to the winter shelter, she discovered it was missing. Holly panicked, not knowing where it had fallen off, and the next day went back to the site to see if she could find it. Unable to, she sat on the beach crying as her thoughts flooded with the day it was put around her neck.

"I want to give you something," Holly's mom said just as the ambulance was pulling up to their home.

Janelle continued to cough hard as she asked Holly to open her jewelry box and retrieve a small blue pouch, and hand it to her. The siren had turned off, and Holly heard her grandparents' voices directing the paramedics to her mother's room. They didn't have much time left together.

Tears flowed down her cheeks, knowing that her mother would soon be whisked away, just like her brother and father were a few weeks earlier. She wasn't prepared for the fact they never came back. Her grandparents had prepared her and her younger sister for the same outcome with their mom, but she was far from ready to say goodbye. Holly tried to stay strong as she handed her mother the small velvet pouch.

Janelle tightly clutched it as she laid silent while the paramedics came through the bedroom door. Her parents stood by, watching as they started to prep her to move when Janelle asked everyone if she could have a moment with her daughter.

"Please, wait just a moment. Just a moment," she coughed and waved Holly to come closer, then opened the pouch, "Put your hand out, my sweet daughter."

Holly cupped her hand as a white-gold heart shaped locket fell into it. She recognized it. It was a necklace her father had given her mother when Holly was first born. She tried hard not to cry more as she opened it and stared at the small inserts. On one side of the heart was a picture of both her parents holding her as a baby, and on the other side, a picture of her wrapped in her mother's arms when she was a toddler.

"It's yours now. Wear it knowing you are and always will be loved," Janelle choked back her tears as Holly hugged her tightly before she was put on the stretcher.

"I will, Mommy. I will never forget and will keep it close forever." That was the last thing she ever said to her as she watched her mother wheeled out of the room.

Rosa took a liking to Holly, having been through similar situations because of the pandemic. They spent some time together working on a couple projects for the shelter, and got to know each other a bit more. After hearing her story, Rosa knew how important the necklace was to her so, despite the fact they'd have to pass through Mr. Chuso's neighborhood, she agreed to help her look for it.

The first time they went to the beach and dug around in the sand, they had no luck, plus Rosa's time was limited as she had to get back for a migration meeting. She promised to go back again and knew it had to be before the snow arrived, or the treasure would stay buried until late spring, most likely ruining the pictures. A few weeks passed before Rosa finally could go back with her. Even though she was getting busier with her plans and the community, she knew she had to make good on her word.

It was a cold, sunny afternoon. The lean-tos were the only things that greeted them as Rosa and Holly jumped off the path and onto the Oakledge community's sandy shore. The structures were built to survive a few winters, just in case folks had to stay in them. The girls found a couple of pieces of driftwood near the water and used it to dig around in the cold, wet sand. Holly and her beach family had lived in one of the tents further up the shoreline. They had already checked that area for the necklace the last time they were there, so they spread out along the rest of the beach.

Out of the blue Holly shyly asked, "Can I ask you something?"

"Anything, Holly. What?" Rosa responded as she bent down and picked up a snail shell.

"How well do you know Darcy?" she paused a moment then timidly added, "Do you know if he has a girlfriend?"

Rosa looked over at her and started giggling as she replied, "Oh, are we sweet on him?"

As she looked up the shore, towards the path they had come down, Rosa spotted a somewhat familiar person standing at the end of it. The person was just watching them. She wasn't close enough to clearly identify him, yet her heart pounded hard in her chest at the thought of who it resembled. Maybe her eyes were playing tricks on her, but she didn't want to take any chances. She told Holly to follow her as they hurriedly walked to the other side of the beachfront and exited through the woods.

He had spotted the girls just a few weeks earlier when they first walked down one of the side streets near his home. He couldn't believe his luck that one of them was Rosa and decided to venture out in the same direction, hoping he'd find her at the beach. And sure enough, he found her, the thief who stole his gun. Mr. Chuso watched as they dug around in the sand, apparently they had lost something. They never saw him, not until that day.

Charles Randolph Chuso felt his blood boil. He assumed she recognized him and watched as they scurried further down the beach, away from him. The arthritis in his knees had acted up, so he was in no shape to tramp after them, but he was determined to get back what was his and not let her disappear again. He was sure they'd be back, and he would wait.

The Beretta handgun had belonged to his younger brother, who served seven years in the military before losing his battle with cancer. On his deathbed, just moments before he passed, Charles inherited the handgun. It was a memory that he would never shake and the only possession he had that kept his brother's memory alive.

Charles and Thomas James Chuso grew up on their parent's farm in a small town just east of Burlington. Even though there were five years between them, Charles and Thomas were the best of friends from the day Thomas came home from the hospital. Charles loved his little brother and vowed to take care of him and watch out for him, as big brothers should. Once out of high school Charles got a job at a local mechanic shop, living his dream. Cars were his forever passion, and he and Thomas remained close. Five years later, Thomas, who had always wanted to travel and wanted more than just local life, joined the Army. It was a bittersweet goodbye for the brothers, not knowing when they would see each other again, but they stayed in touch. Seven years later, Thomas was home for his final time. Just a few months later, he died from cancer.

Charles was devastated, and even though he moved on with his life and his family, he lost a part of him he could never find again. From that point on, whisky, who was already Charles' friend, became his best friend, forsaking all others, just to help erase the emptiness he constantly felt, if just for a short time. But it backfired on him, as the alcohol took away any new memories that he could have and should have created with his own family while they all were alive.

Shortly after Mr. Chuso's wife and kids passed, he pulled the gun out of his bureau drawer where it had been since he got it and kept it on the end table by his chair in the living room. He was obsessed with it, just knowing it was there, next to him, gave him some comfort, and he just wanted it back.

Mr. Chuso went back to his condo and waited for the girls to surface from the beach area. If they came his way, he planned to follow them and find out where Rosa was staying so he could get the gun back. But as the sun started setting and half a bottle of whisky later, he knew it wasn't happening that day.

Thereafter, almost every day for the next week, he strolled down by the beachfront and waited, knowing she'd eventually return since there was something there they had been searching for. And just eight days later, his patience paid off. He followed them back to the beach. Mr. Chuso felt his heart pulsate in his throat. Excitement and anger flooded throughout his entire body as he stood for a moment on the sandy shore, noting how close they were. They had not seen him yet, and knew he had to play it out just right, as his legs wouldn't be able to run after them, if they saw him. As they dug in the sand for the lost possession, he slowly crept closer.

Rosa and Holly were suddenly aware of the man's presence as they heard the ground crunching from his overweight body sinking into the damp sand. As they turned and glared right at him, he stopped dead in his tracks. Rosa immediately tensed up knowing, without a doubt, it was Mr. Chuso standing just five feet in front of them.

The familiar, sickening voice danced in her ears as he half chuckled, "Well, who do we have here? Oh, wait, it's the little fucking thief!"

He was just as she remembered, the miserable, filthy, disgusting man, now basking in his glorious discovery. For a moment, she thought she was going to pass out. Holly had no no clue what was going on or who the man was, but sensed he was trouble.

She nervously whispered, "Rosa, who is that?"

Rosa put one arm out to block Holly from taking any more steps forward, then mumbled under her breath, "Just stay back and don't say a word."

"You little bitch, I knew I'd catch up to you. I want the fucking gun back that you stole from me, and I want it now!" Mr. Chuso's face got beet red, and his spit flew everywhere as he stepped a bit closer, excitedly yelling, "I bet you are looking for this!"

At that, he opened up his clenched fist and revealed a shiny heart locket swinging from its chain.

"Oh my God!" Holly exclaimed, "That's my mother's! Why do you have it? Give that to me!"

Mr. Chuso laughed as Holly tried to push past Rosa's arm, then spitefully said, "All in good time, pretty girl. She has something I want, and I have something you want! So let's get this done with. Hand over my fucking gun and you're little friend will get the necklace."

Rosa firmly held her back and instructed, "Holly, stay back! You don't want to mess with this man. Please!"

Not taking her eyes off of him, she sarcastically replied, "Can't say I ever thought I'd see you again, Mr. Chuso," hoping her voice didn't sound too shaky as she swung her backpack on the ground in front of them both, "You want to make a deal? Well, let's do it. I have your gun."

With that, Rosa opened her backpack and pulled out the Beretta M9. Holly gasped with astonishment, and Mr. Chuso's eyes grew wider, not believing he was that lucky she had it with her. He watched as she held it in her hands, surprised by her knowledge in doing so.

"You never fail to amaze me, Rosa. But if you know what's good for you and her, hand it over right now and she'll get her necklace," he demanded as he dangled it in front of them then stuffed it in his pants' pocket.

After the first time he saw them at the beach and realized they were digging around for something in the sand, he had decided to check out the area and do some digging of his own. He picked up one of the sticks they had left behind and grazed it across the beach for several minutes when he saw a shiny object reflecting the sun's rays. He picked up the locket, opened it and saw the faded picture of a woman holding a small child. His heart momentarily filled with sadness as he remembered the one he had given his wife with their two boys in it. She had worn it for years. He wasn't sure if the locket was what the girls were searching for but put it in his pocket just in case, to use as a bargaining chip. And was glad he did.

Two things Rosa knew for sure at that moment. Either she was going to have to shoot him, or he was going to shoot her if he gained control of the gun. Either way, she knew it was going to be used once again and felt panic flood through her entire body.

She took a deep breath and stated, "I'm not giving this back to you, Mr. Chuso. But you do need to hand over that necklace and then get the fuck out of my sight."

It took a minute for it to sink in what she was saying, then Mr. Chuso felt anger take over as he yelled, "Why, you no good piece of shit! You will give that back to me! It's mine!"

Rosa knew all too well the tone he had copped, and the way he slurred his words, signaling he probably finished a bottle of whisky before he arrived there. Then he flung his arms about, seemingly losing control over his own self.

"Mr. Chuso, just give us the necklace and go home," Rosa calmly demanded, "You don't need this gun and I'm not giving it to you."

"Yes you are you little twit. Give it to me now or I'll kill you with it myself!" he yelled, as he started to step closer to them.

Still keeping her eyes on Chuso, expecting he was going to pounce at her, Rosa instructed Holly to turn around, face the lake in a low yet stern tone, "Holly, stay back, in fact, turn around, face the lake and cover your ears no matter what happens. Do it now."

Just as Holly turned, Rosa watched Chuso's body explode in rage as he let out an ungodly, angry growl, then lunged forward at her, "Give it to me now! You little piece of ..."

Just before he could grab her, shots rang into the air, and the sounds of the waves roughly plunging against the shore, escorted them away.

Mr. Chuso's body laid in a lump not more than a couple of feet away. Rosa heard Holly's whimpers as she stood there,gun still in hand, looking down at the selfish, crude bully that she never felt deserved to walk the face of the earth. His reign of terror had come to an end. It certainly wouldn't erase any of the nightmarish moments she had encountered with him in his home or all that he had done to his family and others, but it certainly saved the next victim destined to cross his path.

Snapping out of the momentary trance, Rosa quickly put the gun away and approached his body with Holly right behind her. His thick coat soaked up some of the blood from his wound, keeping the rest hidden under it.

"Oh my God, Rosa, what just happened? Who is this man?" Holly hysterically asked, "You just killed him?"

"I'm so sorry you had to witness this. He was a very bad man from my past and did some very bad things to others. We will be okay. Nobody needs to know what happened here. We're just going to leave and forget about it. It is what it is. Trust me," she softly said, cusping Holly's face, wiping some of her tears away.

Then Rosa bent down, reached in Mr. Chuso's pocket, and pulled out the locket. She gently put it into Holly's hand, wrapped her arms around her, and said, "Here you go, my friend. It's back where it belongs."

Once Holly regained some composure, Rosa picked up her backpack, and the two left the beach, leaving Mr. Chuso's body lying in the sand near the lakeshore. The sun was slowly going down over the horizon, casting some reddish-orange rays across it. A couple seagulls sang out as they flew overhead. Maybe both were a symbol that God already forgave him and carried his soul to a better place where, maybe, his family welcomed him.

The Nightmare

After their traumatic outing at Oakledge, Holly hung around Rosa more. She admired how Rosa stayed strong and appeared to be unaffected by what had happened that day on the beach. She was thankful her mom's necklace was back in her possession, safely around her neck, but couldn't shake what they went through to get it. The chilling moment she realized Rosa shot Mr. Chuso, gave her recurring nightmares. She'd wake up in a cold sweat after seeing Chuso's lifeless body laying in the sand with his eyes wide open, blankly staring right at her. There were times during the day that she'd closed her eyes and still heard the gunshots, just as clear as that day. She and Rosa never spoke about the incident again, yet it had silently fused them together.

During the next several weeks Holly started hanging out with Dora and Chad Kinley, a couple in their late 20s. Dora first noticed her when they were together at the Oakledge Beach community. Holly had stayed to herself, rarely hanging around anyone but her grandparents and little sister. But when they arrived at the winter shelter, Dora noticed Holly spending more time with Rosa and Darcy. She couldn't help notice there were times where seemed alone and sad, haunted by her silent thoughts. Dora felt she could use another friend and after discussing it with Chad, made an effort to get to know her. Holly liked her, so they started hanging out on a daily basis.

Dora and Chad had met on a dating site just five years earlier. For most of their young lives, they had been focused on travel and careers; neither had been interested in a serious relationship until they laid eyes on each other. A year later, just before the virus made its debut, they married. They were at the point they were ready to start planning a family until the second wave hit, changing everything in their life. They eventually found themselves part of the green band community.

Dora was strikingly pretty, model-worthy, and only in heels, was a bit taller than Chad. She had a thin build, long blonde hair, and mesmerizing sea-blue eyes that almost glowed when the sun reflected in them. She was full of energy and loved to be the center of attention but didn't demand it. People just seemed to gravitate toward her open, fun-loving personality, and she brought the party wherever she went, just by being there. Dora had a big heart and looked out for others, whether they were family, friends, or strangers. Holly became one of them.

Chad was a tall, thin, yet well-built guy who also had lots of energy. He kept his dark black hair pulled back in a small bun, had a close-shaven beard, and big brown eyes that smiled when he did. He didn't like creating any attention around himself but held his own when Dora created it around them. He had spent his early 20s traveling and working in various orphanages and villages, helping those who were in need. His compassion spilled over to Holly as well.

"Hey Holly, we're going to take a jaunt down to the library and look up some of the articles on the better lands that Rosa recently shared with us. I know you're interested in that as well. Care to join us?" Dora asked her as she sat alone on the side of the auditorium stage, just swinging her feet back and forth.

Holly's eyes lit up when she saw Dora. She knew her friendship was genuine, and enjoyed being in her company. Even though she loved her sister and grandparents, there was something about Dora's presence that calmed her, like her mother used to.

"That would be great, Dora! Sure, I'll go with you guys."

"Good," Dora replied and added, "Chad is already there saving us a seat. Hopefully, it's a day the internet gives us some access."

Darcy also took an interest in Holly and had since he first saw her walk into the auditorium. She was a bit younger than him, just on the verge of turning 16. He loved her long jet black hair that she mainly wore in a braid draped over her shoulder. Her Latino descent and big brown eyes combined with her five-foot-one-inch bundle of energy made his heart melt every time she was in his sight. Because of his own short height, he loved the fact he somewhat towered over her, giving him confidence that he could just scoop her up in his arms and be her protector.

As Holly started spending more time with Rosa, Dary came into the mix. Eventually the two of them did a few things on their own and occasionally met up in the library when Holly went with the Kinleys. Other times they hung out in the auditorium playing games and talking for hours. As Holly's interest in the migration grew, Rosa had asked her to join in on some of the planning sessions. It was obvious to others that Holly and Darcy had become close, and a relationship was brewing. Eventually, Darcy asked her to move from the green band section to his, which confirmed their relationship. Many nights they laid awake talking and giggling into the early morning hours. They became inseparable.

But Holly's nightmares continued and were getting worse. One particular evening, they both had fallen asleep in each other's arms. She woke up in a sweat as Mr. Chuso stood over her and had a gun pointed directly at her head. Holly heard the safety latch go off and saw him start to pull the trigger when Darcy rolled over and put his arm around her. His movement startled Mr. Chuso, and the gun fired. The bullet missed her and hit Darcy. Holly frantically screamed as she grabbed Darcy's body, holding it tightly against hers.

"Holly! Are you okay?!" Darcy exclaimed as he woke up to her hysterically crying, holding him tightly.

He had been through this before with her as the nightmares seemed to come often, but this one was different. It frightened her more. She'd never talk about them, and all he could do was just hold her close until she calmed down.

Holly's sobbing woke up a few folks next to them and one, "Hey, everything okay over there?"

"Yeah, we're fine. She just had a bad dream, all good," Darcy quickly replied, then wrapped his arms tightly around her and said, "It might help to talk about it."

"It was just a bad dream," she softly responded as she snuggled closer. "I'm sorry I woke you. I'm okay, really," then planted a soft kiss on his lips.

She had no intention of sharing the reality behind her nightmares with anyone, not even him. What scared her most about them was how real Mr. Chuso seemed, and that he kept coming back. Holly found herself wondering, on many occasions, if he had found a way to reach her from the other side, to haunt her for the rest of her life for what had happened that day. She was curious if he was doing the same to Rosa, but didn't dare ask.

Finally feeling more relaxed, Holly softly kissed Darcy as she whispered, "Let's just go back to sleep. All is good. Really."

As they snuggled up, Holly prayed that Mr. Chuso had enough fun with her, at least for that night, and eventually fell into a peaceful sleep.

The Teams

At long last, the migration team lists were in place, and it was time for Rosa and Darcy to make the big announcement that would introduce the team leads. Despite the enthusiasm for that day, there was still some discontent among the community over who initially was going and who wasn't. Everyone wanted to be the first to go, but Rosa wasn't going to change the plans no matter what their reasons were or the disruption it created. She knew the plan was well thought out and would benefit everyone in the long run. Rosa also knew when something was finalized and put into action, the worst thing to do was get wishy-washy and let others persuade it in a different direction. That was something she learned at a very early age, thanks to her father.

Rosa recalled the evening she hung out with him in their living room while her mother was off doing some volunteer work. She was reading her book, and her father had just gotten off the phone with a disgruntled client. The soap factory was having some issues with the client's soap line. She recalled hearing him say they were done; he wasn't going to do what they asked.

Bill had come home that evening very distraught after a meeting with his most valued client. They suddenly weren't happy with the current production numbers and wanted them at least tripled. The client told Bill he needed to do whatever it took to make it happen, even if it meant building a new addition or shutting down other client lines. Although Bill wanted to keep his lucrative client happy, any new adjustments of sorts would have temporarily stopped all production for other clients and was something he refused to do. He tried to work it out with them to no avail and eventually made the tough decision of telling them to find another soap maker.

"Daddy, why didn't you just help them out, like you do everyone else?" seven-year-old Rosa recalled asking him.

"Because my dear Rosa, they are just one account, and if I disrupted everything for them, all my other clients wouldn't be happy. In the end, I needed to do what was right for everyone.

I couldn't give up what was already working because one demanded me to do so."

"I guess I get it, Daddy," she had replied, trying to put it all together in her head.

His words never left her, and as she played them over in her head, she finally understood them. "The one thing you must remember, Rosa, in order to be a strong leader and keep things consistent, you must keep control. You must stick to your guns, your instinct, your knowledge, and not let anyone drive you off that path, or in the end, you will lose it all."

The meeting to announce the Team Leads was held on the university campus just up the hill from the auditorium. The makeshift stage was set up in the middle of the common grounds near an old corroded fountain. A little over 1,000 folks had already gathered by the time Rosa, Darcy, and the rest of the migration team arrived. Bodyguards from all the communities were assigned to help patrol the area. Blitz and Trap had formed their own task force, keeping a close eye out for expected testy protesters.

"Okay, folks, can I have your attention. We have lots to share today," Darcy shouted into a megaphone at the enthusiastic crowd as he stood on the platform with Rosa, Jimmy, and a few others.

The scene could have been mistaken for a big festival, with lots of music, people dancing around, and several food stations spread about. The vibes were a bit unsettling, and Rosa felt anxious as she stood watching all the unexpected commotion. The crowd was the largest yet, loud and wild. She knew it could easily get out of control, as it seemed nobody initially acknowledged Darcy's first attempt to gain their attention.

"Listen up, folks, it's time we get our migration teams in place and start preparing for the journey, which is just around the corner," he announced, a bit louder than before, finally getting people to listen.

But before Darcy could say another word, the expected chaos started, and the same old shout-outs were fast and furious from the protesters.

"This is bullshit!"

"We all should be able to go!"

"You can't stop any of us from going!"

"If we don't go, none should go!"

A constant underlying chant came from their supporters, added to the growing tempers, "Go Rosa, Go Rosa, Go Rosa," and the audience quickly became more unruly as they fought to verbally drown each other out.

Then, before anyone knew what was happening, Blitz jumped up on the platform, grabbed the megaphone from Darcy, and belted out, "Enough, people! A plan is in action. If you don't like it, then take your filthy punk asses out of here!"

Silence quickly erupted among the crowd and most knew that Blitz was extremely agitated with them as he yelled, "Don't test me! If you don't shut your fucking mouths and listen, then, by all means, I'll do it for you. Now let these good people talk; otherwise, get the fuck out of here!"

A silent hush remained in the air as Blitz continued to look across the crowd waiting to see if anyone was going to challenge him.

"We hear you, dude!" a daring individual yelled out, followed by a couple of others in agreement, and the supportive chanting slowly started again, "Go Rosa, Go Rosa, Go Rosa," which was only an invitation for another unrest to burst out within the crowd.

Before it could gain momentum, Blitz let out a giant whistle that once again silenced the masses then replied, "Come on, people! Rosa and Darcy have worked hard for this, for all of you. To help bring you to the better lands. Just because you can't be first in line doesn't mean you won't get there. Act like this, and I'll make sure none of you get there!" then he pointed at a large group who continued ignoring him, then hollered, "You all, get the fuck out now!"

Immediately several bodyguards forcefully raced toward the group, who quickly turned and high-tailed it out before they got close. Rosa and Darcy watched as almost a quarter of the crowd also turned and headed off the campus with no further conflict. The rest of them remained silent with all eyes on Blitz as he handed the megaphone back to Darcy.

Then, quite unexpected but well received, a change emerged among the rest of the people as they started clapping and chanting, "Go Blitz! Go Blitz! Go Blitz!"

Blitz looked over and winked at Darcy, who in turn shook his hand and for the first time spoke to him, "Thanks, Blitz. I truly mean it."

Blitz replied, "You got it," then jumped off the stage.

At that point, Darcy laid out a few rules and expectations for those that would stay behind then handed the megaphone to Rosa to announce the first four teams.

Rosa and Jean-Pierre still planned to lead the first team of 100 travelers. Among them were Blitz and some of his chosen bodyguards, along with Tony Roswell and George Rudder. They planned to leave in late March and expected to arrive in the better lands sometime in early May. Following them, just a week later was Team 2, led by Bill Wallington; then Team 3, led by a local couple, Don and Marie; and Team 4 put Sam Hatfield at the helm.

Each one of the team leads had their two minutes of fame as they got up on the platform and introduced themselves, then had a chance to mingle with the crowd after the meeting was over.

"I think that went well," George said to Tony as they headed back down the hill to the auditorium.

"I agree," Tony responded, "For now. I expect we will get some push back if someone doesn't like the team they're assigned to or some other bull crap. Can't please them all. I'm just glad that Rosa asked us to be on her team."

"Me too," George replied.

George Rudder & Tony Roswell

Jean-Pierre and Rosa agreed that George and Tony would be a good fit for some of the first travelers and wanted them on their team. Both had some medical knowledge that would benefit the team and the migration plan. Although George was only a massage therapist, his capabilities of helping folks went far beyond those limitations. The plan for him was a bit different. He would only travel with Team 1 to the Cleveland hub then would then stay behind to provide his services to the next two teams as they passed through. George would then migrate the rest of the way to the better lands with Team 4.

George Rudder was a mid-20 Generation Z laid back guy who was born in the mid-south, where he lived with his parents and two older siblings his first eight years. He was a tall, lanky black man who wore blue, round-framed eyeglasses and his curly, thick hair cut just above his ears.

During his middle school years, his parents moved the family to upstate New Hampshire, where his father transferred his orthopedic surgical practice to a local hospital in Lebanon. By the time George got to high school, his two older brothers were attending colleges in different states. During his junior year at the University of Vermont, the pandemic hit and the next year forced the schools to conduct virtual graduations.

Right afterwards, his parents gifted him with an office space near Lake Champlain, where he started his own business as a massage therapist. Even through some of the second wave of the pandemic, his business continued to grow. He generally only worked on patients who had incurred muscle injuries and there a lot of them since transportation shut down and they had to get around on foot. Then the evacuation orders came down.

George met Jean-Pierre when he first arrived at the winter shelter, just after the Christmas holiday. They immediately hit it off, sharing the love of basketball and playing some hoops together at a local park when weather permitted. George's six-foot-five lanky body frame had helped him excel on both his high school and college teams and was no match for Jean-Pierre, but they had fun.

George's professional skills kept him quite busy catering to the many different community folks, tending to their back and muscle issues. In fact, he was so busy he was given a small room in the auditorium basement to work out of. Despite the underlying circumstances, George was happy.

Shortly before George had arrived at the auditorium, Tony Roswell had made his debut on its doorsteps. He also was a Gen Z 20-something, educated, professional male who had a career as a pediatric nurse. Tony had worked at the local hospital before its building had been overcome with the uncontrollable virus particles. Once the evacuation order closed its doors, Tony no longer had a job and, months later, found his way to the auditorium.

He was one of the first ones that greeted George when he arrived. Tony had spotted the tall, modestly nerdy guy, looking lost as he made his way through the auditorium. Nobody seemed to notice him, despite the fact he towered over them all, so Tony introduced himself and brought him to Jean-Pierre to see if he could stay. Tony then offered to take George under his wing, show him the ropes, introduce him around, and get him settled.

They both had some healthcare medical schooling in common, which helped them relate well to each other's profession. George admired Tony's six-foot-two muscular, well-toned physique and his preppy style. He also noted how excitement flooded through him when their eyes connected. George believed they understood each other yet wasn't quite sure if Tony's personal life paralleled his.

George knew, from a very early age, that he was different from the rest of his family and friends, not only his race, but his sexuality. For the most part, the small remote NH town he once lived in left him with good childhood memories. Except for a few of the bullies that roamed the hall of the middle school and had called him out for his skin color and his awkwardness due to his almost six-foot height at an early age. But once he got to high school and found his place among the basketball team, the bullies left him alone.

When all his friends were dating girls and goofing around, he chose to go to the local gym and shoot hoops or stay at home and study. Not that he couldn't get a date, he was just more interested in maintaining his honor roll status to get into medical school and follow in his father's footsteps. But there was one girl he had been close to from the time they had moved into the town. They rode bikes together, grabbed pizza, sometimes studied together, and just hung out.

One time, the summer between eighth grade and high school, they were in her backyard, sitting behind the storage shed just talking, when out of the blue, they kissed. It was a very awkward moment for George, and as soon as their lips parted, he ran home. She had her suspicions about why he did, and years later, when he came home on a college break, he confirmed them.

During the beginning of his junior year at college, he finally met someone that he wanted to be with. They had a lot in common, from hiking the nearby mountains to shooting hoops together. Unfortunately, several months into their new connection, the pandemic arrived, and eventually the school was forced to host online classes. His new love interest ended up flying back to his home in California, and they continued to chat for the next couple of months. Distance eventually killed the relationship since there was next to no chance they'd see each other again. George resigned himself to the fact that was the only relationship he'd ever have and, from that point, chose to keep his gender preference to himself.

As time went on, Tony and George spent more time together. George had a sense something was developing between them but was still not sure if Tony was feeling the same pull or if he was even gay. At one point, George was sure Tony had his eyes on one of the community gals, but he never pursued her. Then one evening, about a week after the migration team leads were announced, George got his answer.

Tony had asked him to join him for an evening walk around the college campus. It was a bit warmer than normal for early March but still had a chill in the air. The sun had just set, and most of the snow had melted. The air smelled fresh as it had been a while since any buildings had been burnt in that area. They laughed and joked most of the walk, sharing stories about their college campus days. They came upon one of the museums near the outskirts of the campus that was boarded up and stopped to admire its unique brick structure.

The university had acquired a collection of art, artifacts, and other old pieces since 1826. Over the years, they had converted one of their buildings into a museum for the public to visit and also used it for archaeology art classes for college students. Before the pandemic, 30,000 visitors passed through it annually.

"Hey, want to be adventurous?" Tony asked George, chuckling while they stood in front of the building.

George looked at him, surprised he would even suggest stepping into the evacuated building, and replied, "Yeah, I don't know about that, Ton, that's a big risk!"

"Well, trust me. There are greater risks out there than going inside that old, abandoned building that's been boarded up for a couple of years. Nothing can be living in there anymore. Let's just take a peek. I want to show you something anyways," Tony replied, a bit more serious as he headed to the back of the building.

It was apparent others had been in the building since the boards were somewhat broken off the back entranceway. George shook his head, not wanting to go inside as Tony pushed the door open, climbed over some of the boards, and escaped the coolness of the night air. George looked around to make sure nobody saw him and reluctantly followed. The room was filled with pure destruction from vandals and animals that had previously tramped through it. Nothing of substance was left anywhere. Any art that was still in sight was ruined and left for mother nature to do as she wished with.

"Looks like there's nothing here to look at," George said as he looked around, "I think we should just leave. I'm sure what you wanted to show me is long gone."

Tony responded as he moved closer to him, "Yeah, you're right. Nothing is here to show you, except one thing," Then he slowly pulled George closer as he softly whispered, "This," then moved his lips closer to his, until they touched and locked into a warm, passionate kiss.

It was the confirmation George was looking for and the start of their relationship. Since they both had been assigned to Team 1, they had ample opportunity ahead of them to explore where it would go.

The Preparation

With all the team members picked, the community scurried around to help prepare them for the upcoming departures. Team 1 had only two weeks before theirs, with still much to be done. For the most part, the community supported the choices for the new teams, others worried if they ever would get their turn once all the teams had left.

The Kinleys continued to visit the library daily, especially after they found out they were leaving with Rosa. Holly continued to tag along with them even though she was going to stay behind with Darcy. A couple of days after the teams got settled in was the first time Holly and Jenny formally met. They had seen each other around, but never really spoke until that day in the library.

"Wow, you like Stephen King novels?" Holly politely asked as she sat down next to her.

"Well, not until recently," Jenny looked at Holly and smiled as she added, "but they certainly help me forget about all that's happening around here, at least while I'm reading!"

"I hear ya, but his books are whole other nightmares!" Holly said as they both laughed.

"And what's your book of choice?" Jenny asked.

"Mainly about the better lands. Just want to know all I can about it before I go there," Holly responded.

"I assume you're going with Darcy since I see you with him most of the time?" Jenny asked.

"Yeah, I'm not in any of the first four groups. It all worked out," Holly answered, then asked, "And what about you?"

"I'm leaving with Rosa, although my heart tells me to stay here with my family," Jenny responded, then continued reading.

"Your family isn't going with you?" Holly asked.

Jenny put the book on her lap as she sadly said, "No, I'm afraid not. My brother and mother aren't doing well, but as soon as they get better, they will travel. I'm hoping if they don't hop on with one of the other three teams that they will go when you do."

"You'll have to introduce me so I can watch out for them," Holly said as she watched Jenny pick the book back up.

"I'd like that," she replied then proceeded to read, signaling she was done talking.

Jennifer North-Livingston was 19 and never had a chance to complete her high school education like so many others, because the reliability of the internet had interrupted all the remote learning platforms. At that point, her education stopped. She was a local, born and raised in the area along with her younger brother. For the most part, they had a comfortable, happy life. Summers were spent at their grandparents' camp on the north shores of Lake Champlain, and winters were spent in their ski condo in the mountains. Shortly after both her parents lost their jobs they had to evacuate their home, and eventually found themselves standing in line at the Leddy Park beach community.

It was just after Jenny's family was assigned to Team 1 that her parents insisted she go by herself. Both her mom and brother had underlying health issues that were preventing them from traveling at that point. Jenny wasn't happy with their decision.

"You've got to be kidding with me. I can't go without you all! We're family, and if you don't go, then I don't go. Please don't make me go," she begged, unable to see the bigger picture they saw for her.

"We're not kidding with you, Jenny," her mom started, "and we can't make you go but believe us, it's best if you do. And you do know if we all could go together we would. Right now, you're the strongest of all of us, other than your dad, and it's important to us that you go with Rosa and be one of the first to see the better lands, and save us all a perfect spot."

"I don't understand! Why would I go without you all? You need me here to help you, if you really can't go," she said as tears streamed down her cheeks.

Her dad stepped in, "We want you safe, Jenny. We'll be fine and we'll get there, but we have to get your mother and brother strong enough to make the trip. The last thing we want is to be half-way there and be left behind in some place we're not familiar with."

Jenny hugged her mom and for the next several minutes, cried on each other's shoulders. Reluctantly, she finally agreed to go. As her dad joined in on the hug, he warmly said, "You'll be in good hands, my precious daughter, and we'll all be together before you know it."

Holly hung out with Jenny more over the next couple of weeks and introduced her to Rosa, hoping to help her feel more comfortable to take the journey without her family. Even though Jenny was older than both girls, she began to trust their support and guidance and started preparing herself to make the trip without her family.

In the meantime, Blitz had gathered some of his newly formed bodyguards for a quick meeting to make sure they were properly prepared for the upcoming departure. Both Trap and Jimmy were staying behind with Darcy to help with the Fall migration but still joined the meeting.

Blitz addressed the team, "We have no idea what we'll find out there. We're going to travel through a lot of different towns. Some may be functioning quite well, or not. Some may be totally vacant. We don't have a clue what this pandemic has created outside of our own space. So we must make sure we're well prepared."

"Yeah, you can drive yourself crazy second guessing it all," Jimmy said.

"Fucking frightful," Trap added, glad he wasn't making the initial journey but not entirely happy that Jeff wasn't either.

"No more frightful than staying here and just letting that damn virus wipe us out," Brandon piped in.

Blitz responded, "Well, we all need to stick together in this. I chose the 20 of you to help me ward off any threats that the team could encounter along the way. It means we'll be the first in and the last out of places. We need to test the temperature of what's going on before we allow Rosa, Jean-Pierre, or anyone near them."

"Especially being in the first team. If it fails with us, all else fails," Brandon added.

Brandon James Richardson had recently turned 20 and had reached his six-foot-three height at age 15. He kept his shoulder length, brown hair pulled back in a ponytail sported by a green bandana wrapped around his forehead. He grew up about an hour and a half drive south of the Burlington area.

During the second wave of the virus, Brandon's home was evacuated. His parents moved further south to stay with relatives, while he opted to stay in the area with a friend. Once the apartment got its burn orders, they decided to head north to be closer to the state's largest distribution hub and ended up at the Leddy Beach community.

Brandon briefly met Jean-Pierre when he initially arrived at the winter shelter. He made his grand entrance at one of the disrupted rallies where he stepped into action and helped contain some of the rowdy protesters. Shortly after, Jean-Pierre asked Blitz to consider him for one of his bodyguards. Blitz did, Brandon accepted.

Blitz responded to Brandon as he yelled out across the team, "It won't fail! We won't fail! We will all get to the better lands safely!"

They all rallied together and loudly chanted, "Better lands, better lands, better lands."

Later that evening, Rosa called a meeting for just the Team Leads, including Darcy, so they could go over final preparations. Don and Marie had something they had to take care of and weren't able to attend. The rest of them met in one of the rooms downstairs in the auditorium, where they could have privacy away from the unsettled community. Even though the excitement of the departure was growing, the changes and the unknown that everyone faced was a harder transition than anyone had anticipated or planned for. Several of the community members, who were among the unchosen, decided to go in a different direction and left the auditorium only to add more anxiety to everyone staying behind.

"Since there's only a couple more days before Team 1 leaves, this may be the last time we all get together until we meet again in the better lands," Rosa said as her eyes slowly scrolled around at Bill, Jean-Pierre, Sam, and Darcy.

Her eyes filled with tears as Darcy said, "And we will meet again, my friend."

"By next year this time, we'll all be together," Sam added, trying to sound optimistic.

"God be willing," Bill softly said, "I hope this isn't a mistake, and there really is a pot of gold at the end of this rainbow."

"There will be Bill!" Jean-Pierre jumped in, trying to create some excitement.

"Let's hope," Bill replied. "Don't get me wrong, I'm all in, but none of us really know, do we?"

William George Wallington was in his mid-30s and had a stocky build covering his six-foot-two body frame. For several years Bill had been part of the Vermont Air National Guards. He had always been intrigued with its history since he was in elementary school. The organization had originally identified itself as the Green Mountain Boys, a militia organization first established in the late 1760s between the British provinces of NY and NH. Shortly afterwards they captured Fort Ticonderoga in upstate New York, they seemingly ceased to exist until they resurfaced through some of history's most historical battles, including the Civil and Vietnam War. The summer of 1946, was when the Vermont Air National Guards came to exist in the state.

Bill had grown up in the northern Vermont area, close to the Canadian border, and first joined the Guards part-time when he attended college in the Burlington area. He remained active, mainly devoting time on weekends and short stints in the summer. He married shortly after graduation and found himself in a rocky marriage that resulted in divorce five years later. Before the virus arrived, he stayed on call for the Air Guards and worked as a part-time history professor at another local college, until it closed its doors.

Shortly afterward, many of the Guards were dispersed to high profile areas to help out pandemic survivors, while Bill was assigned locally. As the second wave took his home, the National Guards pulled out of Vermont and basically ceased to exist. He eventually ended up at the Oakledge Beach community.

Upon joining the winter shelter, he immediately befriended Rosa, already knowing of her, and jumped in to help out around the auditorium. Because of his background, Rosa asked him to keep a watch over the community during the night hours and help with the ongoing hunt for essentials. Folks took a strong liking to him and felt safe when he was around. Bill went out of his way to help anyone in need; it was just his nature. He was good at what he did, but he wanted more. Rosa saw his drive and knew he would make a good Team Lead and when she asked, he gladly accepted.

Rosa responded to Bill, "No, you're right. We don't know what to expect out there, but if we don't take this plunge, and just hang here, we don't know either. Which is the worst of the two evils?"

"I think staying here and just letting things happen, would be the worst of the evils," Jean-Pierre chimed in.

Everyone agreed then proceeded with the final preparation details. Just as they were about to wrap up, Sam asked if could say one more thing.

"I just want to emphasize how important it is that we all stick to the same route no matter what happens. That is the reason why we are trailing behind each other. If we veer off even just a little, things could go bad real quick."

"Yes, you're right, Sam," Rosa agreed, "and if something goes wrong, we have no way of finding each other if we don't stick to the same route. So let's make that clear right now. Once we get on the road, we don't change direction. Are we all clear on that?"

Everyone agreed.

"No matter what happens, guys, we can't sidestep the importance of this," Sam added.

Just a few years earlier, before he arrived at the auditorium, Sam Hatfield had been part of a local police force. He stood about six-foot-three, was in his mid-30's, and extremely fit. Sam kept his head shiny, shaved down to the bare skin, which seemed to accentuate his big blue eyes. At times, his personality stood out more than his appearance. He had a loud yet calming voice, even when he talked softly, and his laugh was highly contagious.

Sam had been engaged to his childhood sweetheart just a few years before the virus had erupted and sadly lost her to a home burglary that went bad. The break-in was related to a past drug bust he had been involved with. Several of them went to prison, but a couple didn't receive any time and swore to get even with him for the others' convictions.

Sam was on duty when they broke into his condo. They raped, tortured, and killed his fiancé. They left her naked, mangled body in the bathtub for him to discover when he got home later that night. Shortly after his painful loss, he left the force, blaming himself for her untimely, brutal death.

Sam got a job working in the local mall at a hobby shop and made just enough money to make ends meet. Once things went awry due to the pandemic, he stayed with some friends up until that winter, when they, too, lost their home. Like many others, he eventually found his way to the winter shelters and ended up at the auditorium where he first met up with Rosa. He had already heard some rumble on the street about her, and as he got to know her more, was impressed how she cared for everyone's well being.

Sam & Blitz

Right from the start, Blitz and Sam did everything they could to avoid each other without ever speaking. Their reasons were personal. Blitz hated cops, and knowing Sam had been one, he didn't trust anything he said or did based on his past run-ins with the law. Blitz knew cops had judged him by association and never listened to his side of things, even if he wasn't at fault. As a result, he had been arrested and thrown in jail several times when he wasn't guilty as charged. Blitz knew one wrong word or move was what cops waited for, and he had paid some ultimate, unnecessary prices at their hands. He didn't trust Sam, even if Rosa did.

For Sam, Blitz initially made his stomach sour at the very sight of him. He knew his type. The bold, boisterous, arrogant, bully gang type. Like the ones that had so horridly taken his beloved away. Sam knew who the street thugs were and couldn't believe he was there. He thought Blitz always had a guilty look and avoided any eye contact after they initially saw each other. Even though he knew very little about Blitz's past, he felt he knew him all too well. It was easy to judge him as a no-good derelict. Sam had arrested enough of them, all drug users, dealers, thugs, and even murderers. He could not figure out why Rosa and the others accepted him into the community and thought she might have been threatened or blackmailed. He needed to get to the bottom of it, but for the time being, Sam didn't trust Blitz, even if Rosa did.

Change was a constant force in the new post-pandemic survival: the burns, the homeless, the fight for survival, and everyone on equal playing ground. There were no more priorities for the rich or poor, bad versus good people, or old versus young. It was a hard adjustment, and many still hadn't given up their once entitled stature, so disputes, even physical fights, were an everyday occurrence on who did what and when.

A few weeks before the migration teams were confirmed, Sam got up just before the crack of dawn to get in line at the distribution hub and wait for a few of the other community members to join him, before the doors opened. He wasn't the chosen one to hold the place in line, but he was tired of all the arguing among some members on who and when they needed to go, so he volunteered for that particular day. Sam loved being out in the fresh, wintery morning air and had always been an early riser, so he had no problem doing it.

As he headed down the main street toward the lakefront, he watched the steam from his breath dance in front of him. Suddenly distracted by a loud screech overhead, he looked up just in time to catch a red tail hawk flying about, looking as though it was circling its prey. Its movement was serene, peaceful, and for that moment, made him forget about all the chaos he had encountered over the last few years.

Just as he watched the hawk disappear over one of the few undemolished rooftops, his feet slipped out from under him. There was no time to think how to stop or cushion the fall, so he landed hard, flat on his butt on the icy sidewalk. On his way down, he felt an excruciating pain coming from his foot that had rammed into a rusty fire hydrant before he went down. When he tried to get up, it caused him to fall back down. He was afraid he might have twisted his ankle or even sprained it.

Sam knew he had to get back to the auditorium to get someone else to go in his place as the pain increased. He scooted on his butt along the ice, closer to the hydrant, then gradually pulled himself up, but quickly realized he couldn't apply any pressure to his aching foot. He looked around and didn't see a soul in sight. It was too early and cold for anyone to be roaming about. So with no other choice, he slowly sat back down on the icy sidewalk, and waited for someone to come along to help him.

It seemed like at least an hour had passed as the sun had started to project some light into the once darkened sky when he finally heard a voice from behind him, “Hey man, you okay?”

Sam felt a sick feeling flood through his body. It was a familiar voice, one he didn’t want to hear, especially then. He sat for a moment, shaking his head in disbelief that of all the people in the entire city, it had to be Blitz.

There was no way to avoid him, and Sam was chilled to the bone so he reluctantly replied, “Not really, man. I think I sprained my ankle on that damn hydrant.”

Blitz approached him, and for the first time, they made real eye contact. He looked over at the hydrant and chuckled as he replied, “How the hell did you do that?” He realized Sam wasn’t going to answer, so he said, “Give me your hand. I’ll help you up and get you back to the auditorium.”

Blitz knew neither of them trusted each other, and even though Sam didn’t immediately grab his hand, Blitz knew he had no other choice, so he chuckled and said, “Don’t worry, man, I don’t bite, really!”

Sam slightly smiled at him then grabbed his hand. He was relieved he no longer had to endure the cold ground. He was also relieved that Blitz didn’t walk past him and just leave him there. Sam wasn’t sure what he would’ve done if the situation was reversed. Arm in arm, they slowly limped back to the auditorium. From that very moment on, the two of them became tolerable, even somewhat trusting of each other.

Rosa' Team 1 – The Departure

Rosa had scheduled one final rally with the community and almost everyone showed up to hear the last-minute details, whether they were part of the initial journey or not.

"Team 1 is scheduled to leave on March 22nd, which is tomorrow!"

The crowd all applauded, many wept in excitement as Rosa continued, "Bill's Team 2 is scheduled to leave on the 29th, followed by Don and Marie's Team 3 on April 5th, and last but not least, Sam's Team 4 on April 12th!"

Again, everyone broke out in cheers and applauded, signaling their approval.

"I'm almost done, folks, so please, give me a couple more minutes here," Rosa exclaimed as she stood up on the Memorial Auditorium's stage, waiting for the noise to tone down a few notches, then continued, "I want to once again go over the five planned hub stops along the way that will hopefully shelter us for a night or two inside their facilities, and replenish our supplies. All the Team Leads have been instructed not to sway off the route at any time, and if you get lost for some crazy reason, you need to look for the closest one to you and wait for the next team."

As the room quieted down more, Rosa continued, "All the Team Leads have an official route map, but I just want to verbalize it to you all. When we leave here, we'll catch the Charlotte ferry and migrate toward Lake Erie via upstate New York. Our first planned stop is at the Fort Drum Army Base, which should have enough room for each group. From there, we'll travel down into Cleveland, Ohio, via a boat ride on Lake Erie, if it's still operational. Our third planned stop is in Ashland and then we move onto Cincinnati. The final indoor hub stop will be at the Fort Knox Army base in Kentucky. Of course, we'll be tenting along the way, and don't know what to expect as we go through all these towns so it's important to stick together as a group."

Jean-Pierre then yelled out, "And the last stop is the better lands! Let's hope it's what we expect! So with that said, tomorrow morning let's get this show on the road!"

The crowd broke out in unison, "better lands! better lands! better lands!"

Music filled the air as the community celebrated their last day together. Shortly after the meeting, Rosa decided to take a walk by herself and ended up down on Church Street, sitting on one of the boulders, staring at the church as the sun began to set. As she sat there, she had reflected back over everything that had brought her to that moment. It was so surreal.

"Rosa, it's time," Jean-Pierre softly said as he approached the boulder she was perched on, "I thought I might find you down here. Are you ready?"

She slowly let go of the last four years as she watched the sun's reflections fade from the church. She looked over at Jean-Pierre and nodded, then glanced back to catch the last light disappearing from the building's bricks. The plan was in place, and it was time to execute. Morning would come fast, and they had to be on the road by the break of dawn. The ferry only ran once a day, and they couldn't risk missing it.

Rosa was anxious to see what the end game was, hoping there truly were better lands out there, and she wasn't misleading her followers. While they all knew that the adventure ahead wasn't going to be easy, the result hopefully would mean a new beginning, one they all needed before the third wave of the pandemic hit.

At the very least, if it were a place they could breathe some fresh air, instead of the smoldering ash from all the constant burning rubble, it would be a success. It was hard to escape the smell unless down by the waterfront, where the occasional breezes blew some fresh air in from the lake. The relentless pandemic remained unexplainable, incurable, and very much alive.

When the second wave had rolled in, vaccinations were developed and given to all the survivors, but many more continued to die. The strains kept evolving, and nothing was stopping them. Only the burnings had slowed its course, and nobody knew what the third wave would bring. It was already gearing up to strike again. There was news it had already landed in other countries, including their neighbor, Canada. People were fearful that the human race was on its way to becoming extinct.

Rosa tried to reassure herself that wasn't the case, that it made no sense for everything to just end, losing a battle against an invisible killer. She questioned God. She wondered if there was one, and if so, what His plan was. The God she had learned about certainly wouldn't have allowed all the destruction, chaos, and death that was alive and well around her.

But, by the grace of research and more understanding of what else was out there, the prospect alone of the better lands rejuvenated most people's beliefs, hope, and trust. At least for the time being, there was more to life than just sitting and waiting for the enemy to destroy what little hope they all had left. Rosa was all in and believed that something more was out there, and now, there were hundreds following her.

"Ready?" Jean-Pierre asked again, holding out his hand to help her down from the rock.

As she grabbed it, she looked at him and smiled even though her eyes welled up. It was bittersweet as she said a final goodbye to what was once so beautiful and simple that had turned so dark and evil.

She took one last look at the church, now darkened from the evening sky and answered, "Yes, let's do this," then jumped down, shoved her blistered feet into her shoes, and headed, hand in hand with Jean-Pierre, down the street toward the auditorium.

***

3:30 a.m. came quick and everyone was up as Trap's voice bellowed out the final roll call, "Len Schiller, George Rudder, Chad and Dora Kinley, John Bouldin, Blitz, Jon and Cindi Cramer, Tony Roswell, Tim Harrington, Jenny North-Livingston, Sandy Fleming, Brandon Richardson, Ralph and Annette Sims, Dennis and Charlotte Cummings…"

"It's finally here, Rosa," Darcy excitedly announced as he put his arm around his trusted friend, knowing it would be several months before they saw each other again. They needed to stay on schedule to catch the ferry that departed later that day and she had no time to wallow in goodbyes.

"I can't believe it," she responded in a low yet excited tone as she stayed focused on Trap still rattling off names, wrapping her arms around Darcy's waist.

"And finally, Rosa & Jean-Pierre. Make sure you gather your belongings and get over to the middle school so we can count you all off and get you on your way."

Trap jumped off the stage and headed over to Rosa, who was already surrounded by the other Team Leads and community members who were staying behind.

"We're excited and nervous for you," Marie said as she hugged Rosa.

"We'll be right behind you," Bill started, "I can't imagine you'll run into too many issues, at least not from what we read about all the other towns you'll be passing through."

"I'm sure it will be fine," Jean-Pierre responded, "And like you said, you're right behind us, so if need be, we will just sit and wait for you."

"Most likely, that won't happen," Rosa added, "It is going to be a long journey, but I doubt we will hit any major roadblocks. We've already gone over this."

"Well, since I'm the cleanup crew," Sam chuckled, "I'll have all your backs!"

"You always do," Rosa said as she gave him a tight hug then proceeded to hug the rest of them.

They headed over to the school grounds, where everyone else was already waiting, saying their final goodbyes to folks.

Darcy gave Rosa another hug as he said, "Well, this is it! You are off on the adventure of a lifetime. Literally, all because of you, my dear friend, we all soon could be in a better place. Godspeed, and I will see you soon."

Then he turned to Jean-Pierre and gave him a big hug, "You take care of her, my friend, and yourself! I'll see you on the other side."

As Darcy stepped back, he felt his eyes well up when they locked with Blitz's. They had traveled a long, crazy path together, going from mortal enemies to trusted friends. Darcy went to shake his hand, but when Blitz grabbed it, he pulled him close and embraced him.

As they stepped back from the hug, Blitz said, "I know this community is left in good hands. You take care and don't take too long to find us!"

After a few more goodbyes, it was time to get on the road. The team assembled with Jean-Pierre, Rosa, and Blitz leading the pack. They turned and waved to the gathered crowd, then headed up the hill, around the corner, and out of sight. Eventually, everyone headed back to their prospective shelters to wait in anticipation for their turn.

Lake Placid – Chad and Dora Kinley

The journey from Burlington to Lake Placid, New York, was uneventful. It had taken a few days to get there, the weather had cooperated, and the air seemed fresher as Team 1 wandered through the countryside's remote areas. Everyone was in good spirits. Although they all were used to tenting in warmer weather, nobody complained much about the frosty evenings.

"Well, we made it to the famous Olympic site here in the town of Lake Placid!" Rosa announced to the team as they stopped to rest and set up camp for the night.

"It is quite the place," Jean-Pierre replied, "I've never been here, but I know it has quite a little history."

The outskirts of the village rested on the shores of Lake Placid. In pre-pandemic days, when it had been fully operational, there were only about 3,000 residents, but winter tourism brought in hundreds more. In 1932 and 1980, it was home to the Winter Olympic Games. During those times, thousands of tourists came to the beautiful surroundings to watch the ski competitions, and many continued to visit the area long afterward, to enjoy alpine skiing and other annual events like Ironman. Once the second wave of the virus hit, most of the iconic buildings that attracted tourists were burned to the ground along with most homes. The town's population dwindled to about a quarter of the folks left living in and around the area. It had become another dead zone, like every other place they had traveled through.

"It's still pretty amazing to be standing in a place that is a part of history," Brandon said as he helped Rosa take supplies off her back.

"I think every place is part of history now, given the extreme condition the virus threw us into!" exclaimed Jean-Pierre as he started pitching his tent.

What he would have given to not be part of it all, yet he was thankful for where he was. For a brief moment, he saw Kate standing in front of him. Smiling. He heard her voice as she said, "Of course you'd say that, big brother! You do love history!" A tear quickly escaped him. He missed her. He shook his head and returned to reality.

"So, this is where we rest for the night?" Jenny asked as she watched a few others take their backpacks off and started preparing their sites.

"As good as any!" Rosa responded, "We're about a half a mile away from the village."

"Isn't there a small distribution hub in town? Should a few of us go and check it out?" Blitz asked.

"No, let's play it safe and wait until we get to Fort Drum. I'm sure we have enough supplies," she answered.

It wasn't long before everyone had their tents up, campfires were roaring, and folks were all huddled together, singing, laughing, and taking in some of the picturesque views of the surrounding white mountains and the semi-frozen lake that could be seen in the distance. The sun was starting to set, and Dora had already planned to approach Rosa to inquire if she wouldn't mind if she and Chad went off to explore the village for a bit. It was their fourth wedding anniversary, and they wanted to make it somewhat memorable. Dora had been to Lake Placid many years ago as a child and had some fond memories of those times. She wanted to share just a taste of them with her husband, who had never been.

One of the rules established before the team left Burlington was that all members of the teams needed to stay together, unless they were in small groups of at least ten, and others knew where they were going. It was a safety precaution since nobody knew what to expect. Of course, if someone did stray from the group at any given time, there was no real consequence for it since they were all out in the middle of nowhere.

But Rosa consistently preached that there was safety in numbers and the only way they would have each other's back was to stay close enough to cover them. Everyone had agreed to the rules before they were assigned to a team.

"You know the rules, Dora, so I'm surprised you'd ask me this. Especially with nightfall coming and we are leaving early in the morning," Rosa responded to her request.

"I know, Rosa, and I'm sorry. We know the rules. But it's our fourth wedding anniversary today, and it just so happened we landed here in Lake Placid. You and I both know we'll never have the opportunity to pass through here again. Ever. I just want to walk through the village with Chad, and then we'll come right back. I promise," Dora softly pleaded with her.

It was four years ago to that day, just a month before the virus played havoc on everyone, when Chad and Dora wed in Bali. Dora had always dreamed of a destination wedding, and both were extremely happy they didn't wait any longer, or it wouldn't have happened, at least not there. Once the first wave of the virus struck, all foreign travel plans were halted.

The Kinleys were extremely impacted by the second wave of the virus. At that point, things went south quickly. They both lost their jobs and struggled to make ends meet. Finally, like most around them, they had to give up their home and watched it be demolished shortly afterward. They eventually found themselves at the Leddy Park beach community and moved on to the winter shelter. They met Rosa the first day they were at the auditorium and were immediately drawn to her leadership, bubbly personality, compassion, and drive. It was an instantaneous friendship. Then they met Holly and kept her under their wing until they were split up, both on separate teams.

"Look, you're asking a lot. But I hear you. If I agree, I can send Blitz or a few of his guys with you so that you'll be safe."

Dora quickly responded, “No, really, that won’t be necessary. It’s a straight shot in and out of there, and we won’t be gone all night. Besides, it wouldn’t sbeem much like an anniversary with two or three other guys tagging along,” she chuckled.

Rosa sat for a few moments, just staring at her. She hated to say no. It was such a special day they’d never get back. So reluctantly, she agreed, “I shouldn’t do this, but okay. Just promise you two will turn around and come back if there is anything that seems out of the ordinary. And don’t go in any open buildings or stay away too long, please. There is so much risk to letting you do this.”

Dora thanked her and gave her a big hug, then went off to tell Chad the good news. Shortly afterward, they hit the road.

When Chad and Dora got into town that evening, they were pleasantly surprised to stumble upon a local pub that was still open for business. Maggie’s Pub’s lights were on, laughter and music could be heard behind her walls. The pub had once been a part of the Lake Placid Lodge, known for its cozy rustic setting and local music. Lots of buildings surrounding it lay in rubble, still filling the air with the familiar burned charcoal aroma that was hard to escape wherever they went.

Once inside, they were surprised to see at least 20 other folks hanging out listening to a couple of guys play guitar, and another on a small drum set while others danced and enjoyed some frosty glasses of beer. The fireplace’s crackling sound blended with the music. The town folks immediately welcomed them and, upon hearing of their celebration, offered them food, and drink. The Kinleys enjoyed the company of their new friends and each other. Just before midnight, they headed back to the campsite to be ready for the early morning departure, as promised. Dora had no doubt that she gave Chad an anniversary present for the memory book.

A couple of mornings later, in the small town of Clifton, New York, Rosa's team had mostly packed up and were ready to move out. It had been another quiet stay. Clifton barely had any life left to it. It was first settled back in 1866 when the Clifton Iron Mine came to the area. The town rested near Cranberry Lake, the third-largest in the Adirondack Park. The team had hoped to have pitched their tents near it, but many of the shoreline camps were recently burned, so the intolerable smell still lingered, coupled with the extremely cold breezes from the lake that wouldn't have allowed their campfires to have lasted through the night. So, they set up the tents in a wooded area about a mile or so down the road from it.

That morning Chad woke up with an awful sore throat, had the sweats but could not get warm. Dora was sure he had a fever and helped him get dressed so he could go sit by one of the dying campfires to try and catch some heat. She continued to pack up their stuff as he sipped on some hot tea, hoping he'd feel better before they left. They thought he might have picked something up from the night at the pub and shuddered, thinking it could be the virus. He worried if that was the case that he more than likely had spread it to a lot of the team. Even worse, to Dora. But he didn't have a cough.

The Kinleys knew if the others learned of his symptoms, their journey would have to end, at least until Chad got better. That was another stipulation the migration teams agreed to. Once someone fell ill enough to either affect the team negatively or slow them down, they would have to stay behind, and if they got better, they'd join the next team that passed through the area. Because Chad didn't have a cough and no real outward signs of anything serious, they decided not to share it with anyone.

Once they were on the road, every step Chad took was more painful than his last as his energy level continued to drain from him. Dora tried to help him along the best she could, but it became obvious they no longer could keep up with the group. About 30 minutes later, Chad stopped and announced he couldn't go any further. Once everyone knew he was sick, the inevitable stared the Kinleys smack in the face, and there wasn't a thing they could do about it.

After Tony checked him over and was unable to confirm what he had, although he didn't think it was the virus, Jean-Pierre said, "I'm so sorry, Chad, but there is no way you're going to be able to continue on with us. You can barely drag yourself along behind the team."

Blitz, Rosa, and several others had gathered around as Chad rested on the side of the road and agreed, "I know, man. This really sucks. I just want to lay down and sleep this off. I know the team can't wait for me to get better, and I have to stay behind and take care of it myself. The good thing is there are three other teams coming through and I know I'll be better to join one of them!"

Then he addressed his wife as she stood next to him with her arms around his shoulders, "Listen, my beautiful bride, you're going to have to continue on with the team without me for now, but I'll hook up with one of the others as soon as I'm able to move again. No need to worry, I'll be okay and will find you again, I promise."

Before he could finish, she gently put her fingers over his lips, then pulled his head into her stomach and exclaimed, "Absolutely not, Chad! That is the most ridiculous thing I have ever heard you say! If you stay, I stay, and I will get you some help! End of discussion!"

"I'm so sorry," Rosa interrupted, "Dora, you have no choice but to stay. You've been the closest in proximity to Chad, and we can't take any chances for the rest of the team. That was something we all had agreed about before we started this venture. Another team will be here in a week, and we'll leave you with enough supplies."

"Besides, two of you together is safer," Blitz added, "If I could, I'd stay with you both."

"Thanks man, but we understand," Chad replied after hugging Dora for a few minutes.

Jean-Pierre informed them, "I did see some signs that pointed toward some medical care just before we arrived in Clifton. I think it was in the town of Colton. My best advice is you should backtrack for about an hour or so and find it. Hopefully, the facility is still open. It's your best bet at this point."

About 15 minutes later, after making sure the Kinleys were well stocked with extra supplies, the team bid their goodbyes and silently watched as the two turned and slowly headed back toward Clifton.

"What's going to happen to them?" Jenny worriedly asked Rosa after they had been on the road for a few hours.

"I really don't know," she replied, locking her arm in hers, then continued to walk side by side, not wanting to think the worse.

Rosa's Team 1 – Fort Drum, NY – 7 Days After Vermont Departure

The rest of the trip to the first major hub stop was mainly subdued as the Kinleys were on everyone's mind. Most everyone felt bad about leaving them behind, but there was no other choice. It was too risky for the team. As planned, it had taken exactly a week to travel through upstate New York toward Lake Erie into the town of Fort Drum. The team had primarily stuck to the main roads to avoid wooded and mountainous areas, even though it could have saved them some travel time.

For the most part, the weather had cooperated with Spring-like temperatures through most of their journey and they had welcomed the warmth of the sun as it beat down on them. But when the group woke up that morning, they found the landscape lightly blanketed with some snow. The early morning skyline had a brightness to it, even though the darkened clouds were as far as the eye could see. New England weather had its own agenda as to when Spring actually arrived. It was no surprise that the end of March allowed Winter to make some last-ditch efforts to stick around. It snowed pretty heavily throughout the day, which made travel a bit more challenging, adding more time on the road. By the time dusk had fallen, the snowstorm had intensified, and the moisture from the warmth and cold air transformed the flakes into multiple sleet pellets that fired at their bodies. The last two hours were the worst as they trudged through it in the dark.

Everyone was cold, wet, and hungry. Some didn't know how much longer they could go on. But then they rounded a corner and saw a welcomed sight. Dimly lit street lights shined down on a snow covered street. Just beyond them, inside a building window, a red flashing message quickly caught their attention: 'Come in! We're Open!.'

"Oh my God, is that what I think it is?" Jean-Pierre excitedly yelled out, barely feeling his frozen mouth move.

"No way," one of the members hollered.

"There is a God!" another screeched out as they all started cheering and headed toward the blinking sign.

As they got closer, they got more excited that the flashing sign led to a large country diner sitting in the middle of nowhere, like it had been waiting for them. The surrounding buildings were darkened from the nightfall. Very few had been burned. Not another soul was in sight. The lights were on inside the diner. They stopped in front of it and briefly assessed its large roof-covered wrap-around porch then without a second thought, everyone got out of the continued snowfall.

"I need you all to be patient," Rosa hollered out to those close enough to hear her as they huddled together, "Jean-Pierre, Blitz, and I are going inside to see what's up. I don't want us all to pile in there until we are sure they can accommodate us. Just hang tight for a few more minutes."

"Did you all hear her?" Blitz belted out as they started to head inside, "Hang tight while we go inside and check things out! Spread the word among you all!"

"At least we're out of the snow," Jenny said, trying to stay positive.

"Yes, that we are," Brandon responded.

Miss Lily

One inside, Blitz, Rosa, and Jean-Pierre were greeted with the warm heat that quickly consumed their cold bodies. Rosa had not remembered ever feeling so cold and didn't realize it until the heat hit her. The blue and white booths and table tops were empty. Bon Jovi music was blasting from the other side of the breakfast counter, where a petite, middle-aged woman stood behind it. She looked a bit nervous as they closed the door behind them, shutting out all the banter on the porch. There was laughter coming from the kitchen area just behind her, indicating she wasn't alone.

The waitress's frizzy, reddish-brown hair was pulled back in a bun covered with a clear hairnet. A few strands fell about her forehead and neck. Her uniform looked like it was from the 1970s: a dark blue dress that zipped up, with a white collar and white cuffs on the short sleeves. It was sported with a worn-out faded white apron. Rosa had thought it was an odd outfit to wear in such an offbeat place with no customers.

"How can I help you, folks," the woman asked with an unexpected bubbly, low, raspy voice coming from her tiny body.

As they moved closer to her, Blitz cleared his throat. He had already taken notice of her delicate facial features and how fragile she looked as her five-foot-five-inch frame stood all alone in the big empty space. The uniform tightly hugged her shapely body, and he noted her tattooed arm sleeve; a colorful Goddess surrounded by a bouquet of flowers. She had his attention.

He was the first to speak after he cleared his throat, "Good evening, Miss. We're sorry to intrude so late. I'm Blitz, and I can't help but notice that beautiful tattoo. It's very becoming on you."

The waitress smiled as she looked at the three red faces staring at her then replied, "Well, honey, you don't wait long to make a move now, do you? But flattery could get you anywhere you want!" she laughed as she winked at him then extended her hand out and said, "I'm just kidding! It's Miss Lily. You all look so cold and wet. What can I do for you?"

Blitz slightly blushed and moved closer to shake her hand. As he stared into her dark green eyes, he felt his heart flutter. It had been a long time since anyone had that type of effect on him that quickly. His last relationship had a quick start but ended badly, which was just as well as he knew she wasn't worth another stint in prison. After her, he had little faith that he'd find any kind of love in his life.

"I'm Blitz," he shyly responded, surprising even himself when he leaned over and softly kissed her hand as she put it in his.

"Hi, Miss Lily, I'm Rosa, and this is Jean-Pierre," Rosa said as she interrupted the flirtatious moment, quite stunned by Blitz's behavior, "We've been traveling most of the day by foot in this terrible storm. We're cold and hungry and the rest of my team is hoping to be able to come in here as well. There's just under a hundred of us," she stated as she rubbed her arms to get some blood flowing through them, then looked around at the empty tables noting there was plenty of seating for all. Then she asked, "Is it okay if they come in to warm up and get a hot meal? I know it's a lot to ask, but we do have money, and we'll pay."

Miss Lily's body tightened up as she let go of Blitz's hand and looked out the windows eyeballing the many snow-covered folks clustered together. She knew they were there as she had watched the group trudge up the snowy street and onto the diner porch. She had heard Rosa's voice instruct them to stay put. There were a lot of people, with only three of them on duty. She was a little worried, not knowing who they were or if they meant trouble, but felt less nervous after meeting Blitz. Miss Lily also knew they could use the business, as it had been hours since the last customer left. She looked back through the kitchen serving window at the two younger cooks who had been peering out it, listening to what was going on.

"They're a good bunch, and I can promise there won't be any trouble," Blitz added softly, "they're all just tired and hungry and cold."

Miss Lily looked at her three guests then asked her kitchen help, "Hey boys, what do you think? Do we have enough stuff back there to put a warm meal together for these cold, traveling folks?"

"Yes, Ma'am! We're on it," one of them replied as she focused her eyes back on Blitz's wandering ones.

Miss Lily was quite aware that Blitz had not taken his eyes off her since they came in. She didn't know whether to be threatened or flattered by it, but in some weird sense, she didn't mind. It had been a long time since anyone crossed the diner doorstep that caught her immediate attention, or elsewhere for that matter. She was taken back by his presence as he stood in front of her. He made her heart throb and hands sweaty.

She had always been attracted to big, burly men. His shoulder-length brown hair and semi-close-shaven beard were finally thawing out from the ice that had built up on them. Miss Lily felt a sudden calming effect that ran through her inner self the longer their eyes stayed locked. Maybe it was his oversized, muscular, tall build, or his dark brown eyes that seemed to pierce through her soul, that gave her that comfort. The leather he wore was just icing on the cake as she had no doubt he had a biker connection. Miss Lily knew that type, her type for sure. And for a moment, she wished there'd be more time to get to know him, but knew he was just passing through.

"We'll get some dogs on the grill and fries going right now!" the other kitchen helper exclaimed as they both darted away from the window to get busy cooking.

"We really appreciate this, Miss Lily," Blitz gently said, aware she was seemingly as entranced with him as he was with her.

He gently touched her hand that was resting on the counter, then broke eye contact with a wink and headed over to the door to flag everyone in.

"This is great!" Jean-Pierre exclaimed as he immediately took off his wet coat and grabbed a seat at the counter. "I can't think of the last time I had a hearty meal from a diner!"

"Me either!" Rosa excitedly said as she sat down next to him.

"We have a fire going at the end of the dining room where folks can put their wet stuff to dry out a bit," Miss Lily stated, getting more flustered as the team piled in and took their seats.

"That will help," Brandon stated as he came and sat next to Rosa, followed by Jenny.

"Here, give me your stuff, and I'll take it over there," Jenny said, collecting all the wet outer gear from folks.

Once everyone found a seat, Rosa stood up for just a moment to address them, "Okay, team, we made it! And a big thanks to Miss Lily who let us all come inside for a bit. And to the cooks who are nice enough to whip up some hotdogs and fries. Jenny will collect your wet stuff and put it by the fire for a bit, although I'm not sure there's room for it all. So just your coats, please. They won't have time to dry out, but at least they'll get warm! And let's please be respectful and pick up afterwards. There are only three of them here, so just help out."

Everyone cheered and said thanks to Miss Lily as they got settled. For the most part, they were quiet and somber, as if defeated in battle. The freezing temperatures had taken a toll on them.

"It will take forever to get that many cups of coffee together, so I hope everyone is patient," Miss Lily hollered out to everyone as she scanned the volume of heads sitting before her, "and I'm guessing most of you will want some water so I'll get going on those while the coffee is brewing," her voice faded off as she quickly headed down the end of the bar to the coffee station, not quite sure what to think about the thoughts dancing about in her head.

It had been about three years since she was seriously involved with someone and Blitz's presence brought back some of those memories that momentarily gut-punched her. At 34, she never married, yet had been in a seven year relationship with a Vice President of a motorcycle club. The Sons of Goddesses were one of the largest biker organizations, spread all across the United States. They weren't well perceived by most locals as chaos followed them around. Smokey had been part of the Rochester, NY club where Miss Lily had lived with him until things got rocky.

It was just before the pandemic hit that Smokey had taken off on a cross-country motorcycle ride with another gal. Miss Lily was fit to be tied, and once he returned, she laid down an ultimatum for him to commit to being monogamous or lose her. Smokey had agreed and wanted to work things out, but in the midst of their issues, the first wave of the virus hit, and the founder of the organization ordered local clubs to move to its home base in the Cincinnati area. She had felt they weren't on that solid of grounds for her to uproot her life and move with him. He had promised they'd work things out, but she never heard from him again.

"Where are you all headed in such a storm," Miss Lily asked as she started filling up some water glasses from the fountains sitting directly in front of Rosa and Jean-Pierre. She had wished Blitz was next to them, but he had taken a seat at a nearby table. It didn't stop them from continuously stealing glances at each other.

"We're headed to the military base for a couple days to rest and replenish our supplies," Rosa answered as Jean-Pierre volunteered to help distribute the water glasses that were piling up on the counter. Jenny also jumped in to help.

"Well, it's a little less than a mile from here, and you won't miss it," Miss Lily replied, still filling the glasses, "Not many military men left there anymore. That damn virus did its job on them and our town, like anywhere else in this fucked up world." She paused for a moment, realizing how young Rosa was, then said, "Pardon my French…"

"No worries," Rosa piped in as she giggled, "I've heard way worse than that, believe me!"

"I bet," Miss Lily chuckled as she quickly looked over at Blitz then continued, "Occasionally, I see a few of them soldier folks down here, having breakfast, or they come in for a late night dinner. They're about our only customers now."

"Well, looks like we changed that for you, thanks to the pandemic, or we wouldn't be here," Jean-Pierre responded as he grabbed a few more waters.

"I suppose that's what you're all running from. They say the next wave is coming soon and is supposed to be pretty nasty. I suppose we all should be running. Where are you all from, anyways?" Miss Lily asked as she looked across the room at the cold, wet bodies occupying the tabletops and scooted off to check the coffee pots.

"Vermont," Rosa and Jean-Pierre simultaneously answered before he headed over toward Blitz's table with the remaining waters.

"Thanks, bud," Blitz said. "This has been one hell of a trip so far, hasn't it?"

"Yup," Jean-Pierre answered, "and let's hope it gets easier the further south we go."

Miss Lily came back with some coffees and placed them in front of Rosa and Jean-Pierre, then asked, "So you've come down from Vermont? All of you?"

"Not so sure it's down, maybe over," Brandon chuckled as he chimed in.

"Oh, thank you, this is so good," Rosa complimented after quickly taking a sip and smiling at Brandon, then answered, "And yes, all of us came from there. There are more coming in the next week and a couple more teams after them." Then she paused and took another sip before she continued, "The storm has taken a toll on everyone. I can't tell you enough how we all appreciate you taking care of my team."

"Well, we have plenty of food here. It's just going to take some time to get it cooked up for you all," Miss Lily stated as she put together some condiments for the tables, then said, "I just have to ask. You have referred to all these people as your team a couple of times, and honey, I can't help notice how young you are. What do you mean by your team? Some of them are old enough to be your parents," she laughed, "and for course, they're probably with you."

Rosa set her cup down as she slowly responded,"No, they're not here. I lost them both to the virus over the last four years."

"Oh, honey, I'm so sorry. I didn't mean to take light of this," she said, feeling embarrassed as she momentarily touched her hand.

"No worries. I've adjusted. "I'm sure having this many people come in here is a bit mind-boggling, but we have a plan. It's a long story. Just know it's been an adventure, and all these good folks have stuck by my side. We all believe in each other and make a good team," Rosa replied, giving her a quick smile, then picked up her cup and took another sip of coffee.

"Well, honey, you surely got it going for you," Miss Lily said, reaching across the counter, patting her on the shoulder.

Miss Lily and Blitz's eyes continued to meet, holding contact just a little longer each time. She felt an uncontrollable passion grow within her. As she stood making some more coffee, she suddenly envisioned both of them, alone in the diner. Blitz slowly approached her, and as their eyes remained tenderly focused on each other, he scooped her up in his muscular arms, threw her on the counter, spread her legs, and embedded himself deep within her.

Miss Lily felt like she was getting a hot flash and was brought back to reality when she overpoured the water into the coffee maker. She wasn't sure what was going on and why the sudden thoughts were tantalizing her. Surely, there were enough people in the diner to occupy her attention, yet Blitz seemed like the only one to capture it in a way she never expected. Quickly, she cleaned up the spilled water and headed over toward Rosa.

She asked her, "Where are you all headed after you leave the base?"

"Well, I know it may sound crazy, but we're headed to some better lands that are immune to the virus. We're the first of four groups that will initially pass through here," Rosa responded, quite aware she didn't have Miss Lily's full attention, watching her continually gaze over at Blitz, so she loudly cleared her throat.

Miss Lily felt like she not only got caught red-handed by Rosa staring at Blitz, but felt he somehow knew what she had been thinking earlier. She broke eye contact with him as Rosa asked, "Miss Lily? You okay?"

She felt her cheeks flush as she replied, "Yes, I'm fine, and what in the world do you mean by a place that's immune from the virus? Somebody might have pulled your chain 'cause honey, there ain't no place in this world that's safe from that shit." She grabbed the coffee pot and poured a few more cups, then hollered, "How's it going back there, boys?"

"Just about ready, Miss Lily," one of them shouted over the Eagles tunes they had blaring in the kitchen.

"No, it's true," Brandon piped in as he sat on the stool next to Rosa, "Rosa spent months of research on this land. We've also talked to several folks who had passed through the area. So, it's as real as can be."

"You don't say," Miss Lily chuckled as she poured another coffee, then shook her head and commented under her breath, "What a bunch of crock."

It wasn't long before the whole team had warm food in front of them, and a content silence fell as they took their first bites. Seeing that everyone was momentarily taken care of, Miss Lily grabbed her coat and headed out on the porch for a quick cigarette break. She still felt a bit flustered and needed some air. She went around the corner to catch a glimpse of the moon as it tried to peek through the sky full of clouds and watched the snow as it continued to cover the grounds.

"I was afraid you left without saying goodbye."

Miss Lily jumped as Blitz's voice startled her. "Oh, I didn't mean to scare you, Miss Lily," he said as he moved closer and gently touched her shoulders.

"Oh, no, you didn't," she lied as she immediately felt more flushed by his touch and suddenly felt a bit giddy, yet nervous.

She never thought he'd follow her outside, although part of her was hoping he would. Now that he was there, she wasn't sure what to say or do as her heart beat faster in her chest.

"Mind if I join you for a smoke?" he asked her in a soft, caressing voice.

"I'd love that," she shyly answered as she grabbed one of her Marlboro's, lit it with hers, and handed it to him. She felt like a school girl with her first crush!

"Why, thank you. This is one smoke I'll never forget!" he chuckled as he took a puff and watched the snowflakes fall then said, "It sure is remote and beautiful out this way."

"That it is for sure. So, Vermont is a long way from here," Miss Lily started but lost her train of thought as their eyes met.

Blitz waited a few seconds, not sure if she was going to say more, then responded, "Yeah, it took us seven days to get here, and we have another 30 something or more to go. I'm actually from Montreal. Me and some buds landed in Vermont shortly after the pandemic pulled its bullshit."

"Bullshit's an understatement," she sarcastically said.

He watched her take another puff on her cigarette, then she flicked over the side of the porch into the fresh fallen snow. They both watched it die out then talked for a few more minutes about all the chaos the pandemic had created. Miss Lily said she needed to get back inside so Blitz threw his butt over the porch rail then gently pulled her close.

"We really appreciate you opening up your place tonight to this many folks. I don't think some of them could've made it the rest of the way if not. And, as you know, I haven't been able to keep my eyes off of you. You are so beautiful."

Miss Lily felt her heart beat harder and faster, excited that she got the confirmation she was looking for. Blitz felt the same as her.

"Well, honey, I'm flattered. I take it you're still trying to make a move on me?" she chuckled as he pulled her even closer, planting a soft kiss upon her lips that passionately continued for the next few moments.

Eventually, Miss Lily reluctantly pulled away and said, "Don't get me wrong. I don't want this moment to end, and from the first time I saw you, I had wished you were a local, so I'd know I'd see you again. But right now, I really must get back inside.

Blitz continued to hold her close and pulled her in for another kiss then said, "Come with us, Miss Lily. Come with me. It's clear there's something here, something worth pursuing between us," and once again they continued to kiss.

"Miss Lily!" one of the cooks yelled at her as he came around the corner of the porch, "We really need your help inside! Everyone is finishing up!"

Miss Lily held her hand up to signal him that she'd be right in, then looked up at Blitz and said, "Oh Lord, as much as I would love to come with you, I just can't right now. I can't just leave the diner stranded with nobody to run it. I can't do that," she softly said, feeling her eyes well up with tears.

"You can. And if it isn't now, you can come with one of the other teams, and I'll be there waiting for you," he softly kissed her again before they walked arm in arm back to the diner door.

Once inside, she saw that everyone was just about done and scurrying around to help pick up. They brought their dirty dishes up to the counter and cleaned up the tabletops. She wished her handful of daily customers would do the same.

As the team prepared to head back out into the storm to their destination at the base, Miss Lily approached Rosa and said, "I really do think you're all crazy in believing that there's some virus free place out there. But if by chance there is, well, don't forget about me here. Oh, and that big man, Blitz, well, tell him not to forget me either."

Rosa giggled, knowing she had already detected something between the two and responded, "Will do, Miss Lily. I can't thank you enough. All of us can't thank you enough, as you heard. And I'll make sure I let Blitz know. I'm sure he won't forget you." The two embraced before Rosa headed outside with the rest of the team.

Blitz waited until everyone had left the diner then approached Miss Lily and gently held her hands as he asked, "Are you sure you won't come with us?"

Miss Lily felt her eyes begin to water as she desperately wanted to say yes, but replied, "Oh Blitz, I wish I could. But I just can't. I wish things were different because I think we got something between us."

"I feel it too, Miss Lily," as he bent down and passionately kissed her.

Blitz knew he had to go but didn't want to so after one last kiss, he softly said, "Maybe, by some luck, our paths will cross again, Miss Lily. You're one in a million. Don't forget about me because I sure as hell won't forget about you." Then he slowly backed away, winked his watery eye at her, then went out the door to join his team.

Miss Lily stood by the window as a couple tears rolled down her cheeks, and watched them all trek up the road. Blitz never looked back and she was equally as happy he didn't but couldn't help wondering if she had just made a big mistake. Had she passed up on what might have been the true love of her life? Well, she certainly didn't believe all the other hogwash the team was talking about, so for now, she knew it was best to stay put and keep Blitz close, in her thoughts.

Fort Drum Army Base

The Fort Drum sign was a welcomed sight for the tired, soggy travelers. Nestled near the shores of Lake Ontario and the Adirondack mountains, the facility was originally established as Pine Camp back in 1908. It underwent a major expansion during WWII, at which time, in 1951, the name was changed to Camp Drum in honor of LT GEN Hugh A. Drum. Then in 1974, it was designated a permanent military base and renamed Fort Drum Army Base.

Up until the pandemic, it was home to about 20,000 soldiers. Like most other bases throughout the East Coast, many soldiers had been dispersed throughout the New England area and Ohio. They were tasked to help control looting, transport the sick, guard distribution areas, and aid with the necessary burning of buildings to prevent the virus from surviving. Many soldiers succumbed to the virus with the loss of family members, friends, and even their own lives, dwindling the military population to a point bases were closing.

As Rosa's team arrived at the base entrance, two soldiers came out of the gatehouse to greet the large group, and one of them asked, "What brings you all here so late and why are you traveling in this storm?"

The team, snow covered and cold, stopped and huddled together as Jean-Pierre greeted the soldiers who didn't look much older than most of them.

"We're passing through this area, on our way to Kentucky, and the storm has taken a toll on myself and my team. We've traveled for seven days on foot and need to rest up, get warm, stock up on supplies, and wait for this storm to pass. We hope you can take us in."

The two soldiers looked at each other and nodded as one responded, "Roger to that! Let's get you all out of this blizzard. First, we'll escort all of you over to the first building just past these gates on the right," he pointed to it, but the heavy snowfall blocked any vision of it.

The other soldier added, "Once you get inside, you'll be asked to sign in and leave any weapons in lockers before we bring you to the shelter facility where you'll find plenty of food and a warm place to sleep."

"Thank you!" Jean-Pierre exclaimed as he motioned for the team to follow the soldiers through the gate.

Once everyone got through the check-in process and inside the warm building to dry out, they were provided dry bedding, clothes, warm food, and hot showers.

Most of the base housing units were burned to the ground when the virus arrived, so a couple of the military dining halls had been converted into shelters for the many transients who sought periodic lodging. A couple of the halls were also used for essential distribution storage areas that were accessed by surrounding towns.

Just before the weary travelers were ready to call it a night, Rosa asked them to gather around her as she said, "Okay, folks, I know we've had a long day traveling in some miserable weather, but we're safe and warm with full tummies, thanks to the kind folks here at Fort Drum. They're also allowing us to stay an extra day so that we can wait out this storm." She nodded and pointed to a few of the soldiers that stood against the wall near the entrance as her team clapped and cheered, thanking them.

One side of the hall was filled with all the teams' wet supplies, spread out all across the floor so it could dry out. On the other side, the team had settled down for the night in their warm, dry bedding. It didn't take long for most of them to fall asleep once the lights dimmed. Some soldiers were scattered about, keeping watch over their new guests.

"Jean-Pierre," Rosa whispered as she laid her head on his chest, "are you awake?"

"Barely," he whispered, kissing the top of her head, then pulling her closer, "What's up?"

She quickly broke his hold by scooching up closer to his face to see his eyes in the dull light that came through the nearby windows as she continued, "I can't stop thinking about Chad and Dora. It's awful that we just left them in the middle of nowhere."

Jean-Pierre lightly touched her face, moving her long blonde strands of hair that had fallen over her eyes as he replied, "I know Rosa, me either. It was a tough choice, but we could not take the chance. He was pretty sick, and even if they could have traveled a distance behind us, it was too much of a risk. We're keeping an eye on a few of the others that were close to them, but I think all will be okay. We just can't afford to take those type of chances, and I know you know that. That was the rule. We all knew it."

"I know," she sadly responded, "I never should've allowed them to go into town that night by themselves. I should've played by the all the rules, but it was their anniversary, and the little getaway seemed harmless."

She rested her head back on his chest as he held her tightly against him, both staring out the windows, watching the snow continue to fall against it.

"What if we never see them again, Jean-Pierre?" Rosa quietly whispered, "What if something bad happens to Chad? And Dora's left all alone? Oh my God, maybe we shouldn't have left them!" Rosa was getting herself worked up, so Jean-Pierre pulled her closer to him.

"Shhh," he quietly whispered as he rubbed the top of her head, "You have to stop this, Rosa, or you'll drive yourself crazy. We did what we needed to do. Besides, I believe we'll see them again. So right now, let's not think that. They both will be fine, and I'm sure they will find one of the other groups to travel with once Chad is better. They promised they would. Get some sleep Rosa, I love you."

The next day there wasn't a cloud in sight, and the sun was brightly shining as everyone woke up, all happy to be inside and able to lounge around for the entire day. Some folks went outside and walked around the base. Among them were George and Tony, looking for a bit of private time, finally away from constantly being surrounded by lots of other bodies. By the time they arrived at Fort Drum, it was clear they wanted to pursue things further, and little by little, others realized they had become a couple and were supportive of them.

"This has been one hell of a trip so far," George commented as the two walked around the base in the winter wonderland, exploring the far side of the campus.

"No shit," Tony replied, "But up until we hit that storm yesterday, it was pretty smooth sailing."

"Well, we lost the Kinleys. That was enough to shake everyone up. I heard some people talking that they had wanted to turn around and just go back to the auditorium at that point. I have to say that crossed my mind too, but what the hell," George said with a heavy sigh.

"Yeah, I hear ya, but there ain't no giving up here!" Tony exclaimed, putting his arm around George's shoulder, "we'll make it and see what all this hoop de la is about. And we'll make it together!"

"That we will," George said as they stopped, looked around to make sure nobody was near, kissed then held each other for a few moments.

Meanwhile, Rosa, Jean-Pierre, Blitz, and a few others met in one of the other dining halls with one of the Sergeants and some officers to fill them in on their travels. Wesley John Fleshman was 36 and had been in the Army for 18 years. He was a seasoned veteran and had been on a few combat tours and stationed at Fort Drum for the last five years, worriedly watching its deterioration brought on by the pandemic. He lived on base with his wife of 13 years and one of his two kids. Their five-year-old daughter had contracted the virus and died just several months earlier.

Like anywhere else, the base wasn't excluded from the deadly virus, and many chose not to leave the gates, feeling they were more protected inside them. However, they all knew that, most likely, no matter where they were, surviving the third wave might be impossible. So, they were intrigued to hear more about Rosa's migration plan to the better lands.

"It's a shame you all have to take off so early tomorrow morning. We'd love to learn more about this mission you're on. Sure, we can't keep you a few more days?" Sergeant Fleshman asked.

"We really can't, sir," Jean-Pierre responded, "We have a schedule all worked out with the three other teams, but I'm sure each of them will provide some more insight as they pass through here."

"Yes, I agree," Rosa added, "and again, we appreciate your help and support for letting us stay here."

Fleshman looked around at the assembled team at the table. He thought about asking how they were prepared to protect themselves and possibly supply them with some help, but they were out of time to organize it all.

Instead, he said, "We like your motivation and determination. It's crazy that you got this many people to follow you. Let's face it, despite all we read and hear about these better lands; they're basically unknown territory. You've accomplished quite a task, young lady, and we'll look more into this with each of the oncoming teams."

Time flew by fast, and the next thing they knew, it was time to leave the security of the base and hit the road. The extra day had helped everyone catch up on much needed rest and replenish their supplies. They made friends with lots of curious soldiers, many of whom wanted to join their crusade, but the rules didn't permit picking up any others along the way, at least not for the first three teams.

"Thank you again, Sergeant," Rosa said to him and the many soldiers that were lined up to bid them goodbye.

Sergeant Fleshman extended his hand out to Rosa and those standing next to her as he replied, "It was our pleasure, and who knows, we may just run into each other again someday. Good luck with your venture, and God speed to our country as this next pandemic hits."

At that, Team 1 left the gates and headed down the road towards the next major distribution shelter in Cleveland.

Bill's Team 2 – Fort Drum, NY – 6 Days After Rosa's Departure

When Bill's Team 2 prepared for departure from Vermont, Darcy had called a meeting with the Team Leads. He wanted to make sure everyone was on the same page and needed to go over pertinent details of things they had not been privy to beforehand. Everything was in place; the departure was scheduled, and everyone was anxious to start their journey to the better lands. Darcy also wanted to introduce Peter Little, a new teammate, to Bill. One of the other travelers had changed their mind, and Peter was taking her place.

Peter James Little, 27, was a southern gent from the Atlanta, Georgia area. He came to Vermont a couple of years earlier and stayed the summer with his grandparents at their home on Lake Champlain. During that time, the pandemic had just gone through the second wave and had hit Atlanta hard, killing off a lot of folks in the neighborhood he grew up in. Unfortunately, it also took his two younger sisters and both parents. With nowhere else to go, Peter decided to stay with his grandparents, but 18 months later, they both passed from unrelated virus complications. He continued to stay in their home until an evacuation order hit that area, and it was targeted to be burned. Shortly afterward, Peter found himself on the doorstep of the Leddy Park beach community.

"Okay, now that we've covered the last-minute details, and we're still good with them, all that's left to say is good luck, man," Darcy said to Bill as he gave him a hug.

"We won't be far behind you," Sam added, also catching a hug.

Since Bill had not been part of any of the beach communities, he didn't have as close of connections to others as some did. It was his background and willingness to be there when folks needed the extra hands and security that crowned him Team 2's lead. There was one gal that he had shared some conversations with over the winter months and was happy to hear she was going to be traveling with him.

Patricia Louise Cunningham arrived at the Memorial Auditorium with the Oakledge green banders and got involved with a lot of the internal community work to help everyone adapt to their new environment. She had been a psychologist at the hospital in Burlington and had been working on her Ph.D., planning to eventually open her own practice until the pandemic crushed those aspirations.

Patti had dated on and off over the years, but early on, she was married to her career, and it seemed to trump any possibility of a long-term relationship. She also had an impatient, blunt side to her that created controversy in social settings and too often, offended others. She had already made a few enemies. Something she rarely apologized for. She stood five-foot-nine-and-a-half-inches and was a soft spoken, red-headed ball of ambition. Thanks to her better qualities, she was involved with some of the community' decision-making.

She noticed Bill when he first arrived at the Memorial Auditorium and made an effort to get to know him. He remained reserved and distant, but she liked his sense of humor and his humanity he displayed to others. She was smitten by his looks and the gentle side he displayed around her. For the first time in a long time, she hoped maybe she would find a connection that would evolve into a relationship. Patti was thrilled that she was picked to be on Team 2, even though she had originally preferred to stay back with the final migration group as the whole better lands' concept was still a bit unsettling to her.

Bill's team safely arrived in Fort Drum a week after leaving Vermont with no mishaps. The sun was barely setting when they got into town and spotted the diner's flashing sign and headed over to see if they could get something to eat before going to the base. As Bill and the team started toward the porch, the big red diner door flung open. Standing on the other side of it was a short, red-headed waitress wearing a dark blue diner-style dress. She greeted them with a huge smile.

"Welcome, I've been expecting you," she excitedly exclaimed. "Come on in! The boys already got some hotdogs and fries cooking for you!"

Miss Lily had been counting the days that they'd arrive, based on what Rosa had told her. And exactly seven days after Rosa's team left, there they were, tromping down the street and headed right toward the diner as she hoped they would. For a brief moment, she flashed back to that day that Blitz and Rosa walked through the door and recalled the initial feeling of being overwhelmed with so many mouths to suddenly feed. She had worried that things could have gotten out of control quickly since it was only her and the two kitchen cooks on duty. But immediately locking eyes with Blitz, her heart had melted, and all her worries disappeared. Even though he wouldn't be walking through the door this time, she knew the new group was still part of him and could not wait to welcome them.

"Why, thank you," Bill said, quite taken back by the unexpected warm welcome. He saw her name tag then added, "Pleased to meet you, Miss Lily. I'm Bill."

It took about 30 minutes to get everyone settled in, and drinks and food soon started to fill their tables. Miss Lily decided to mingle a bit and went over to Bill's table, knowing he was in charge of the group, and started up a conversation.

"So, I suppose you're all from Vermont too?" she asked, looking over at Patti and noting her hair color, almost matching hers.

"Yes, that's right," he answered as he took another bite of his hotdog.

"And I suppose you're headed over to the base like Blitz's group did?" she coyly asked.

"We are Miss Lily," he answered as he took a sip of coffee then asked, "By the way, do you recall who else was with Blitz?"

"Oh, honey, there were a ton of folks, just like you have. I only got to really talk to a few of them," she responded.

Patti took a sip of water then replied, "Yeah, it's sure lots of people to deal with all at once, and you're doing a great job. But what I think Bill wants to really know is if Rosa was here with Blitz."

"Like I said, there were a ton of people here; most I didn't get to talk to. But yes, Rosa, the pretty young gal who was in charge of the whole kitten kaboodle, she was here. She's something else," Miss Lily responded then took a moment as she watched Bill eat some fries and added, "She sat at the counter with another guy who stayed pretty close to her, John something," then she slightly whispered, half-jokingly, "I think they were a thing."

"Well, not only do you serve food, but you're a romance detective too," Patti said sarcastically as she took a bite of her hotdog.

Miss Lily wasn't sure how to take her comment or tone, detecting a bit of hostility in her. Bill was getting used to Patti's ways and knew she didn't mean harm with the comment.

He quickly responded to Miss Lily, "That's great news. Can you recall who else was with the team?"

"Like I said, honey," she replied, quickly eyeballing Patti, then continued, "there were about a hundred of them. We had no time to get acquainted," she winked at Bill. "My boys were pretty busy in the back kitchen. But that John guy was pretty helpful. I even offered to hire him as my waiter," she giggled.

Patti rolled her eyes as she corrected Miss Lily, "You must mean Jean-Pierre."

"Yeah, that was it, Jean-Pierre. Jean-Pierre. It's got a bit of romantic flair to it; no wonder Rosa was all goo-goo over him." Miss Lily paused and smiled at Patti, then started laughing as she added, "and of course there was Blitz. That's one hunk of a man right there." Once again, she winked at Bill then headed back behind the counter.

"Oh my God, she is a tad annoying," Patti mumbled as she ate her hotdog, "I never thought she'd leave. She is full of questions and much to do about nothing."

"Come on, Patti, she's doing her job and being friendly. She didn't have to welcome us all in here."

Bill had known about some of Patti's ups and downs of her personality before he made his moves on her. But there was something about her that he couldn't resist. The first overnight migration stop in Lewis, New York, was when their relationship left the friendship station.

The small town of Lewis was established in 1805, named after the third governor of New York. Before the pandemic, its population neared about 1500 but had since lost over half to the virus. It was not known to be a hustle-bustle type of town, rather a perfect place to raise a family, retire, and generally just enjoy life.

The air was cold and brisk that evening, and most everyone else was fast asleep in their tents. Bill and Patti shared a blanket to stay warm as they sat around the campfire and watched it until the flames died down. They were the last ones to turn in and decided, for the first time, to forfeit separate sleeping areas. Most folks shared tents with other team members, except for Bill and a few others. He liked his own space, but that evening, he invited Patti to lay next to him and every night thereafter.

Bill could not have been more thrilled that Patti accepted his invitation that night. Since his divorce, he only had a few short-term relationships and one night stands up until the pandemic hit. Before he came in contact with Patti, Bill had no interest in anything long-term with anyone, and at the first sign that things were getting too serious, he'd bow out.

Patti was different, and that night at the campfire, when they snuggled together, it had hit him like a ton of bricks, and he jumped in with both feet for what he hoped to be the long haul. He felt she was on the same page as him. However, they had their moments, especially when her snippy side came out to play. Patti was very opinionated, and for the most part, thought she was always right. But the warm and passionate side he experienced when they were together certainly outweighed those moments.

As they all were about to leave the diner with full bellies, Bill asked Miss Lily to pass on a message to the next team.

"So that's Don and Marie?" Miss Lily asked as she giggled, "kind of like a brother and sister duo?"

"Of course not," Patti said, not amused by her joke.

Bill chuckled then said, "They're a married couple and you'll like them, easy to get along with," he smiled, then asked Patti, "Okay, are you ready to go?"

The team bid their final farewell to the diner while Miss Lily and her kitchen boys watched as the door closed behind the last guest and they tromped up the street, out of sight.

Just like the diner, the base was already on alert for Team 2's arrival and welcomed them with open arms. Once everyone got settled in their sleep quarters, some went to another dining hall to grab desserts and snacks then mingled with a few of the soldiers. Bill, Patti, Peter, along with a few others were sitting at one of the tables when Sergeant Fleshman approached them. They had briefly seen each other earlier.

Bill immediately stood up to salute the Sergeant as he introduced himself, "Captain Bill Wallington, Vermont National Guard unit."

"Sergeant Wesley Fleshman," he reciprocated, "So sorry to hear that the Guards folded up that way, Captain. I heard what you and others are doing as I had the pleasure of meeting young Rosa and her team when they came through here a week ago. She's quite the ball of fire. If times were different, I'd enlist her! Hell, she just about convinced me I should be taking the plunge as well," he chuckled then added, "We could use a few brain powers like hers about now. Did you fly?"

Bill smiled as he nodded in agreement, then answered, "Yes, sir. I was a fighter pilot. I graduated from Norwich then the Airforce selected me for flight school training. I actually did a couple of combat tours in Afghanistan."

"Good on you, Captain. Well, we want you and your team to be comfortable here, and anything you need, let us know. I certainly wish you all the successes at the end of this journey! Will you be staying an extra day also?"

"No, that's not in our plans. Did Rosa?" Bill asked.

"Yeah, but the weather they endured the day they got here literally wiped them out."

They went on to discuss some more of the migration travel plan, and the Sergeant chose not to offer any additional soldiers since Rosa had told him the rules, that no other folks were supposed to travel with the first three teams. He planned to discuss some options when Team 4 arrived.

As the Sergeant got up to leave, he said, "Well, get some rest, and who knows if our paths will meet again, and if they do, we can share some of our war stories."

As he was about to head out the door, Peter rushed over to him and said, "Excuse me, sir."

Fleshman stopped and asked, "Yes, what can I do for you, young man?"

"Well, Sir, I'm Peter. Peter Little and my family are originally from Atlanta."

"I'd say you're a ways from home, son," Fleshman responded.

"Yeah, well, thanks to the pandemic. But I was wondering if you might be able to help me find someone since I have no other way to at this point. I lost all my family and only have my uncle left and don't know where he is. Thought you may know him or of him since he's a highly decorated Major in the Army. The last I knew, he was stationed at Fort Benning."

"Hard to say, son. What's his name?" Fleshman asked.

"Major Brentwood Charles Holdridge, sir." Peter replied.

Major Holdridge was Peter's mother's brother, but the immediate family had distanced themselves from him years earlier due to some disagreements they couldn't seem to resolve. But Peter still carried around fond memories of him and hoped the Sergeant could help find him.

"Brent, yeah, I kind of sort of knew of him. Not sure it's the same guy. But I'll certainly keep an eye out and get info to you if I find out anything," Fleshman carefully replied, knowing the one and only Major Brentwood Holdridge who was no longer active in the service, for which he was thankful. Fleshman decided to spare Peter the details, as none were good, so he left it at that.

Peter was excited to hear there was a possibility to be reunited with his long lost Uncle Brent and asked, "If you find anything out at all, can you send a message with Team 3 or 4?"

"Will do, son. Safe travels," Fleshman responded as he headed out the door.

"Thank you, sir," Peter replied as he left.

The next morning arrived sooner than everyone wanted. They were basking in some of the much needed creature comforts and wished they could stay longer. Their send-off was over the top. As Team 2 bid their goodbyes to their new friends, they were greeted with soldiers lined up and down the base's main street, standing at attention, rendering a salute to Bill and his team as they went on their way.

Trap's Team 3 – Fort Drum, NY – 2 Weeks After Rosa's Departure

Team 3 had some last-minute changes and ended up with Trap as their new Team Lead. Don and Marie backed out at the last minute after deciding they no longer wanted to be involved in the migration plan. Some distant relatives had traveled to the area, found them, and shared news about some other locations in Maine, so they joined them on that venture instead. The couple felt it would be an easier journey for them as Don had some minor physical issues with bouts of sciatica that could've impacted the team staying on schedule. It was something Darcy had been concerned about even before they resigned from their duties.

When they initially told Darcy of their new plans, even though he knew deep down it was better for the team; he went into panic mode. The team's departure was less than a week away, which left him little time to find a replacement. That afternoon, Darcy sat in his usual spot on his sleeping bag in the corner of the auditorium, partially reading his book and partially watching Trap up on the stage, making a big production as he helped Holly, Sam, and some others with last-minute details for Team 3's departure. He, of course, was being Trap, loud and obnoxious, but in a friendly way.

"Come on guys, let's put some better thought into this, I mean really," Trap said, his voice a bit raised yet free of obscenities. He wasn't in agreement with how the first aid packets were put together, and despite his fuss over it, everyone kept doing what they were doing.

Darcy was pleased how far Trap had come from the miserable, lost soul he had first witnessed, to the considerate, caring, almost fatherly man who seemed to genuinely care about others. He also managed to put a lid on his once uncontrolled, vulgar 'trap.' At least for the most part. It was nice to see folks periodically engage with him just for conversation and a few laughs. Trap had been a good addition to the winter shelter, and he wanted him in his final migration group. At least that was the plan until that moment.

Darcy let out a power whistle that echoed through most of the auditorium, something he had learned from Blitz. He didn't mean to capture everyone's attention, but did. He flagged only Trap to come over and join him.

"What's up, Boss Man?" Trap asked as he got closer.

"Well, my friend, have a seat," Darcy said, watching him plop down on the bare floor even though he offered a part of his sleeping bag for comfort, "You know that Don and Marie changed their mind about the Team 3 leads, right?"

Trap nodded his head in agreement then asked, "But what the fuck, what are they thinking? Knowing all we know, why would they bail, really?"

Darcy shook his head, showing he disapproved as well but then responded, "They have some personal things going on and really just want to be with their family, so it's okay. They need to do what they need to do. But I need someone to lead that team to the better lands, and I could not think of any better person than you, Trap, to lead the folks safely there."

Darcy watched as Trap shifted his body around, giving himself a second to let the offer sink in, then watched as Trap's face lit up with excitement as he responded, "Really, Boss Man, me? Lead the team? You mean it?"

Darcy nodded with a big smile as he said, "Yes, Trap, you!"

Trap was overwhelmed that he had been chosen for such a responsible task. He knew his presence over the past couple years was far from desirable, even for him. He hated every moment of his disruptions and if it weren't for Blitz standing up for him that day, he might have continued down that dark path. It felt good to find himself again, although not the same self as when he had his loving family around him. But he now had others who he started to care about, like family, and wanted to do all he could to help out.

"You got it, Boss Man!" he exclaimed. "This means the world to me! I won't let you or anyone down!" Trap stood up and then shook Darcy's hand and headed back over to share the news with Holly and Sam.

Shortly after, Darcy called Jeff over. He was equally impressed how Jeff had taken on a different attitude since that day with Blitz and Trap. He toned down his obscenities, joined in with a lot of the group efforts and made himself available for any task that needed to be done. Darcy even caught him having lunch with Trap a few times.

"Hey what's up," Jeff asked as he approached Darcy.

"Hey, I wanted to talk to you about something as I'm sure you've heard Don and Marie are no longer Team Leads and I just asked Trap to take their place. I know you two had your issues, but you both have been doing great and are two strong leaders that I believe could work well together for the team's sake. And Team 3 needs a second lead. So, what do you say? Can you fill that spot?"

Jeff was hesitant at first. Even though he had to make amends with Trap, only because he was afraid of Blitz's wrath, he despised the guy. He couldn't imagine running a team side by side with him, but at the same time he wanted to get out of the community setting and to the better lands sooner than later. He had been assigned to Darcy's team so it was still months away. He agreed to fill the spot.

Just a week after their departure, Team 3 arrived in the town of Fort Drum and were munching on Miss Lily's famous hotdogs and fries. The group was much rowdier and less friendly than the others that had passed through, and Miss Lily felt tension among them. She had not been worried prior to them, but something felt different this time.

She wished that Don and Marie had showed up instead, as she got a bad vibe with the Team Leads.

There were quite a few conflicts the team had encountered before Fort Drum but were mainly between Trap and Jeff. Being forced to be in closer quarters and to work together without Blitz as their constant referee made it quite clear that bygones weren't bygones as the hours and days dragged on. First, they didn't agree on little things like where they were going to pitch their tents for the night, who was responsible for night watches, and distribution of essentials among everyone. Jeff continually opposed Trap's directions, even though he initially went with the flow. But it wasn't long before the arguments grew longer and more intense. Their conflict was heading down a dark tunnel with no light at the end of it.

Scott tried to remain as neutral as he could, although when push came to shove, even though he favored Trap's marching orders, he followed Jeff's. He tried to deflect some of the issues among the restless, somewhat divided team by occupying their attention in different directions, especially when things got contentious. Most of the time his efforts fell short. Jeff always wanted the last word even if things didn't go his way. A major storm was brewing, and there was little that Scott could do to stop it from happening. Jeff was gathering some followers while others had Trap's back, committed to honoring his commitment to the migration plan.

As they all sat in the diner, it was clear the group was divided and frustrated. Trap's following took over one section of it, while Jeff's groupies sat in another part. Miss Lily stood behind the counter and listened to banter that confirmed there was trouble ahead. Jeff and a couple of others were seated at the counter, noticeably disgruntled, and didn't try to keep their conversation low enough so others wouldn't hear. Miss Lily made sure she stayed within ear range as much as she could to catch the scoop. After all, nothing else exciting was happening in the town, let alone in the diner.

"I'm telling you this is such bullshit. There's no need to go to that base just to be in an inside shelter for the night. There are plenty of other places to set up tents on the way. Why should we stop now? We could walk through the night or at least until we get more tired. This whole base shit is only adding several unnecessary hours. It's ridiculous!" Jeff stated while he jammed a handful of french fries into his mouth.

"Yeah, Trap has his head up his ass and is no leader for sure. He can't make independent decisions over and beyond what he was told to do. Your plan is so much better than all of them. Even that annoying teen, Rosa. She thinks she has it all down but really doesn't have a clue either. It's pathetic that everyone follows her around like a bunch of hungry puppies," Grey growled, gobbling down the last of his hotdog.

He looked over at Miss Lily and politely asked, "Can I have another, darling?"

Grey Edwardsen was a big supporter of Jeff, not because he liked him, more because he had his own agenda. Jeff was easily riled and Grey could seamlessly manipulate and run the team through him. He was in his mid-50s, one of the oldest men among the group, and copped an attitude because of it. He felt he was much wiser than the rest of the pack and nobody, other than him, had a clue. He blew into Jeff's ear, hyping him up, letting him take the lead on his ideas, pushing him to do so. He was a true instigator, and Jeff was an easy target. He didn't care for many people. Trap, Rosa, Jean-Pierre, Blitz, and others were never on his 'let's be friends' list.

When Grey first came to the auditorium, he stayed to himself, watching the interaction that went on between everyone, especially Trap and Jeff, even when they appeared to be friendly. Grey weighed out his options, and once the formal announcement for the new Team 3 leads was made, he started luring Jeff into his devious plan.

"You should have just taken control of it all from the beginning. Everyone would've listened and followed you over her," piped in Ralph, sitting on Jeff's other side, "but somehow she got the control."

Ralph had been part of the Oakledge Community from day one and was always into everyone's business, drawing his own conclusions on what should or shouldn't happen, sometimes expressing them. For the most part he kept a low profile. Once he arrived at the auditorium, he started hanging around Jeff more only because of the proximity of their living space. Eventually, they became friends of sorts.

"No kidding, and our time will come. For now, we just play along," Jeff added, filling his mouth with more fries then gulping down some water.

"Thanks, darling," Grey said to Miss Lily as she placed another hotdog in front of him.

Miss Lily couldn't believe what she was hearing. She thought Rosa was one of the most independent, strong, young leaders she ever had laid eyes on and knew the amount of respect she got from every one of her team members as well as from Team 2. After all, she was the one behind the whole migration, no matter who else decided to take charge or not. Miss Lily wasn't one to keep her thoughts to herself even though there were times she wished she did.

"Wow, I can't help but overhear what you boys are saying," she said, looking directly at Jeff's already confrontational eyes as she filled his water glass. "I met Rosa, and I have to say I'm overly impressed that someone that young could put together all this. Who wouldn't be thankful that you all have the opportunity to find some better lands that will hopefully keep you safe from whatever else is out there? Thanks to Rosa," she politely said, even though she still wasn't behind the whole better land theory. She watched as Jeff's face got red, and his body tensed up as he threw his fries back on his plate.

Then he gruffly said, "Mind your own business bitch," then he forcefully pushed his plate across the counter, got up, grabbed his coat, and slammed the door behind him as he headed outside. Grey, along with the rest of his posse, quickly got up without saying a word, and followed him.

Scott quickly approached the counter, apologizing to Miss Lily for Jeff's rude behavior, and then turned to Trap and said, "Hey, Boss Man, let's pack it up. I think we overstayed our welcome here."

Trap agreed and extended his apology to Miss Lily. The group was even more unsettled with some of Jeff's guys still inside, glaring over at the counter. Miss Lily wasn't quite sure what was going to happen next. She did have a handgun hidden under the register in case of any emergencies and thought about grabbing it, but luckily Trap got everyone out the door with no incidents. He left Miss Lily an extra big tip on his table.

Outside, the tension had accelerated, and an argument between Trap and Jeff broke out.

"You're one piece of work!" Trap hollered at Jeff as he stood across the empty parking lot with several of the others, "there was no reason to call that lady any names! You owe her an apology and you need to go back in there and give it to her!"

"Fuck you, old man. You're the one to talk!" Jeff shouted back as he started moving closer to him, "and that bitch needed to mind her own business and so don't you!"

Grey joined in and yelled over at Trap, "Look it, asshole, you're costing us time, and you know it! There was no need to make this stop here! We could be a couple of hours or more down the road right now, especially if we didn't take this long way around! These people are tired and this route is more miles than it needs to be! But you're a piece of shit who can't figure that out!"

Trap yelled back, "Yeah, well, we're following the plan, as promised. You have no fucking business trying to change things up and create such a riff as you have here! As it is, half these people didn't even finish their meal!" He started walking toward Jeff.

Scott knew if he didn't do something quick, the situation would get out of hand, so he ran between them and yelled, "Enough! Not here, not now! Let's move on. Come on!"

By then, everyone had formed a semi-circle around the three of them, and Miss Lily and her kitchen staff were peering out one of the diner windows, not sure what was going to happen next.

Scott continued as things seemed to calm down a tad, "We can't afford to fall apart here or divide. Come on, guys. You both have a responsibility here to get the team to the better lands safely and the way Rosa has planned." He looked over at Jeff, knowing he wouldn't be happy with him.

"This is bullshit. You're bullshit, Scott. Rosa is bullshit, and this piece of shit right here is bullshit!" Jeff hollered at the top of his lungs as he pointed to Trap then demanded, "Let's go, boys!" He motioned his posse to follow him as he abruptly started walking off in the direction of the base, taking almost half of the group with him.

Trap wasn't sure where they were headed, and at that point, didn't care as he gathered up the remaining folks and headed in the same direction. Miss Lily was quite relieved that nothing took place in the parking lot or in her diner and watched as the last one walked out of sight.

"Holy crap," she said to the two cooks, "let's hope Team 4 isn't anything like these guys."

Sam's Team 4 – Fort Drum, NY – 3 Weeks After Rosa's Departure

It had been four weeks since Rosa's team had left Vermont, and the day finally came for Sam and his group to make the same trek. Team 4 was crowned "the sweepers,' and were the last of the folks to depart until Darcy's team, later that Fall. Sam's team was to help anyone who had fallen along the wayside and pick up some others along their journey, if they were deemed fit. They also decided to add 15 more folks for added protection, not knowing what to expect along the way.

Jimmy was excited that Sam convinced Darcy to let him travel with him. He didn't want to wait another several months to join up with Rosa, George, Tony and the others. Sam had argued that Jimmy would be an added value to his team since he had close relations with the migration power team, and already knew the expectations. Sam made him his right-hand man.

It was 3:30 a.m. when Jimmy enthusiastically jumped up on the stage and started calling off Team 4 names to prepare for their departure. His voice sounded a bit shaky through the megaphone as he read the list, "Erika Stiles, Bob & Louise Morrie, Brian & Phyllis Smith, Derek Wright, Marilyn West, Jill Packard, Roger Hatfield,..."

Marilyn was standing next to Sam when her name was called. She had been with the winter community just before the Christmas holiday and celebrated her 30th birthday in January along with Rosa's 16th. Marilyn had migrated to the Burlington area from the small rural town of Plainfield, about 48 miles southeast and had lived there for three years. She had shared an apartment with a couple of roommates and, shortly after receiving her master's degree in economics, worked at the state capitol.

Like everywhere else, when the pandemic hit after the first wave, things changed for her. She was put on furlough from work only to be let go once the second wave arrived. Her two roommates also lost their jobs, and both ended up going back to their homes out of state. With no means and a final evacuation notice, she packed up some belongings and headed to Burlington, then landed on the steps of the Memorial Auditorium where she met and fell in love with Sam.

Marilyn had short curly, auburn hair and occasionally pulled it back in a tiny ponytail to tame its frizz. Her eyes were bright green, and her face and arms were covered with freckles. Sam towered over her five-foot-seven-inch moderately thin body and was enamored with her upon their first meeting. He had not taken an interest in anyone since his fiancé had been murdered. The two of them quickly became inseparable, and it was a hands-down decision that she would be on Team 4, so they could travel together.

Meanwhile, Darcy and Holly tried to catch up with everyone as they left the auditorium doors for the last time. Holly had gathered some small shells down by the lakefront, painted them all a bright red, and was handing them out to folks to carry in their pockets for good luck. She had wished she thought of it earlier so the other teams could have had them as well. Sam was already over in the middle school's yard, checking everyone in as they arrived. The air was cool but not as cold as when Rosa's team left. It was almost the middle of April, and Spring had truly sprung.

A full moon was still casting its light over the city, and unlike most early mornings, silence was hard to come by. Most of the communities were there, represented by over a thousand folks gathered in the yard and on the streets, cheering on and waving to Team 4. As they made their first trek up the main street and turned right, one by one, they dropped out of sight and marched forward to the ferry to begin their venture.

Darcy looked over at Holly, who had tears in her eyes as she said, "I wish them all the luck in the world, and hopefully, they find nothing bad along the way. I wish it were us going."

Darcy wrapped his arms around her and held her close as he said, "It will be us soon, I promise. And everything will work out. This is all so crazy and still hard for me to wrap my head around. We've gone back in time in so many ways and really are becoming pioneers all over again. Almost like time travel, going from one life to another in a short time. I struggle with it every day, but I know in the end, we'll find that rhythm again. I have to trust that."

Holly squeezed back, responding with, "Me too, babe. We're all in this together and it can only get better, I hope."

As planned, one week later, Sam's team arrived in Fort Drum. The trip was uneventful, and like the other teams, were unaware that Chad and Dora had departed early on from Team 1 and the trouble that was brewing with Team 3. Just as they entered the town, they saw the diner sign and headed over, all 115 of them.

"There's certainly a boatload of you here!" Miss Lily exclaimed as she watched all of them happily eating the diner's hot dog and fry special.

Sam, Marilyn, and Jimmy were seated at the counter, with several others, all engaging in conversation with her.

"Yeah, we have about 15 extra of us as we're the last team coming down this way for the next three months or so. We don't know what to expect as we follow behind the other teams, but so far, so good," Jimmy responded, sipping his coffee.

"Well, one thing for sure, you certainly are a friendlier bunch than the last one that came through here. Believe me. I was a bit worried at one point," Miss Lily blurted out.

"Why, what happened?" Sam asked as he put his hotdog down and looked at her.

"Well, they weren't happy campers with each other, that's for sure," she replied, "now I know why that couple bowed out of traveling with them."

"Let me guess, I bet you're talking about Trap and Jeff," Marilyn said as she wiped her mouth with the napkin. "They can be quite overwhelming for sure and offensive depending on the moment, but hopefully, they keep it together for the team's sake."

"Yeah, and they were doing fine when they left. Must have been some other mishap that got them going," Jimmy stated.

Miss Lily nodded and smiled as she filled up a few empty water glasses, "Yeah, Marilyn is spot on about them being offensive. Jeff sat right at this very counter, and I heard most of the conversation, and it wasn't pretty," she paused as she grabbed another coffee pot.

Sam held his cup up for a refill as he replied, "Oh man, Miss Lily, I can only imagine what went down in that group. There's a lot of bad blood from the beginning between a few of them, especially those two. But last I knew that they had made amends like Jimmy said. Otherwise I can't imagine that Darcy wouldn't have put them together. It's probably something we should've seen coming, especially since Blitz wasn't around to keep them in line."

"Yeah, well, Blitz was the only one that controlled those two fuses," Jimmy added.

"Well, had we known it was a disaster waiting to happen, we would have never let them travel together. God only knows what it means for the rest of the team. Hopefully, they can keep it together so they can reach the better lands in peace," Sam replied, then looked at Miss Lily and sincerely said, "But let me apologize for it all."

"Hey, honey, no worries. I'm a big girl with equal mouth power," Miss Lily playfully replied, momentarily thinking about Blitz after hearing his name then said, "But yeah, it was a tad tense there for a bit. Especially once they all got outside. I thought there was going to be an all-out brawl! The group was pretty damn divided and angry and if you ask me, I'm surprised they all left in the same direction."

Sam never expected to hear that Trap and Jeff's differences led to such erratic behavior, especially during the migration journey. He shook his head in disgust as he said, "Well, if they did any damage or didn't pay, I'll take care of it. We'll try to make up for that bad encounter."

"Nah, don't worry about it. They paid me, in fact, tipped me well over the top," Miss Lily responded, "But I have to tell you, no group beat the first one that came through here."

Miss Lily slightly smiled as she poured Jimmy another cup of coffee. She put the pot down in front of them, leaned into the counter, and said in a dreamy tone, "Rosa was great! They all were, but one guy in that bunch was quite the eye candy. Can't seem to stop thinking about him."

"Hmm, I wonder who that could be?" Jimmy curiously asked as he stirred some sugar in his coffee.

"Me too!" Marilyn excitedly said, "Do share!"

"Hmm," Miss Lily teasingly mumbled, contemplating her next move.

She had been fortunate enough to work at the diner for a few years and never missed a day. Since her relationship ended with Smokey, she had kept to herself and not dated since.

The few people that were left in town weren't her type, even though they were friendly, some head-turning material, and even had asked her out on dates which she turned down. Miss Lily knew her life was at a standstill and lived moment to moment, but if the pandemic continued and the next wave hit harder, she knew she'd be vulnerable to its wrath and be out on the streets.

Since meeting the three other teams and listening to their plans about the better lands, she thought about taking the same chance they all were. She thought about the choices she had, to stay and wait things out or join them and see if there was a real pot of gold at the end of that rainbow, like Team 1 had joked about. She wasn't sure if either choice promised a fairy tale ending but felt there was nothing to lose if she took the risk. And for that risk, maybe there would be something new, eventful, and possibly life-changing for her, including the big burly hunk.

Miss Lily knew this was her last chance to get on board, if possible, so she took a deep breath and said, "Hey, look guys, here's what I've been thinking about," she tapped her fingers on the counter and continued, "Since Rosa was here and first talked about those better lands, well, at first, I really thought it was a bunch of bullshit, and well, maybe I still do. But if it's for real, and I could live in that place not scared that damn virus is coming for me anymore, well, I'd like to take a chance on it. Maybe it's true, maybe not. But if there's any chance you can, I'd like you to take me with you."

Miss Lily felt her face flush, her hands got sweaty, and couldn't believe she really asked, even though she had rehearsed it in her head several times. She anxiously waited for an answer as she looked at the three of them watching her. Nobody said a word for a few moments. Jimmy took another bite of his hotdog as Marilyn put her half-eaten one back on the plate while Sam cleared his throat.

"Well, Miss Lily," Sam started, glancing over at the others, who quickly gave him a nod of approval, "it's a long journey that we have left. Do you have any family members you were thinking about bringing as well?"

"Just me," she quietly replied.

Sam nodded then asked, "Do you really think you'd be up to it, and do you really understand what it all entails?"

"Yes, and yes," she quickly replied in her low, raspy voice, "I've got the picture loud and clear and I'm in pretty good shape, if I say so myself.

They all chuckled as she twirled around, then Sam said, "Well, okay then, why not! We'd be delighted to take you along with us, providing we can pack up some of those dogs to take with us!" They all laughed.

"Really!?" She quickly shouted as she ran around the counter to give all three of them a hug.

"Oh, one more thing," Marilyn added as she smiled at Miss Lily, grabbed her hand, and asked, "Who's the guy?"

"Yeah, inquiring minds want to know," Jimmy laughed

"Why, there's only one it could possibly be, honey," Miss Lily teased as she smiled, then winked at them both and skipped back behind the counter.

"We're waiting, Miss Lily," Marily giggled.

Miss Lily leaned over the counter, closer to the three of them as she whispered loudly with her raspy voice, "That one dreamy, big hunk of a man, I believe his name is Blitz."

Since Miss Lily lived half-way between the diner and Fort Drum, the plan was for her to meet them the next morning on base. In the meantime, Team 4 headed over to settle down for the night, leaving Miss Lily to wrap up her business so she would be ready to set sail to the better lands in the morning.

Once on base and settled into their living area, a couple of young soldiers approached Sam while he and Marilyn sat at one of the tables, nibbling on some chocolate cake and reflecting on the day.

"We were wondering if we could talk to you, sir. I'm Private Hansen, and this is Private Stone. We understand you head up this team?" Hansen asked as Sam checked them out. They weren't in uniform and looked young enough to pass as teenagers.

Sam stood up and shook both their hands, "Nice to meet you soldiers. Yes, I'm Sam, and this is Marilyn," then he motioned for them to take a seat.

Hansen cleared his throat and said, "We wouldn't normally approach anyone like this, but in short, the base is closing its doors in a few weeks, and we were told we're all on our own when it happens. Not many of us are left here, and hardly any activity is happening, except your groups that have passed through. We are going to lose everything when it shuts down. We had previously approached the first two groups, but they said their hands were tied. We contemplated talking to the last one, but they were very disheveled, and some of our officers had to step in at one point to break up a few fistfights. We eventually had to separate their sleeping quarters."

Roger Eugene Hansen was all but 19 years old and had joined the Army right as he turned 18. It seemed like it was his only choice and was heavily encouraged by his father, shortly before he passed away.

Hansen grew up in the Michigan area, the middle kid of four brothers. All of his family, other than his father, were wiped out when the second wave of the virus came, along with their home. For the next few months, they both shuffled around from couch to couch at various friends' homes. It was during that time that his father decided Roger should join the Army so as to be insured of shelter, food, and medical attention. Although it wasn't Private Hansen's first choice, he hopped on the bus. Shortly after, he got word that his dad had passed. Just a year after enlisting, he found out most bases were closing down, leaving him once again, nowhere to go. Hands down, he wasn't passing up the opportunity to get to the better lands one way or another.

Sam looked over at Marilyn as she said, "I'm so sorry guys, this is such an awful time. And sorry about Trap and Jeff's team. We're hearing about the blazing trail they're leaving behind them. But I didn't expect to hear that a military base is closing, especially through these hard times."

Then she addressed Sam, "This is crazy, Sam. What's happening? Bases closing? What about Darcy's group coming through? They'll have no idea until they get here. Then what? Or maybe he'll be able to find the news on the internet, if it decides to work."

She was rambling a mile a minute, clearly upset by the news, so Sam grabbed her hand as a cue for her to stop talking, then slightly whispered that he had the conversation from there.

He turned to address the Privates, "I, too, am sorry and shocked to hear this news. But it makes sense it's closing, given all that is going on and what's coming, and not enough folks here to run the base. I respect you all so much, but guys, the deal is we're not supposed to just willy nilly pick up any other travelers right now. We already have extras with us and don't know if we're going to run into any of the other team members. But we will have another team coming down in the Fall, maybe that timing will work out."

They both bowed their heads as Private Stone replied, "We understand, sir, no worries. We just thought we'd ask and I doubt we'll be here come Fall."

Sam hated to see the disappointment on their faces and said, "Well, I'm not saying no, and I don't know if I can say yes. But, let me ask, how many more of you are there that want to hop on this train?"

The Privates both looked at each other feeling a glimmer of hope then Hansen replied, "Only about 15 of us, sir."

Just as Sam was about to respond, another soldier in uniform approached the table extending his hand out to him. Sam immediately recognized the stripes on his uniform and immediately stood up.

"Hi sir, I'm Sergeant Fleshman. Thanks for taking the time to meet with us. I'm sure my Privates have already filled you in," he said.

"It's an honor, Sergeant," Sam said as he gave him a salute then sat back down, inviting him to do the same. "I'm Sam Hatfield. I was a Lieutenant for ten years on the Vermont State Police squadron, and this is Marilyn, my girl." Marilyn nodded at him.

He nodded back then said, "I met Captain Wallington a couple of weeks ago as he directed his group through here and was quite impressed with how he led the team. Quite unlike the last disaster that plowed through here a week ago. Your group looks bigger. How many do you have with you?"

"Oh, there are 115 of us, 15 more than the other three teams as we're the last ones coming through here for a few months," Sam paused for a moment, "Yeah, about that last team, sorry about them. We should have never placed Trap and Jeff together. Miss Lily, from the diner, filled us in on some heated stuff that went on there as well. So, they're shutting down this base?"

"Yes, sir. We saw it coming for the last year, and with the pandemic on the go again and not enough folks here to run or maintain it, the decision was made at the federal level. There are many others closing too. But the bad part is when they do, there's nowhere else for anyone to go because of the massive closures. A lot of the soldiers are taking their families, at least those that have any left, and heading west, where they heard the lands were less susceptible to the virus. Kind of like the better lands you're all headed to. Others are heading up through the Canadian territories. Hey, come to think of it, one of the guys with Captain Wallington, Peter, I think his name was, shared that he had an uncle who was a Major out of Fort Benning. Have you ever heard the kid's story?"

"No, can't say I have. There were hundreds, close to a thousand of us up in Vermont, all targeted for this migration. Everyone kept to their own clique if you will," Sam responded.

Fleshman cleared his throat and said, "Well, just as well. I feel bad for the kid since he's his only family out there, but that uncle is bad news. He was stripped of his rank for a bunch of shenanigans that brought disgrace among the military. Don't think Peter knows about any of it, and I certainly didn't share that info with him. He's a good kid."

The Sergeant shook his head for a minute and looked around the room before he continued, "So, after talking with Rosa, Captain Wallington, and with some of my squad and a couple from another, we'd very much like to team up with you. It would be a handful of us, just 20 or so. We wanted to offer earlier, but Rosa had shared that nobody else could go with the first three teams, so I let it be. And certainly had no interest in getting in the middle of the last dust storm."

"Wow!" Sam was taken off guard by the proposal coming from the Sergeant. At that point, he felt it was a worthy consideration and more likely a done deal the more he heard.

Fleshman smiled at Sam as he continued, "And we come with lots of advantages for you and your team. As you know, we're a light infantry unit, part of the tenth mountain division, and can supply everyone with protection, including our soldiers. I've been doing this for 18 years and don't want all my abilities and knowledge to be all for nothing. I'm not ready to close shop if you will."

Without thinking twice, Sam humbly replied, "Wow, you know, I'd be honored for you all to join us. It's not what we're supposed to do, as I stated to your Privates, but it makes sense. We're only at the start of our journey and have no idea what we're facing as we move on. So, 20 or so is the magic number?"

"Thereabouts. A few of us have some family members that would be joining. My wife and my nine-year-old son for one. We just lost our five-year-old daughter several months back to the damn virus," he paused for a moment in silence, then said, "And a couple other ranked officers have wives, and I think a few teenagers would also travel with us."

Sam wasn't excited about bringing any kids on the journey as the migration team had agreed it wouldn't be a good idea, at least not initially. It would take at least another day or so for Sergeant Fleshman and his troops to prepare for their final departure from the base. In the meantime, Sam's team was able to catch up on some rest and good food while they waited it out. Miss Lily showed up the next day, as planned, and was invited to stay with them at the base until departure.

The day before they left, they all started preparing for the integration. Sergeant Fleshman talked to Sam about adding more supplies to the team, such as food packs, water supplies, and M16s. None of the other teams had been privy to receiving any of it. At first, Sam was hesitant. The M16s were serious business and he wasn't sure how well the others would accept them. He needed to make the team understand that the assault rifles along with the many soldiers to travel with them, meant a life line, especially if they got into any serious conflicts.

And he succeeded. The more the team learned, the more it made sense. As it stood, if they ran into something life-threatening down the road, they had no real protection. Only about ten of them on each team packed handguns, the rest carried a hunting knife or mace of some fashion. The new plan meant that most of the team would carry an unloaded M16 with no intent to use, unless the need arose and there'd be plenty of ammunition along for the ride.

"God only hopes we don't have to ever use these," Marilyn said to Sam, a bit wigged out when the weapons were distributed, "But I get it. One never knows and better safe than sorry."

Team 4's early morning departure three days later welcomed 20 soldiers, all dressed in their camouflage attire, along with seven family members that included three kids. Most of them knew who Miss Lily was, so she felt a bit more at ease with her decision to travel with the team.

As all 143 of them left the base, the street was lined with the remaining soldiers, standing at attention and rendering their salute to some of their own who were leaving them for good.

Rosa

Team 1's next stop was the Cleveland stadium, and everyone was excited to get to the inside shelter. That morning, just ten hours away from the hub, all the tents were packed up and the team was eating breakfast around a few of the campfires. Rosa decided to wander down the small hill to a nearby river, then sat on a rock and just watched as the water flowed by. The sound was mesmerizing. The air was fresh and clean. The sun had begun to lighten up the sky.

She thought about her parents and how long it had been since she last felt her dad's hug or her mom's warm kiss on her forehead. She thought about the days she sat for hours on their dock on Lake Champlain, just watching the waves gently lap to the shore. It was a peaceful time; a time her little life had nothing to fear.

As Rosa continued to watch the water move down stream, it was hard to comprehend that life had morphed itself into something she didn't recognize yet she was a big part of. So much had happened in such a short time, perspectively. Her fear of the unknown had grown into a hope of something bigger that would eventually shine a brighter light into all of their lives. Rosa had no doubt that things would have been so different had she not walked out of Mr. Chuso's front door that day. And if it wasn't for the Beretta M9, she just might not have.

"Are you ready, Rosa?" Jean-Pierre asked as he came down the hill toward her.

Rosa looked at the river, took a deep breath and as she hopped down from the rock said, "As ready as I'll ever be. Let's get the team to Cleveland."

CPSIA information can be obtained
at www.ICGtesting.com
Printed in the USA
BVHW080006060821
612957BV00002B/9

9 781647 196455